## THE COMPLETE CASES
## OF THE RECKONER

*Carroll John Daly*

CARROLL JOHN DALY

# THE COMPLETE CASES OF
# THE
# RECKONER™

## CARROLL JOHN DALY

### ILLUSTRATIONS BY
### JOHN FLEMING GOULD

ALTUS
PRESS

BOSTON • 2015

© 2015 Steeger Properties, LLC, under license to Altus Press • First Edition—2015

EDITED AND DESIGNED BY

Matthew Moring

PUBLISHING HISTORY

"The Curtain of Steel" originally appeared in the February, 1933 issue of *Dime Detective* magazine. Copyright 1933 by Popular Publications, Inc. and assigned to Steeger Properties, LLC. All rights reserved.

"Drawn in Blood" originally appeared in the June 1, 1933 issue of *Dime Detective* magazine. Copyright 1933 by Popular Publications, Inc. and assigned to Steeger Properties, LLC. All rights reserved.

"Blood on the Curtain" originally appeared in the December 1, 1933 issue of *Dime Detective* magazine. Copyright 1933 by Popular Publications, Inc. and assigned to Steeger Properties, LLC. All rights reserved.

"Answered in Blood" originally appeared in the March 1, 1934 issue of *Dime Detective* magazine. Copyright 1934 by Popular Publications, Inc. and assigned to Steeger Properties, LLC. All rights reserved.

THANKS TO

Jay Daly, Joel Frieman, and Rick Ollerman

# TABLE OF CONTENTS

# THE CURTAIN OF STEEL

FROM BEHIND THE METAL CURTAIN IN THAT MYSTERY ROOM CAME THE DREAD VOICE OF THE RECKONER— PRONOUNCING DANGER EDICTS, DEATH COMMANDS. AND MARTY DAY— GENTLEMAN ADVENTURER, MASTER OF THE STRANGEST WEAPON IN THE WORLD— SHUDDERED AT THOSE ORDERS. WHAT WAS THE AWFUL SECRET OF THE UNKNOWN'S POWER? WHY DID DAY HAVE TO LISTEN AND BLINDLY OBEY?

# CHAPTER ONE

# THE MAN IN THE MASK

**F**EET WERE coming down the stairs. Marty Day snapped out his electric flash, pushed the small safe door almost closed and dropped back in the deep blackness of the library. He didn't need anyone to tell him that his position was extremely delicate; that he had no right in that house; no right by that open safe from which he had just lifted a long, pale-blue, linen envelope held tightly by a thick elastic band.

Morally Marty believed he had a right to that envelope; at least, a right to lift it from its present resting place. But legally—well, man-made laws did not look too closely into the motives of the individual, except when those motives established a reason for convicting a man of crime. Now, the judge would simply look over his glasses and recite, in the dull monotone of constant repetition, the little speech that would deprive Marty of his liberty for five or ten years.

Marty smiled grimly as such thoughts went through his head. He carefully adjusted his black mask tighter and stepped back closer to the window. Feeling along the arm of the deep, overstuffed chair he found his cane. A strange affectation, that cane, for a man on such an errand? Not with Marty Day. That cane, to an outsider only, was part of a gentleman's equipment. To Marty it was a weapon of defense, a weapon of attack, a plain black stick that would pass without comment anyplace. In the hands of Marty Day it was more deadly, certainly more surprising and silent, than a gun in the hands of a desperate man.

Marty reached the window as the footsteps crossed the hall outside the library door. Hastily slipping the envelope for which he had risked his freedom into his jacket pocket, he pushed back the curtains and turned to the slightly raised window he had prepared for a quick retreat.

Marty's breath sucked silently into his lungs as he drew hastily back and dropped the curtains. A man stood almost directly beneath the window. The whiteness of his face was faintly visible in the dull glare of the distant street light. But that dull light showed more to Marty Day. It also shone upon brass buttons, the blue of a uniform. One thing was sure: that silent figure beneath the window was not a city fireman. Marty cursed softly.

He swung suddenly and faced the sudden glare of light above a flat desk, faced also the figure that now stood in the doorway. A heavy-set man, thick-joweled, with smooth soft skin, through which ran thin pencil marks that were really blue veins. The eyes were two, round beady holes, snapping little shoe buttons of grayish brightness, that were both greedy and cold. And Marty faced one more thing, a thing more impressive than that face. The black snub nose of a high-caliber automatic that the man held in stubby but steady fingers.

Those beady little eyes shot quickly from the slits in Marty's mask to the partly open safe, then back to Marty again. Then placing his left hand behind him he closed the door by which he had entered.

"I see you have accomplished your purpose." The man spoke for the first time, and Marty Day was surprised at the calmness of his

Rierson fired as Marty
struck with the cane.

voice. "Now, I must ask you to return to me that envelope. Shall I say 'Before I place a bullet between your eyes'?"

"I don't think you'd do that." Marty tried to make his voice as calm as that of the owner of the house; he also tried to disguise it, speaking deep down in his chest.

"We won't mince words," said the other. "You wanted certain documents that are in that envelope. Since you risked your life to get them I presume you have some idea of their value, at least, to me. If you have, you must realize that I wouldn't hesitate to shoot you to get them. There! Don't come a step nearer."

Marty's body, that was moving forward, settled back—back even closer to the window. "I don't think you'll shoot," he said. "There's a policeman beneath the window. Under certain circumstances, he'd be as dangerous to you as to me."

" 'Certain circumstances'." The owner of the house nodded. "Again, there are policemen and policemen. But we waste time. You know who I am, of course."

"You are," said Marty Day slowly, his voice still husky and forced, "Joseph Ellison Rierson, the unknown quantity in politics." And with a bit of sarcasm which he did not try to hide, "Formerly Joe Rierson, saloon keeper, ward heeler, common thug, gunman, killer."

The big man smiled. "You are not," he said, "very tactful. You will return the envelope at once, or—" The gun raised slightly, the flat nose centering just between Marty's eyes.

"You wouldn't dare." Marty tried to put confidence into his words, a confidence he did not feel.

Broad shoulders shrugged, thick lips parted slightly. "You are very stupid, my friend," Rierson said. "You were caught in the act of robbing my house; attacked me, and I fired in self-defense. With my—shall I say 'influence' in the city, the authorities would find only praise for my act. Now, I'll give you one full minute to decide if you will hand that envelope to me, living, or if I shall take it from your dead body. To be perfectly frank, I'd be rather sorry to kill you."

"Why?" Marty was startled into the question.

"Because I would very much like to know who 'The Reckoner' is."

Marty straightened slightly. He was about to speak when Rierson cut in sharply, his chin shooting forward, his beady eyes snapping.

"I have gotten where I am, Mr. Burglar, by always carrying out a threat—never bluffing." The gun shot forward in his right hand; his huge body moved quickly, placing the long high-polished desk table between himself and Marty as he dropped the flashlight he carried upon the desk. "The minute is up. Place that envelope on the desk—at once."

**THERE** was no threat to kill in his words now. Nothing of the melodramatic in his voice or actions. But Marty read the truth in his eyes, as he had read it in the eyes of other men before. The will to kill—yes, the lust to kill. He was facing death—instant death—and he knew it.

Mechanically, he dropped his cane over his left arm. Mechanically, his right hand slipped slowly into his jacket pocket and just as slowly came out again as those beady eyes watched him and a thick finger tightened upon a trigger.

Marty's tongue licked at dry lips. Then he laid the envelope upon the flat desk. He hated to do it; he didn't want to do it. But there was no other way. He had failed. He had to do it.

A pudgy hand lifted the envelope and placed it carefully in the inner pocket of the gray suit. "Now, my friend, sit down. You will remove your mask."

Marty's hand went slowly to the strip of black which hid his eyes and nose and partially covered his mouth. Then his hand dropped back to his side again. He was seated in a big chair across from Joseph Rierson. His cane was across his knees. The desk was between them, but there was still hope. At least, he liked to think that there was hope.

"Well," Rierson went on, "I could even spare you that, for I think I might guess who you are. You, of course, work for The Reckoner. Whether through fear or for money, or both, I am not sure. I am going to make you a proposition." He jerked his head toward the phone. "Will I turn you over to the police or will you tell me the name of The Reckoner?"

"And suppose I don't know it?"

Again the beady eyes flashed and the lips parted. "I will be the judge of that. But if you name The Reckoner I will let you leave this room masked. I will let you go free."

"You must fear The Reckoner," Marty said. "Remember that; if you turn me in he will strike, and strike hard."

Heavy lips set tightly but trembled slightly at the corners.

"If you know the truth you know that that envelope would not bother me." And then suddenly, "Yes, I do fear him. The very uncertainty of the man! Who is he? A stranger to me? A warped mind who imagines he is righting wrong, dispensing justice? I have seen men go down who were threatened by him. I have seen careers wrecked. Is he an associate who greets me at my office? Is he a friend who meets me at the club? I fear no political enemy, no state investigator, no living man that I know. But this phantom, with his terse warning notes, his fantastic name! He knifes men in the back and follows their ruin with the message—'The Reckoner'." The man was talking quickly now. Marty was surprised at the excitement in his voice, at the vehemence behind the words.

"Tonight was the one night it was necessary for me to have certain papers here. Of course it was not exactly a secret that a meeting of prominent people was to be held at my house. You understand! You understand enough to know that certain papers, certain cancelled checks, perhaps, would influence men who are not fully aware of what is to the best interests of the city."

"To the best interests of you, Mr. Rierson!" Marty cut in.

"Very well. Have it that way. How did The Reckoner know of my plans? Of course, any one of the men might have talked. It was to their best interest not to, but they might have talked. All of them did not arrive in time to have a private talk with me. And tomorrow's papers may have an account of the dinner. My secretary, Miss Cordet, will be here any moment to see to that. We have nothing to hide. But The Reckoner knew the envelope would be in my safe tonight. Mr. Burglar, your liberty depends now on giving me his name."

Beady eyes were twin points of hatred. Marty Day almost gasped at the power of this unknown man, The Reckoner, for whom he worked. He was able to shake even one with Joseph Rierson's standing, influence, political power.

"And if I don't know him?" Marty sparred for time.

"I won't believe you. Don't you see what he means to me? Any minute he may put the finger on me as he has on others. What is he to you? What does he mean to you? Come! Fall in line with me. I'll give you your freedom." Rierson came to his feet.

"Suppose I try to discover who he is. Suppose I—" Marty was watching the man; letting his hands slip from the table onto his knees, his left hand gripping tightly the bottom of the cane close to the ferule; his right hand caressing the curved handle as he flexed the stick slightly.

**JOSEPH RIERSON** shoved back his chair and was around that desk. "I could tear that mask from your face." He fairly shot out the words. "But I'm sparing you that for the moment; saving your identity, that perhaps I can more than guess at."

"What do you mean?" Marty gasped. He had never seen such sudden, animal-like hatred in a man's face before. It hid fear, he thought. Real, gripping fear.

"I mean that I'll satisfy myself of your identity—dead. The Reckoner can't hurt me personally, at least, yet. But he has struck at me through my friends. It has always been said that those with Joseph Rierson behind them are safe. And The Reckoner struck, and a state senator killed himself. That didn't hurt me publicly. No one but myself knew that on the day he died I received a card with a single name on it. Then a police inspector and—and still another went. That hurt. Ate at the very foundation of my influence. I was behind them; the right people knew I was behind them. Now, tonight it was to be several— several who would know that the information which ruined them must have come through me. The Reckoner can't strike at me, so he strikes at the thing I have built up. My friends, my associates, my influence." He paused for breath, his gun shot closer to Marty's head, his thick lips slipped almost into a snarl. "So if I can't strike this Reckoner, I'll strike his associates, his agents. You!"

"Good God!" said Marty, "you're not going to shoot me down in cold blood, like that."

"Just like that!" said Joseph Rierson. "It'll give The Reckoner something to read in the morning papers that may make his coffee taste as bitter as mine has tasted. Now, who is The Reckoner?"

Marty's black eyes widened. He was going to die; he knew it. He thought of his servant, Knight, and wished for a moment that he had brought a gun. He thought of that mysterious, hidden figure who called himself The Reckoner and who gave him his orders in this adventure he had taken up for excitement. Or was it the excitement? Wasn't it the girl; the girl, Tania, who first got him into this? He needed money, of course, and the chance to do good and be paid for it appealed to him. But, after all, wasn't it because of those steady brown eyes, the determined little chin, the straight lips; the girl who had brought him first to The Reckoner? The girl he knew only as

Tania? Thoughts! Yes, like the thoughts of a condemned man. That multitude of kaleidoscopic brain flashes that seem endless, yet are really of a single moment. But one thought was dominant, one thought that overshadowed all the others. He was going to die.

Though both his hands gripped his cane tightly; though, through habit, that cane was now flexed to the beginning of an arc in his two strong hands, he knew it was useless. Beady eyes bored down at him, cruel lips twisted, harsh words came from between wide, uneven teeth.

"Who is The Reckoner?" The gun came closer to Marty's forehead. The left hand stretched out and fat, stubby fingers hooked around the string that held the mask. Another moment now, and the mask would be torn from his face and his identity disclosed. But what did it matter? In another moment he would be dead.

Marty Day did not answer. He could not answer. Sweat broke out on his forehead. He would never see Tania again. He would....

Distinctly from the hall came a dull click, then the slightest thud of a closing door. For the fraction of a second Joseph Rierson's eyes wandered toward the hall. Just a split second, maybe. But in that split second Marty Day acted. His left hand gripped the cane the tighter; his right hand opened, releasing the curved handle. There was a soft, whirring hum. Beady eyes shot back to those of Marty Day.

There was a dull thump as the steel handle of that cane landed flush on the protruding jaw of Joseph Rierson. Beady eyes grew dim and foggy. For a moment, only, there was a surprised hurt look in them. Then Rierson toppled forward, his left hand dragging the mask from Marty's face.

It took Marty only a moment to come to his feet, duck a hand beneath that jacket, remove the tightly bound envelope and let the huge body of Joseph Rierson drape itself across the arm of that chair. Light feet crossed the hall without. A soft, hardly audible rap came upon the library door. Marty quickly stretched up his hand, and loosening the single globe in the light socket plunged the room into darkness.

## CHAPTER TWO

# THE CURTAIN OF STEEL

**T**HE FOOTSTEPS in the hall were light, the knock on the door was hardly more than a scratch. It was a woman, Marty thought. It was the secretary, Miss Cordet, of whom Rierson had spoken.

That knock was not repeated. The knob turned softly, the latch clicked, and Marty felt rather than heard the door open. Then footsteps crossed the room—slow careful steps, but steps familiar with the library. And as those feet moved, Marty moved. He would not leave by the front way, as the girl had come. The policeman made that too dangerous. He would go through the kitchen, across the rear yard and over the fence, to the yard behind. Marty knew his way. He had a plan of the house. It was stamped in his mind now as he moved toward the door and safety.

The lamp clicked and there was a little gasp, but there was no light. Then the thud of a body hitting the floor, a dull groan, and the voice of Joseph Rierson. "Good God! What happened? He's gone."

The girl must have found the flash upon the desk, for light splashed across the floor, fell almost at once on the misty eyes of Rierson. And the girl screamed. The light came up with a swift jerk, and as Marty looked back into that room it shone full upon his face.

"It's he, and he's got the envelope," Rierson shrieked, and then, "No mask, no mask. I have it here. I saw his face. I saw his face. But it was blurred, indistinct. Miss Cordet, you saw him too. You saw him too?"

What the girl answered Marty did not know. He was darting through the dining-room. He struck his side against a chair, but a dull light through the window showed him the pantry door, and he knew that a step or two away was the kitchen door.

Marty was down the back steps when the library window went up and Rierson shouted to the policeman. He was across the rear court and swinging onto a wooden fence when the heavy feet reached the back of the house. He heard the shout to halt, Rierson's cry for the man to shoot, and then the roar of the heavy police automatic.

A splinter of wood left the top of the fence and bit in between

Marty's fingers. Then he dropped to the stone yard behind, dashed across it and along the alley to the street beyond.

A window went up; a man called hoarsely. There was another shot and the window slammed shut again. Marty was on the sidewalk, running down it around the next corner and to the car he had parked there. But he didn't breathe easily until he had slipped from second into high and had joined the few cars that formed the late traffic on Fifth Avenue.

His brain began to work. He told himself that he was safe, then argued it out that he wasn't. Rierson had not seen him plainly. He had cried out that he hadn't, and Marty could believe it as he glanced down at the cane beside him. To Rierson, his face would have been just a blurred whiteness. As to his voice—well, he faked that in the beginning. Had he forgotten later to disguise it? He grinned and thought not. Caution had started that voice deep down in his throat, but fear had kept it there.

And the girl? Had she seen him? And if she had, would she ever be likely to see him again? No. And he frowned. Rierson had hinted that he guessed who Marty might be. Lord knows he had seen Marty enough. They lunched at the same club very often; there was some distance between their favorite tables though. But Marty wouldn't have known Rierson, remembered him at all, had not The Reckoner told him to watch him, study him.

There was enough scandal about Rierson. But that was in the past. If, as very often was the case around election, some tabloid hinted that Rierson had killed men back in the old days, there was no proof. Plenty of accusations against him, but never any evidence, for Joseph Rierson had never been in prison. That he had ordered men killed, had even killed men himself before he became so prominent, was underworld knowledge.

Rierson had influence. It was said that, unless the crime was too much in the public eye, Joseph Rierson could even spring a man arrested for murder.

**BUT** the girl, the secretary! Had she seen Marty's face? Marty thought not, or he hoped not. She had picked up the flash. It splashed its light almost at once upon the foggy eyes of Rierson. Then she had cried out and involuntarily raised that flash. It was simply an accident that it shone directly on Marty's face. Only a second it was there, and he was gone. Now, had the girl's eyes followed the flash, or had she simply stared unseeingly down at the crouched figure of her boss, on the floor?

And the answer to that question Marty didn't know for sure. But he felt that he was safe. It was logical to believe that her eyes had not followed the sudden upward jerk of the flash.

A block from his destination, well downtown, Marty stopped the car. Switching on the little dashlight he took the envelope from his pocket and slipped off the elastic band. Memorandums, some of the papers. Quick, sharp sentences with figures; a city contractor's name beside that of a public official, and the amount of the graft paid. Nothing to go on there, Marty thought. No proof. A disappointment for The Reckoner in that. Joseph Rierson must have used it simply as a reminder that he could produce proof if he wished. But here and there were one or two notes to work on. Then, there were a couple of cancelled checks. Though made out to bearer, one was endorsed by a well-known magistrate.

Marty whistled softly. Insidious graft, when it begins to lifts its head cautiously, doesn't take long to grow brazenly defiant. There were a few more notes; one with the name of a man Marty had thought beyond reproach. He was just about to study it under the tiny light when a voice spoke close to his ear.

"I don't think he'd fancy that much." And when Marty looked up startled, the girl laughed, then added: "And I don't think I'll tell him."

The girl was tall and dark, and in the dim light Marty thought, very beautiful. But though her eyes shone and sparkled with youth, there was something cold about them; something perhaps almost sinister. For a moment Marty had thought that it was Tania. Then he laughed. The comparison was absurd.

"Who are you?" He slipped the envelope back into his pocket.

"I'm here to save you a trip." She held out her hand. "Direct from—" and she lowered her voice to almost a whisper—"The Reckoner. Give me the envelope."

"But I can't do that." Marty picked up his cane and opened the car door. "I don't know you—and can't trust you."

"I know you," she said. "Marty Day. I knew where you were to stop the car, and at about what time. Besides," she indicated her bag, "I can pay you."

Marty stepped from the car and reaching out a hand fastened it on the hand that was holding the bag. "Don't open that bag," he said.

"Why?" She laughed. "What do you think is in it?"

"I don't know." Marty looked steadily at her. "Maybe money. Maybe a gun."

"The second guess is right." She jerked herself free and stepped back a pace. Her movement was quick as a panther—but not quicker than the movement of Marty's cane.

She stood looking at him, her eyes wide; her mouth opened in amazement as Marty unhooked the bag from around the curved handle of his cane, and opening it took out a small automatic.

"The second guess was right," he said, looking at her. "Now what?"

"Now I'll go with you to—to him." She came close and hooked an arm through Marty's. "It was simply a test. You're very strong, aren't you?" This as his fingers bit into her wrist and Marty held her in a viselike grip.

"Very strong!" he said. "You'll lead the way, of course."

"Of course." She mimicked the emphasis in his voice. And without another word she guided him down the street

**MARTY** knew the little pawnshop well. The entrance on the Avenue; the door on the side street. Now, without the least hesitation, the girl led him past the front of the shop, around to the side entrance and quickly into the vestibule. In the darkness she looked up at Marty, and he thought that she smiled.

"Convinced now?" she asked.

"Who are you? I never heard of you."

"There are a lot of things and a lot of people you never heard of. But don't worry. I like you." And after a moment's pause, "Women would like you, I guess. I am the only person who does not fear The—him." She jerked a small white hand toward the inner door.

"I don't fear him," Marty told her.

"No," she said. "But you will. You're young; you need money. To you it's all a glorious adventure."

"What manner of man is he?" Marty almost whispered the words.

"He's not a man. That is, not in the human sense. He's an idea—a living idea. A mind with just a single thought, and without a body. Some day maybe he'll realize he has a body, and then—" She shook slightly, Marty thought. "But there!" She tapped quickly on the inner door.

Almost at once the door opened. A bent little figure peered through thick glasses at Marty and the girl. The girl nodded as the little figure bowed low and rubbed his hands ingratiatingly.

Marty hesitated when the girl turned toward the street. But he let her go and stepped into the dimly lit hall beyond. The door closed at once, a heavy chain thudded into a bolt, the bent figure straightened slightly.

"He's expecting you," the old man said. "You know the way. No tricks, mind you."

"No." Marty smiled down at that lined face. "I know what to do."

He walked to the left of the stairs, along a narrow hallway. To his right was an open door which led to the rear room of the shop. A heavy iron curtain cut off this room from the shop itself. There was a huge safe in the corner, a barred and shuttered window across the room. But Marty didn't notice these things. He closed the door softly behind him. He knew that the key was in the lock on the outside of the door and resisted the temptation he always had to remove that key before entering the room.

It was the counter at the rear of the room that held his attention. It was an ordinary counter for customers who wanted to do business with the owner of the pawnshop without being seen from the street, or by casual purchasers or clients. But after business hours no hard-visaged face looked up from that counter and assured you that eighteen dollars was the very limit that could be given on such an article.

Now a steel curtain ran from the ceiling to the top of that counter, so that the room behind was shut off with thick wood and thin steel. Although Marty had not visited the shop often and only once before, alone, he knew exactly what to do. Yet, as he did it he got the same thrill; the same feeling of approaching evil as he did the very first night Tania had brought him there, and The Reckoner had looked him over and spoken to him.

Funny, that sense of evil, when everything that The Reckoner did was good; for the good of others. Yet it was there just the same. An eery, cold feeling, though the room was always too warm.

Marty walked to the chair that was pushed close to the paneled wood of the counter, below the curtain of steel. He sat down in it and looked straight at the grayness of steel. Soon it would move. Then—

There was the dull click of a key being turned in the door behind him—the door he had just entered. His body stiffened. That always happened just before The Reckoner appeared. Appeared! Marty smiled to himself.

The light went out. A moment of darkness, and then the slow creak of moving steel. A section of the thin curtain was moving back. Marty riveted his eyes on the spot that sound came from, but he could see nothing. Always, he could see nothing. When the moment came that his eyes seemed to be used to the darkness and he felt that he saw a slowly widening hole, the whiteness of a face behind finely meshed wire—it happened.

THERE was a dull click and the sudden stab of light. The small brass desk light on the edge of the counter, before the curtain, shone directly on Marty's face. To look at it meant temporary blindness. Not to look at it meant not to look at the opening in the steel where the voice of The Reckoner would come from.

So Marty blinked his eyes and looked straight ahead, at the iron-shuttered window. There was a soft cough, and The Reckoner spoke.

"You have visited Rierson and returned with the envelope?" a metallic voice asked. And that voice was always a shock to Marty. There was nothing natural about it, no attempt to make it sound natural. It might be a man's, it might be a woman's, it might he the voice of a child. It sounded exactly like the cracked voice on a dicta-phone record that was speeded up too high.

"Yes." Marty wet his lips before he spoke. "I have the envelope. Here!" He raised his hand, laid the envelope on the narrow ledge, hesitated a moment, then took his hand away.

Almost fascinated, he watched the envelope upon the counter. The lights blazed and burnt into his eyes, and still he watched the blue envelope dance before his watery orbs. He couldn't help it. His eyes were glued there. And they came. The groping fingers; the hand that seemed a pinkish red, with skin that shone, skin that seemed to be so tightly drawn over the bones that there was not a wrinkle or a crevice, or even a line on its glossy surface. That always puzzled Marty. It was unreal, unnatural. Uncanny, even. But he explained it as an illusion caused by his burning, water-filled eyes.

"All right." The metallic voice came again. "This package is yours. You've done well." And as Marty stretched up his hand and lifted the tightly bound flat thickness of bills from the counter, "Ten thousand dollars. I pay well, Mr. Day. I like your work. I shall make you a rich man again." And suddenly, in even a quicker rasp, "Did anything untoward happen? Were you suspected or seen?"

Marty Day's tongue again moistened his lips; then he told everything that had happened. Before he had finished his story he heard fingers drumming lightly on the wood behind the steel curtain.

When he stopped, The Reckoner said: "Rierson didn't recognize you, of course. If he suspects who you were, he cannot be certain. If his suspicions are correct, then you favored him with too much attention at the Empire Club. But he is far from certain of your identity, else he would have cried out your name. Still, you have your alibi. Frederick Strome is an eminent banker. His life is blameless." And with a slight emphasis, Marty thought, "Publicly blameless. Your lawyer is Max Arnold. Tomorrow, lunch as usual at the Empire Club. Have absolute confidence in me. If you should be arrested on Rierson's guess, you will be released so quickly that there will be no time to question you—forcibly. You are too valuable a man for me to lose."

"But the girl—the secretary! It's her identification that I fear."

"You may dismiss the girl from your mind. Your conclusion that her eyes did not follow the flash is correct. She would have spoken then. There, there! The question of the girl is no longer debatable. Is there anything else?"

"Yes." Marty set his lips tightly. "It's Tania. She brought me into this—this business of yours. It's partly because of her that I— I have not seen her lately."

The Reckoner laughed. At least Marty thought it was a laugh.

"You will dine with her tomorrow night at the Café Madrid. Eight o'clock. She will be there on time. You are fond of the girl—in love with her, Mr. Day?"

"I—I am interested in her," Marty answered.

"Of course. Of course. Never commit yourself regarding a woman. She is the type that would appeal to you temporarily. You are a valuable man to me—a very valuable man. Continue to be so. It is quite possible that your reward may be Tania."

"I think," said Marty stiffly, "that will be between Tania and me. Things must be as she wishes."

"Tania will do as I wish—as I say." And as Marty would have cut in, "Remember that, Mr. Day. There can be no wish in the life of Tania or in the life of anyone whom I use, but the wish of The Reckoner. I tolerate no decisions. Only service."

Hot, angry words flowed to Marty's lips. But he did not speak them. There was a dull click as the steel curtain closed. Blackness for a moment, and again the single dim light from the ceiling. Then the ringing of a bell, a telephone bell in another room.

## CHAPTER THREE

## ALIBI

**M**ARTY DAY came quickly to his feet and swung toward the single door. But he did not reach it. With a shrug of his shoulders he dropped back in his chair again. It would be a full five minutes before the key turned in that lock. It always was.

But this time it wasn't a full five minutes; hardly more than two minutes when the lock clicked and the door flew open. The little old man fairly burst into the room.

"You're to go at once, sir. The car to take you is down the street. Your own is on its way to your garage. Make speed."

Marty didn't stop to argue. Something had happened. He didn't know what. But it was something that put him in danger. The door being unlocked so quickly. That telephone call!

But he was out the door, down the street toward that shining, expensive roadster parked by the curb. A white hand waved to him; a motor raced, and he jumped in the open door.

The car was off, almost bounding from the curb.

"What's wrong? Oh! it's you." Marty recognized the woman beside him. She was the girl of the bag—the gun. Queer, amber-colored eyes flashed at him for a moment as she took the corner, skidded dangerously, missed a taxi by inches, and straightening out went dashing uptown.

"The police!" she said. "But I think we can beat them. You see, Rierson telephoned a friend in the department. He couldn't chance a direct accusation because he doesn't know for sure. But the captain from your precinct will check up on you tonight; whether you were in all evening or not. That means that Rierson's guessing. You've apparently got money. You've got a good lawyer; you're a respectable citizen, and they won't take chances.... Damn! That was close."

The car swerved, struck the curb, righted itself and sped on. Looking back, Marty saw the white face of a man they had almost struck.

"You must be pretty close to The Reckoner." There was half a question, half a statement in Marty's voice.

The girl did not answer at once. Then, with a straight stretch of clear road ahead of them, she turned her head slightly and said: "Yes. So close that sometimes it strikes me with terror."

After that there was a silence. But Marty was thinking. The Reckoner had built up a great system. It must cost a tremendous sum to keep it going. Certainly he was a very wealthy man. There was the garage, owned or controlled by The Reckoner. To Marty, just an ordinary place to park his car. But he knew that if the police inquired, they would be informed that his car had not left its place tonight; that Marty had not come to the garage. An expense that—a big city garage? Marty didn't know. It appeared to do a good business. Then there was the cheap, walk-up flat building behind his own pretentious twenty-two story apartment. Did The Reckoner own that, or—

And they shot by the front door of Marty Day's apartment. Marty drew well back in the seat, but the broad back of the man who was talking so earnestly to the doorman never turned. Yet Marty knew the man. It was Captain Geary, of the police.

Calls were pretty close tonight. Had the captain been upstairs and just come down, or had he just arrived? Would he question the doorman before or after visiting Marty's apartment? Marty shrugged his shoulders. That question would be answered as soon as he looked across at Knight's window. For Knight was the most trusted servant a man ever had.

The car rounded the corner, then another, and drew up near the walk-up apartment on the block behind.

"Good luck!" the girl said as Marty jumped from the car. "I like you, Marty Day. If you're ever in a real jam, come to me. And my gun?"

Marty hesitated, then thrust the tiny automatic into her hand.

THE CAR was gone. Marty dashed through the apartment door and was speeding up the stairs. Five floors he raced, stuck a key in a rear apartment, pushed open the door, breathed a sigh of relief that he had met no one in the hall, and closing the door softly passed into a bedroom.

A moment later he flung up a window and looked across at the red brick wall of his own apartment house, towering far above him. Here and there dark blotches of windows broke the blank brick, and an occasional lighted one stood out like a beacon at sea.

But just one window, a window that was in darkness, held Marty's attention. It was perhaps six or seven feet across from him and two feet above his head. That window was in Knight's bedroom. Marty's eyes searched for the long black bar that would be stretched before it on heavy iron supports. It was the bar that Knight put in place when Marty took these midnight excursions of—well, adventure Marty liked to call it. Yes, he was an adventurer and, as he felt for a moment the flat package of bills in his pocket, a professional adventurer.

Just one quick glance Marty cast down in the narrow alley between those two buildings. The home of the rich and the home of the poor. The one facing a wide and beautiful thoroughfare; the other, the humble unassuming block behind. But, like the rich and the poor of a great city, almost rubbing shoulders.

No dark figure stood in the shadows below; no white face was turned upward. One more glance Marty took across at his own window—the length of the bar standing well out from it. Then jamming his felt hat down on his head, buttoning his jacket tightly about him and gripping his strong flexible steel cane in his right hand, he swung quickly and silently onto that window ledge.

The strong and well-clamped but unused awning rod gave him his support as he closed the window behind him. Then cautiously straightening himself, his back pressed against that window, he faced the red brick of his own apartment across from him. But he didn't see that building. He saw nothing but the black round bar standing dimly visible far out before the darkened window of Knight's bedroom.

Marty Day stiffened upon that narrow window ledge, both his hands stretched far above his head, his cane clasped tightly in them, the curved handle moving slowly and cautiously out toward that iron bar. For a moment he hovered perilously above the yawning gap that meant death five stories below him.

His eyes riveted upon that black horizontal bar; his body moved slowly forward, his feet still planted firmly upon that narrow stone ledge. When it seemed he would pitch straight to his death, the curved handle of that cane caught the bar, and Marty's body swung easily and gracefully toward the red brick of his own huge building.

For a moment, only, Marty hung suspended in the air, his two hands tightly gripping his cane. Then hand over hand, he climbed up that cane, his feet straight out below him; his body hardly swaying in the air.

An upward stretch of his left hand, and he gripped that bar. He released the cane with his right hand, and with a lunge sent it into the room through the open window. Then, with the easy grace of one long familiar with the horizontal bar, he swung himself up and through that window.

Knight was in the room almost the moment Marty was. He spoke, his words catching in his throat.

"The police!" he said. "They're on their way up." Then he went directly to the window. Rapidly and familiarily Knight worked. In less than a minute the bar that had been before that window was now holding a curtain across a small alcove in Knight's bedroom. The side braces that had held it were clamped firmly in place above the legs at the foot of Knight's specially constructed bed.

"Mr. Strome is here?" Marty paused as he stepped into the long hall which led from Knight's bedroom to the living-room in front.

"At the table. There've been thirteen moves to this game. You lost a rook and a bishop and—" Knight stopped. The private doorbell of Marty's apartment rang sharply.

"It won't be as close as that." Marty smiled. "Go to the door at once, Knight." He tossed his hat onto the costumer in the hall, and dropping his cane in a corner entered the living-room.

"Ah! good evening, Mr. Strome. I'm sorry to have kept you waiting. I see. I'm the white, and the move is yours."

MARTY dropped quickly into the chair opposite the corpulent, bald-headed man who drummed noisily upon the table, almost upsetting the chess men that had been removed from the board. When he spoke there was a huskiness to his voice that was not assumed.

"I hope," he said, "that I have not let myself in for anything—anything criminal. Before, there never was any trouble."

"I don't know the reason you favor me with an alibi, Mr. Strome," Marty said coldly. "I presume that it is a good and sufficient reason to you. This is the first time you have been called upon to play your part. If it will ease your mind—you are with the law, but the law doesn't know it." Marty grinned. "Ah! The cigar I have been smoking." He quickly lit the half-smoked cigar as voices came from the hall.

Marty Day raised the half-filled glass of Scotch and soda, took a sip, let the ice cubes clink against the side of the glass, and looked up as Captain Geary entered the room.

The police captain smiled broadly at Marty Day and said: "Sorry to disturb you, Mr. Day, but—" He stopped dead as Frederick Strome turned his head. "Ah! Good evening, Mr. Strome. A game of chess, I see. Play a bit myself. He studied the board for a moment, and then, "Been here quite a while?"

"Most of the evening." Strome's thick eyebrows rose slightly, but the steady cold eyes of the banker remained unmoved. Then, "Why?"

Marty frowned, then smiled. After all, Strome's question was a natural one.

Captain Geary grinned. "Four ears are better than two, I suppose. Don't want to alarm you, but there's been trouble in the building." And with a laugh, "Maybe not exactly trouble, but queer-looking people in the house—seen in the hall. Haven't been disturbed, have you?"

"No." Marty's expression had just the correct amount of interest. "Didn't hear anything. Who made the complaint?"

"A couple of tenants, I think." Captain Geary dismissed Marty's question. "High-class house, high-class people. Expect high-class police protection." He scratched his head and laughed. "Doorman said you were still up, Mr. Day. Thought I'd look around."

"Very considerate. You'll have a drink, Captain?"

The captain eyed the bottle upon the table, hesitated a moment, and then: "No, no. I think not. Might have to talk to some long-nose. You didn't hear a scream, Mr. Strome—and you've been here all evening?"

"That's right," said Frederick Strome. "All evening. Still—" he nodded toward the chess board. "If you play the game—"

"Sure. Sure. Well, I'll be going along." He picked up the Scotch and tilted the bottle, holding it before the light. "If you were to ask me again, Mr. Day, I mightn't say 'No.'"

"I won't corrupt the department." Marty grinned. "But there's ice and a glass on the stand."

Captain Geary turned. A minute or two later he placed the bottle back on the table, held a half-filled glass in his hand, whirling ice around in a swinging motion.

"May you never see the back of your necks, gentlemen," he said. He tossed off the liquor, coughed once, then rubbed the back of his hand across his mouth. "See you some more." He smiled cheerily. "Don't worry about my visit. Probably some dame with a nightmare." Then he turned and pounded heavily from the apartment.

"Captain Geary," said Frederick Strome, getting up abruptly from the table, "is an honest, efficient officer. You wouldn't try to make me believe that he is corrupt! He came here to see if you were home. That's it, isn't it?"

"I presume," said Marty, "that is it. And I wouldn't try to make you believe anything, Mr. Strome." And as Strome prepared to make his usual speech, "And I wouldn't try to make you explain anything. You have told me that an unknown friend helped you out in a very delicate matter and you are most graciously returning that kindness by coming here. Neither one of us has anything to explain to the other. We see too little of each other. Good night."

**STROME** took his hat and stick from Knight, puckered up his lips once or twice and made queer noises. But he was at the door before he spoke.

"I have no intention of offending you, Mr. Day. None at all. I'm quite sure our mutual friend would not— Well, I am sure that nothing unpleasant could happen."

"Such words from a banker!" Marty nodded his good night. "Surely you know that nothing can be certain in life; nothing but death and taxes." He closed the door, spun the key in the lock, and seeing his cane picked it up and carried it into the living-room.

"Everything all right, sir? A close call tonight—very close." Knight followed him into the room, his eyes fastened on the cane. "You'll keep the cane, sir?"

"Always." Marty balanced the stick along his fingers. Then suddenly, like a military officer giving a command, "Twenty feet, Knight. Attention! Eyes closed; arm extended—and keep those eyes closed tight. I need no help now. I'm back in my old form. So—"

Marty rested the cane upon the floor, placed the fingers of his right hand upon the curved handle, lifted those fingers suddenly, and the cane sprang like a living thing across that twenty feet and dropped almost gently against Knight's chest, the curved handle slipping itself around his folded arm.

"Just an illusion, done with mirrors!" Marty said, as Knight opened his eyes and grinned his appreciation. "Bred from the finest steel in Sheffield, made in Sicily and finally educated in Algiers. It's the flexibility of the thin outside steel that does the trick, though Martinia, who made it, is sure that it is the coils of heavy steel inside. But the heavy coils, that seem to act as a spring, I had Martinia put there for the weight. Damn it! Knight, you must bow to my stick as superior to the gun. It does everything but talk. You've been worrying about me too much lately. Sometimes, Knight, I think you're getting old."

Knight looked at Marty Day. "You make me feel that way, sir. On the continent you took me with you. In Algiers you—"

"Surely, Knight, you're not going to desert me. When the time comes I know you'll be ready."

"Always, sir." Knight straightened. "Even to murder. I want it like the old days, when it was 'Day and Knight.'"

And before he fell asleep Marty thought of the servant who had been with him now close to five years. Marty had met him on the streets of London; met him for the first time when he looked down the black nose of Knight's gun and listened to his gruff command to "fork over your money." The cane had won then, sending the gun flying from Knight's hand and breaking two of the small bones in his fingers. Since then— Well, Marty was glad that he had not followed his first inclination to turn the man over to the police.

Other thoughts, too. Disturbing thoughts. Joseph Rierson suspected him all right. But he could not be sure. Yet he had sent, or arranged to have sent, Captain Geary to see if Marty were home.

But as Marty Day slept, one thought overshadowed all others. He was going to see Tania again.


## CHAPTER FOUR

## A CASE OF IDENTITY

MARTY DAY was quite conscious of the big flat-footed man who took the table directly opposite and studiously avoided looking at him. It was Lieutenant Frank Bradley, of the detective bureau. Occasionally Marty glanced over pis paper and saw the detective's eyes drop to his plate. Bradley, he knew, was a hard, grim, unimaginative hunter of men. But he was honest, like the great majority of men in the city's gigantic police system.

Rierson was doing the thing right then. He was going to have Marty arrested. He had not been fooled by the elaborate alibi Marty had prepared. But would the judge, would the jury be influenced by it? And Marty began to be apprehensive of the results. He wished now that he had called up Max Arnold. But that was only a precaution. He had never met Arnold, though he knew him as one of the most successful, if not the most brilliant, criminal lawyers in the city.

But where was Rierson? Surely he would be there. Marty looked over at Rierson's usual table. It was unoccupied.

Then Rierson came. He walked easily across the dining-room and sat down in the chair beside the lieutenant. The conversation, at least Rierson's end of it, was in a loud voice. Marty knew that he was meant to hear it. While Rierson talked he grinned over at Marty, and Lieutenant Bradley studied him with hard, steady, unemotional eyes.

"No!" said Rierson, as if continuing a conversation he had left off shortly before. "I turned my head and the man struck me. His hand, I think. He didn't have time to get out a blackjack. So, of course, where I can't be positive of his identity, I think that I know the man. Anyway, you have talked to my secretary. She looked straight at the man's face. She had never seen him before. But she would know him again, beyond a doubt."

"If she points him out, that's that," Lieutenant Bradley said. And in a lower voice, "I wouldn't lay it on too thick. He might not be the man. Contrary to general opinion, crooks don't go around looking like crooks, and they can't be startled into sudden guilty looks. You may be wrong. You don't want trouble over it."

"I may be wrong, but Miss Cordet can't be. The light was directly on his face. Excuse me! There's Mr. Day." Rierson rose suddenly and came over to Marty's table. He stretched out his hand. Marty regarded that flabby hand with its thick stubby fingers a moment, then with a shrug let it grasp his.

"I've neglected you, Mr. Day," Rierson explained as he leaned over the table. "Seen you here many times and often thought of speaking to you. One should be more clubby. I know the Empire doesn't go in for that sort of thing, but it should—it should. I have had a narrow escape from death. A burglar attacked me last night." He leaned even closer. "Do you know, Mr. Day, I suspect—perhaps more than suspect that he is in this club." He jerked a thick finger back over his shoulder. "That's a detective at the table with me."

"And why am I indebted to you for this confidence?" Marty was coldly attentive. He didn't know what was coming.

"A question of ethics, Mr. Day. You're a man of the world. If you were attacked by the hireling of a dangerous international menace, would you give that hireling his freedom for the return of the valuables stolen and the name of the man who hired him?"

"I'm sure I don't know," said Marty. "Would you?"

"Surely. Surely. My secretary is in the lounge now. She saw this prowler who attacked me; looked directly into his face. She has assured me that, beyond a doubt, she would recognize him. Indeed, that his features are distinctive. Like yours, Mr. Day."

**"REALLY!"** Involuntarily Marty glanced toward the side door. He knew now how a professional crook must feel when cornered. The inclination to jump from the table, drive his fist straight against those sneering thick lips and dash for freedom was there. But even before he saw the broad shoulders of the detective, in the doorway, he decided against that move. Maybe it was Rierson's purpose to talk him into a panic. No. There was nothing to do but sit tight and wait for the girl's identification. Maybe Rierson's talk of the girl seeing him was bluff. He'd brazen it out.

"Well," Rierson said suddenly, "what would you do?"

"I hope," said a high-pitched, squeaky-voice behind Marty, "that I'm not intruding. Good afternoon, Mr. Day. Good afternoon, Mr. Rierson." A damp hand clutched Marty's; a sharp face with close-set eyes that seemed to look off the end of a beaklike nose was between Marty and Rierson. Then a tall, lanky figure dropped into the seat across from Marty.

"Ah!" Rierson's teeth bit into a thick lower lip. "Mr. Arnold. Max Arnold."

"If you're asking Mr. Day's advice on financial matters, you couldn't have come to a better man," Max Arnold, the criminal lawyer, went on. "A week ago, Mr. Rierson, I'd have laughed at you. Which all means, Mr. Day—"narrow eyes twinkled; thin rips parted—"that you were right about those bonds. I bought them today at that ridiculous figure you offered. That explains why I'm late for lunch. There, there! Mr. Rierson, don't leave us. We have no business to discuss. Just a luncheon in celebration. Mr. Day has made a shrewd investment."

"No business to discuss!" Beady eyes were bright buttons as Rierson snapped out the words. "Well, I have. I want Mr. Day to meet a friend of mine."

In a daze Marty knew that Rierson had stepped aside, that Lieutenant Bradley was coming slowly toward his table. He knew, too, that Max Arnold had laid a hand upon the table, the fingers of which had touched his wrist for a moment and pressed against it. He felt that narrow eyes were on him, warning eyes. This was the moment. How would he act? Would he look guilty? Over and over to himself Marty repeated the words he would speak—must speak.

"I'm afraid the young lady is mistaken. I never saw her before." Then, should he become indignant if a direct accusation were made, or should he laugh at the absurdity of the accusation—the arrest? Did Rierson intend to make it a public disgrace? Would they all adjourn quietly to one of the private rooms, to the lounge even, or—or—

Marty didn't look up. He heard the light steps; even felt the presence of the woman. She must have come through the side door then, the door which led to the billiard-room and—

Rierson was speaking. "Mr. Day, I want you to meet my secretary, Miss Cordet. I think—I think you have met before."

**MARTY DAY** came slowly to his feet. He wondered if the hands he placed upon the table trembled. He did not look at them. Those hard eyes of Lieutenant Bradley were focussed on his face. He felt them rather than saw them. And then he slowly turned his head. A woman was there—a girl.

"You're quite mistaken, Mr. Rierson." The girl's voice was low and steady. "I never saw Mr.—this gentleman before."

"Not—not last night?" Marty could have laughed at the hurt, surprised, almost amazed note in Rierson's voice. But he didn't. He raised his eyes and looked straight into the soft brown eyes of the girl as she spoke again.

"I'm sorry, but this is not the—that man. I never saw him before in my life."

Marty Day gulped. He was looking straight at the face of Tania.

Tania, who— And he knew the truth. Tania was Miss Cordet. Tania, who worked for The Reckoner, was Joseph Rierson's secretary.

How had he taken it? He knew that he bowed stiffly and said something. He knew that Max Arnold had him by the arm and was talking. He was saying something about all lunching together, calling to a waiter, pointing out a larger table in the center of the room.

Joseph Rierson was stammering. He started to speak to the girl, thought better of it and turned to Marty. There was an apology in his voice, a nervous laugh.

"No, no. The fact of the matter is, I've made a grave mistake, a very grave mistake. Mr. Day reminded me of someone I met—had business with years back. Nothing to Mr. Day's discredit, of course. Just thought he could tell me something about a certain party. A—a—" and again the nervous laugh. "He's travelled a great deal, I understand. You'll excuse me."

And that was all. They were gone. Twice Rierson looked over his shoulder before he reached the main room that led to the lounge. He was holding Tania's arm, talking to her in a low voice. At the door the three paused. Bradley was coming back. Without a word he dropped into the seat at his table and tackled the steak he had left. Distinctly Marty heard him tell the waiter to bring hot coffee. And he understood. The hunting of men was Bradley's business. Because a mistake had been made was no reason why it should interfere with his lunch.

"Very good. Very good indeed." Max Arnold was talking as he and Marty took chairs opposite each other. "Just the right amount of surprise and amazement under the circumstances. But, there! Lieutenant Bradley has big ears. We are to lunch together, by appointment. You have travelled extensively, Mr. Day; I have seen some of the world. We might even perhaps interest each other."

Max Arnold talked and Marty listened. He didn't know much about the man, except that he had come up from the streets of the East Side. Now, he spoke of the great cities of the world with the same familiarity as he spoke of his own. Charming little villages of Normandy—secluded spots of the Orient—hidden, dangerous resorts of Paris—unknown rendezvous in London, that Marty had entered only through Knight.

"It isn't as if I had spent my life traveling and searching for little-frequented spots," Max Arnold explained. "You see, I have friends, peculiar friends, who were once only clients. I could step on a boat in New York today and within the week be in places in Paris that even the great French Surete do not suspect. A quick trip across to London, and in a single night I could startle Scotland Yard by the names of the people I have talked to."

When they rose to go, long after Lieutenant Bradley had left, Marty realized that, after Max Arnold's few remarks as to his actions, he had not once spoken of the reason he was there. Nor had any hint of the name of The Reckoner crossed his lips.

## CHAPTER FIVE

## AT THE CAFÉ MADRID

**T**HE CAFÉ MADRID did its best to look prosperous despite the small crowd and the absence of open drinking and the former well-filled pails of ice on the tables. There was now a *table d'hote* dinner and a gorgeous array of unpaid talent. The Café Madrid was hanging on by its teeth.

Marty looked up from his table, far in the rear of the room, every time a woman swept through the entrance. Ten minutes after eight, and Tania had not arrived. The Reckoner had said she would be on time, and The Reckoner was always right. Twice Marty snapped out his watch. Eight-fifteen, and no Tania! Wasn't she coming? Had The Reckoner changed his mind? Had something detained the girl? Had—

And Marty's eyes stayed on the entrance to the dining-room. The broad figure of a man stood in the doorway. Beady eyes searched rapidly about the room, flashed by Marty, hesitated and swept quickly back to him again. Lips parted and Joseph Rierson walked quickly down the length of the room.

Involuntarily Marty's hand slipped from the table and rested upon the handle of the cane which he always carried. Then his fingers relaxed and came back to the table again. There was no doubt of it. Joseph Rierson was coming straight to his table.

And Tania! She would come. Rierson would see her, would— As the thought flashed through Marty's head, Rierson pulled out the chair across from him and sank his huge bulk slowly into it.

"This table," said Marty, coldly, "is already engaged."

"I know, I know." A huge hand, with great blue veins running back from the knuckles, drummed softly upon the table. "I wanted to talk to you, Mr. Day. I wanted to apologize to you for my conduct at the Empire Club this noon. I think we should better understand each other."

"But I'm expecting company now." Marty was trying to decide the best thing to do. Tania should be warned. A note with the girl in the ladies' dressing-room! Marty was half on his feet when that hand moved from the table and settled on his wrist.

"What I have to say, Mr. Day, will be very much to your interest, and to the interest of another. Sit down. I can assure you we won't be disturbed." There was certainty, almost a finality in Rierson's words— and perhaps a warning, Marty thought. But though the lips were parted in a smile, the beady eyes were hard, with a gray coldness.

What did Rierson mean? What could he mean? But Marty dropped back into the chair as Rierson talked, leaned forward on the table, waving the waiter away and seeming to choose his words carefully.

"I was so sure, Mr. Day, that you were the man who visited me last night, stole some important papers and—well, struck me on the chin, that I planned to have you arrested by an officer whose honesty could not be questioned. And what would that gain me, you think? How would I recover the documents you had stolen? Simple. If I could make a charge, I could also withdraw that charge for a return of that envelope.

"Now, those papers did not, on the face of them, affect me personally. Not one of the men that they would—er—embarrass, could possibly harm me. Of course, there was my pride in protecting my friends. But there was more than that. Those friends formed the foundation of an influence, a power that I have built up over the years. When you destroy a foundation, Mr. Day, you weaken, of course, the structure it supports. And to the extent which you destroy that foundation, to that extent do you weaken the—"

"Why do you tell me all this?" Marty glanced over that huge head with its flabby jaws and blue-veined cheeks. But no woman stood in the entrance.

"I tell you all this, Mr. Day, so that you may realize what importance I attach to those papers, and to what length I would go to have them returned, or to what length I might go to retaliate on those who caused my loss. Are you beginning to understand me?"

"I am afraid not." Marty tried to make his voice indifferent.

**RIERSON** went on, those beady eyes fastened on Marty's now. "You see, I was quite surprised and perhaps somewhat chagrined when my secretary, Miss Cordet, did not identify you at the club today. She saw your face last night. Yes, your face, Mr. Day! She told me she would know the man again. I thought I had recognized your voice. I had noted the attention with which you favored me at the club; I had often seen you stroll by my house. But when she refused to identify you, I thought for the moment that I had been wrong. Then, a little figuring.

"Miss Cordet has been my secretary for some nine months. Her references were perfect, her life apparently an open book. I trusted her as much as I trusted anyone. But I began to think back. With the coming of Miss Cordet came The Reckoner. Miss Cordet was in a position to know of the meeting last night. The man who opened my safe was not a common burglar. Miss Cordet was also in a position to give him the combination of the safe. And Miss Cordet had the opportunity to make a telephone call last night. She had the opportunity of letting you know that the police would visit your apartment to check up on you. Again, she refused to identify you today. Miss Cordet. Miss Tania Cordet." And with a curve to those lips, "Don't try to twist your face into imaginary contortions of amazed incredulity. I took from her the note telling her to be at the Café Madrid at eight o'clock. I came here and found you. Miss Cordet will not disturb us tonight. Miss Cordet may never disturb me again."

Marty came slowly to his feet. He leaned heavily on the table. The fingers of both his hands clawed the cloth. His face changed from a dull white to red, then quickly back to white again. Twice he opened his mouth to speak, but no words came. Slowly his hands were rising from the table; his black eyes were hard and cold. For a moment he knew that he was no better—at least, no different—than the men he hunted. The brain in him warned him to be careful; the man in him cried out to clutch Joseph Rierson by the throat and strangle from him information as to Tania's whereabouts. But he did nothing, said nothing.

"Sit down." Rierson was very calm. "If they are needed, I have friends with me. Even so, you could not possibly do me a great deal of harm here, before there would be interference. Sit down, Mr. Day.

People are already looking at you. Sit down, if you want to see Tania alive again."

"What have you done with Tania?" Marty dropped slowly back into the seat. "If you harm her, Rierson, I'll kill you."

Rierson smiled. "Just so. Tania's very words. The Reckoner has instilled within you the very melodrama he himself creates with his strange selection of a name that is supposed to strike terror. Tania told me you would kill me. You tell me you will kill me. Very noble, very brave, very understandable, and perhaps even commendable in a young man in love. But let us speak plainly—face facts. I dare say you know that I have killed in my day." Thick fingers opened and closed. "And I will kill again, Mr. Day. Rest assured of that. I will kill again! But let us talk, later, of what you will do to avenge Tania. At present the question is: what will you do to save her life? After all, we are all very human. I have taken from you the thing you perhaps care for most. Perhaps you haven taken from me the thing I care for most. My influence, my power, my personal pride in my own greatness. There, there! I am not flattering myself. I'm simply telling you the truth. You have thoughts of killing me brutally. Perhaps I, too, might have such thoughts when Tania's time to die comes. Her death, then, might be far from the Sudden gentle sleep the poets speak of." And suddenly leaning forward, he snapped: "What will you do to save Tania—now?"

"Anything. Anything!"

**MARTY** heard the words, but it was several moments before he realized that the voice was his. Then he broke into a torrent of words. Threats of violence from The Reckoner. Assurance that he, Marty, would personally hunt Rierson to the end of the world if Tania were not set free at once.

Joseph Rierson laughed easily. "You are talking like a book, Mr. Day. I am speaking of life—and of death. You will return to me the envelope you stole last night. I am not interested in how you get it. In return for that envelope, with its contents intact, I will give you back your Tania alive. You must act at once."

Marty looked straight at those beady eyes, the smooth skin with its pulsing blue lines. Here sat a man calmly threatening to murder a girl; he sat opposite him in one of the better known night clubs of the city. Impossible! Yet, since Marty had joined forces with The Reckoner, many impossible things had happened. Somehow, Marty knew that the man spoke the truth; that if he failed to return the envelope Tania would die.

"At once!" Marty felt the words choke in his throat. "How long will you give me?"

"A reasonable time." Joseph Rierson nodded and smiled to a passing acquaintance.

"And," asked Marty, "just what do you call a reasonable time?"

"I would suggest that you get the envelope tonight. But I will give you a little time—a very little time." Joseph Rierson came to his feet. "You may call me at my house, and if I am not there simply say you have a letter to return to me. I will receive the message."

Marty came to his feet and clutched Rierson by the sleeve as he turned to go. "How will I know how much time I have?" There was no threat in Marty's voice now. Just a plea, and perhaps a feeling of fear that was reflected in his eyes.

"You read your papers, Mr. Day. From them you will be able to determine if you have delayed too long. The papers, of course, will tell you when the body of a young and beautiful girl has been found drowned. Another thing. You believe, Mr. Day, that I have five hundred dollars, don't you?"

"Five hundred dollars! Yes. Why?"

"Nothing. Nothing." But just before Joseph Rierson swung on his heel and departed, he said: "If I had any cause to fear you, Mr. Day, remember that I could lay my hands on fifty men who would be willing to—to remove you for the sum of five hundred dollars. Good night."

## CHAPTER SIX

## "TO HIS DEAD—"

**M**ARTY PACED that little room back of the pawnshop for the better part of an hour. Would The Reckoner come? Marty had never sent for him before. But he had been told to, though only under the most pressing necessity. Well—this was pressing enough. The life of Tania!

Twice Marty went close to that curtain of steel; twice he ran a hand along it, even felt the unevenness where the sliding panel must have been. Then, when he was almost desperate with anxiety and fear and about to beat upon the locked door and demand that the little old man do something, the single light in the room snapped out.

In the darkness Marty groped for the chair; had his hand stretched out toward it when the brilliant light on the protruding edge of the wooden counter below the steel curtain flashed up. Almost the moment Marty dropped into that chair the panel began to move.

Though light burnt his eyes and blinded his vision, Marty stared directly at it. But he saw nothing. Then the voice of The Reckoner came. It was just as metallic, just as clear, but not so pleasant, Marty thought.

"Well," he said, "it seems you saw fit to send for me."

And Marty told him, hardly noticing the slur in his voice, the air of superiority in his manner. Quickly Marty related every word he had had with Rierson.

"Now, that is too bad." The Reckoner's voice was very low. "Be assured that I will take the proper steps to punish this man. Sometimes, Mr. Day, the time between the first note of The Reckoner and final retribution is very long, but retribution is very sure. Joseph Rierson will live to regret tonight's action."

"But Tania!" Marty cut in quickly. "What of her? You haven't used those papers yet?"

"No," said The Reckoner, "not yet. They must be studied. Each one carefully verified, and then the best method of using them chosen. It might be a day, it might be a month."

"You'll give them to me?" And when The Reckoner didn't answer at once, "I took them for you. I'll return them to him and free the girl. There will be other opportunities, other ways of striking at Rierson. Well? Well!" And, in a panic, Marty almost raised his voice to a shout. "You're there? You haven't gone? You're not going to leave Tania a prisoner of this man?"

"I haven't gone." And there was a new note in The Reckoner's voice; for a moment the metallic sound left it. "You have come here, Mr. Day, to ask that I give you the envelope to return to Rierson in order to save Tania. My answer to that will be very clear. No!" And when Marty would have talked, "Would you have me sacrifice the many for the one? There are things in that envelope which, if properly used, will safeguard many people. There is a certain judge whose time is about up. There is proof of the robbing of widows and orphans by a man in public life." He paused a moment, and then, "No. Tania is but one. She made a mistake. She should have denied seeing you in the doorway."

"But we can get the evidence again. I got it once. I can—"

"No, no. Such a chance might never come again. But no more, Mr. Day. I will do what I can. I will send Rierson the final threat—one of death. More, I cannot do. More, I swore never to do when I first decided on my course of righting wrong, punishing evil. Besides, Rierson will not, I think, kill her."

"But he will!" Marty cried out. "I saw the man. I talked with him. I looked into his eyes. He will kill her because he hates you. She worked for you. She is giving her life for you, and you won't raise a hand to save her."

"I am sorry," The Reckoner said. "Sorry and sad, indeed. You can do nothing. I will bend every effort to save her, of course. But go to your apartment, so that I can send you word if you can help her."

Marty's mind was working on a single track. He said: "Give me that blue linen envelope, or I'll never raise a hand to help you again. I'm through."

"No, Mr. Day, you are not through. I know you; you do not know me. My hand is far reaching. No one who works for The Reckoner ever leaves him, living. The Reckoner has only allies, or enemies. There is no 'in between' course. Good night."

**MARTY** came to his feet. His hands sought desperately to stop that moving panel, but only smooth steel scraped against his nails. The brilliant light snapped out, a few minutes of darkness and again the ceiling light. Marty was alone with his thoughts. They were not pleasant ones.

And this time Marty beat on that door a half-dozen times before it opened. The stooped old man drew back as he saw Marty's blazing eyes.

"No, no," he half covered his face with his hands. "I could not come sooner. I dared not come sooner. I—"

But Marty was gone, barging down that hall to the street door, almost tearing the chain from its bolt. Then he was out in the air. One thought—just one thought. Not of those The Reckoner would save, but of Tania. To save Tania!

What would he do? What could he do? He gripped his cane tightly, then threw it in the corner of the car as he stepped on the starter. Marty's eyes narrowed. He would go to Rierson. He would tell him he had the envelope. And then—then he'd threaten him. He'd kill him if he did not tell where Tania was; if he did not free Tania. He glanced down at his cane, then shook his head. This time he'd need a gun. It wouldn't do to shake a cane in a man's face and threaten to kill him. But a gun! A gun in his hand and Rierson before him. Marty nodded grimly. Yes, he had murder in his heart all right. He'd get a gun from Knight.

Marty reached his apartment and waited impatiently for the elevator to carry him to his floor.

"I want a gun, Knight!" he said abruptly, and seeing the startled look on his servant's face, "Yes, a gun. I think, Knight, I'm going to need it, I think—I think— My God! Knight, it isn't so hard to kill a man."

"Mr. Day, sir. You better sit down; you'd better have a drink. You're not yourself. A lady called and said you were to wait here to see her."

"Who?" Marty snapped.

"I don't know, sir. She said it was important." And after a moment's pause and seeing the anxiety in Marty's eyes, "No, sir. It was not Miss Tania."

"No, no. It couldn't be. The gun, Knight. A big one. A vicious-looking one."

Knight looked at him a moment and shook his head. "This business, sir. This unknown voice on the phone, with the queer label—The Reckoner. I told you no good would come of it."

"You were right, Knight. Absolutely right. No good has come of it."

Knight waited a moment, shook his head, then left the room.

Almost at once Marty lifted the receiver and called Joseph Rierson's number. A few minutes later he was talking to Rierson.

"I am ready to return the envelope." He tried to make his voice calm. "I can bring it to you at once. At once! You understand?"

There was a moment of silence, and then Rierson's voice. "You work fast, Mr. Day, very fast. Let me congratulate you. It's hardly ten. I have to go out for a few moments. Say eleven o'clock sharp. No, no. I can make it no earlier. And, Mr. Day, it would be very unfortunate for a certain party if your visit to me proved a subterfuge for intended violence."

Marty gulped. Words stuck in his throat. He finally said: "I don't understand."

"No, perhaps not. But it would be impossible for you to see me if you were armed. You are susceptible to sudden impulses. Are you sure you have the envelope?"

"Absolutely." Marty's voice was very low. The assurance, the anxiety for quick action had gone out of it.

"Good! Eleven o'clock sharp, and alone."

**THE RECEIVER** clicked. For a long moment Marty held the instrument in his hand, then as he dropped it back in its cradle, he sank heavily into a huge chair.

"Knight," he looked up as his servant entered, "I won't be needing—wanting a gun." And his eyes shot to his cane resting against the wall.

Just the same, Marty was going to see Rierson. What could he do there? He didn't know. But, something. Yes, he'd do something. He couldn't just sit home and wait. If he could be alone with Rierson! Well, he had his cane and he had his two hands, and he had six feet of trained muscle.

Marty Day watched the clock, and Knight occasionally put his head in the door and watched Marty.

Was Marty in love with Tania? He liked her, of course. Admired her courage, and wondered, too, about the sadness back in her brown eyes. Well, maybe not exactly sadness, but a hidden something. A deepness of feeling that occasionally pierced through, and made Marty wonder if she was in this thing, in with The Reckoner just for the adventure. Yes, he liked her, and now he wondered if—

The clock struck ten-thirty. Marty came to his feet. He couldn't sit there any longer. What if it were too early to go to Rierson's house? He'd do better pacing the streets than sitting there thinking. Thinking! And Marty Day laughed. Not a constructive thought had come into his head. As yet he didn't know exactly what he'd do when he was alone with Rierson. But he'd do something.

And the apartment phone in the hall rang. A minute later Knight entered the living-room. "It's the woman who telephoned. She's on her way up. Said you were expecting her. Mrs. Clarke."

"Who!" Marty had never heard the name before. "Who is Mrs. Clarke? And I don't want to see anyone now."

"She said it was important, sir. She—"

The bell rang. Knight hesitated, then Marty waved a hand. "Show her in, of course, Knight." But for the life of him Marty had no idea who Mrs. Clarke might be.

She came, stood for a moment in the broad doorway. Marty knew her at once. She was the girl of the bag and the gun, the girl who had stood beside his car and gone with him to the pawnshop.

"You—you want to see me?" For a moment Marty's eyes darkened. Here was someone sent by The Reckoner. Someone to bring him information, or— And the thought in his head came out in words. "The Reckoner sent you to watch me," he said.

"No." She waited in the doorway until Knight disappeared down the narrow hallway. "No one sends me any place, Marty Day. I come and go as I please. And I'm not here to watch you, but to help you. Do you love Tania Cordet?"

"Tania Cordet. Is that her real name?" Marty asked.

"That is her real name. I'm just plain Zee Clarke. Do you love this woman?" And for a moment Marty saw the thin lips tremble slightly and the amber-colored eyes narrow.

"I don't know," he answered truthfully enough, and suddenly, "Why do you ask me that? Why are you here?"

"What would you give in return for the life of Tania? What would you give, Marty Day, for the blue envelope that will set her free?"

"You know about that?" Marty was surprised and showed it.

**ZEE CLARK** moved a foot across the soft rug. "I know everything. I suppose I'm a fool not to force you into promising anything I ask. But I guess I don't want that. I'll save Tania."

"You like her too?" The words just slipped from Marty.

Zee Clarke's lips tightened. "I'm not saving her because I like her. I'm saving her for you." And quickly, "Or perhaps I'm saving her for myself. You think you love her now. If she dies you'll be sure you love her. You see, I don't want the dead between us."

"Why?" Marty was startled into the question.

"Because," she said, "I may want you for myself. Don't get the absurd notion that I have fallen violently in love with a man I hardly know. I've watched you, Marty Day. I've never had much use for men, but I have a feeling now that if I ever did, ever could love a man, that man would—might be you. Queer thought? Well, I'm a queer person. Here!" She flipped open that gray bag with a single motion, put her fingers into it, and taking out a long blue, linen envelope tossed it over to Marty.

Without a word Marty tore the elastic bands from the envelope. Hurriedly, clumsily his fingers went through the contents. All there, just as it had been the night before, when he studied it under the dashlight on the car. Then he looked up. "You—" he stammered. "The Reckoner gave you this?"

"No." She shook her head. "I stole it. If the question ever arises, you must say that it came to you by messenger and you thought it was from him. Otherwise, he might kill you."

"But you. He would—would kill you."

Zee Clarke shook her head. For a moment those amber eyes were hard, those thin lips a single straight line. "He knows me. I don't think any man, knowing me as The Reckoner knows me, would dare to kill me."

"And what do you want me to do? I haven't thanked you; I can't thank you. But I'll do anything in return. Anything! Just—" And thinking of what the woman had said about loving him, he stopped short.

The girl smiled at him now. There was a touch of sarcasm to her voice. "Don't let my little display of honest passion disturb you, Marty. When I make my decision that you are the man I want, then I'll take you."

"You are very sure of yourself." Marty could not help but say it as he thrust the envelope inside his jacket pocket.

She nodded. "I am always sure of myself. Now—"

But Marty had grabbed her hand, thanked her again, and with his hat in one hand and his cane in the other was dashing toward the door. The clock had just finished striking the quarter hour.

But before that door closed behind him, Marty heard Knight enter the living room and say: "What is he doing and where is he going?"

And plainly, too, Marty heard Zee Clarke answer: "I am afraid he is going to his death."

## CHAPTER SEVEN

# WHO IS THE RECKONER?

**T**HE MAN who let Marty into Rierson's house seemed the usual well-trained servant. "Your hat and stick, sir," he said extending his hand.

"I won't be here long enough for that." Marty tried the voice with the smile, and then the usual story which all his friends knew and believed. "Besides, my cane is more than simply an ornament. I have a weakness in my left leg, an old affliction. Not noticeable, but at times it's rather apt to let me down."

The man looked doubtfully at the stick, then shrugged his shoulders. Without another word he turned and preceded Marty to the very room he had robbed the previous night.

"Ah!" Rierson turned the book he was reading over on his knees and removing spectacles placed them upon the desk. "That will be all, Hartley. Sit down, Mr. Day, sit down."

Marty remained standing, his cane in his right hand, his left hand leaning upon the desk. "Is Tania here?" he asked abruptly.

"She will be. She will be." Rierson nodded vigorously. "You have brought the documents? Really, Mr. Day, I doubt that you have them."

"I have them!" Marty was emphatic. "Now, what assurance have I that you will set Tania free?"

"You have my word, Mr. Day. That should be quite enough between gentlemen—gentlemen who play outside the law." And ending his laugh abruptly when Marty did not smile, "Besides, what use would I have for the girl? Come, come!" he stretched out a huge fat hand with pudgy fingers, "you are not in a position to bargain. I might any minute repent of my proposition."

"Here!" Marty thrust his hand toward his jacket pocket.

"Don't!" With almost a scream Rierson was on his feet, then he tried to smile, but his lips made only a grimace. He rubbed a hand across his moist forehead, then snatched the envelope from Marty's hand.

"I thought you were going to draw a— But no matter. All here—

all here?" He was backing further away from Marty now. "No, I didn't think you had them."

But Marty was thinking of one thing. Where was Tania?

"Tania! Certainly." Rierson kept those beady eyes on Marty's hands. "To be sure. We have a bargain, Mr. Day. You have completed the first part of it. Now for the second."

"The second—" Marty stammered. What 'second'? You have the envelope. Your word! Where is Tania?"

"Ah!" Rierson's lips parted. "Is it possible that I forget to make clear to you the second part of the bargain? Well, it's not too late to rectify that mistake. We will take up things where we left off last night. Who is—The Reckoner?"

"You're going to keep the girl! You're not—" The truth suddenly dawning on Marty that he had been duped, he clutched his cane tightly, stepped forward—and stopped.

Rierson waved a hand. A voice spoke behind Marty. It said: "You make a move and I'll put a hunk of lead through the back of your head. Up go your hands."

Marty stopped dead. Feet crossed the floor. Something round and hard and cold was pressed against the back of his neck. Marty hesitated the fraction of a second before his hands went above his head. Should he retain the cane? And he thought not. With it raised above his head, it would be recognized by both Rierson and the man who held the gun as a weapon. No. He might get a chance to use it later. He let it slip from his fingers against the table before his hands shot into the air.

**RIERSON** searched him carefully.

Satisfied that he was not armed, he drew back. Opening the drawer of his desk he ordered Marty to lower his hands. Then he slipped steel cuffs upon his wrists, placing the key in his vest pocket.

"You can leave me now, Hymie. But wait outside the door. If I need you I'll call." And sharply, "Keep the gun in your hand, you fool."

The door closed, Joseph Rierson turned to Marty, a gun in his right hand. And Marty watched him closely as he dropped into the chair Rierson indicated.

"You fooled me tonight, Mr. Day. Fooled me most pleasantly. When you telephoned me I didn't believe for one instant that you had the envelope." He jerked a thumb toward the blue envelope on the table.

"No, it was not your voice that convinced me of that. It was the voice of The Reckoner."

"The Reckoner?" Marty gasped.

"Yes. He did me the honor of telephoning me. He told me that if the girl died a hundred deaths I could not save my friends. He told me that the envelope would never be returned. He also threatened me. When you telephoned and then came, naturally I expected only threats and perhaps attempted violence. So I was prepared. Now, Mr. Day, I want the name of The Reckoner for the life of Tania and for your life. I am not fooling. I may tell you truthfully that, despite my bravado in the matter, I do fear The Reckoner. He has an uncanny way of gaining knowledge. Come! What do you say?"

"I do not know the name of The Reckoner. Nor does Tania."

"That Tania does not know, I believe. But you know him. Else, how could you steal that envelope. That envelope that only a little over an hour ago The Reckoner did not know was missing. He doesn't know that it is missing now, probably. You must be very close to him, closer even than I thought. Tania is in this house now." And when Marty started, "Yes. She is, and you are going to see her; going to talk to her and going to tell me the name of The Reckoner, or—" The heavy-jowled face, with its streaks of blue, shot forward. Beady eyes were once again little buttons of brightness.

"You will have cause to fear The Reckoner if you harm Tania." Marty tried desperately to make his words carry conviction.

Joseph Rierson laughed. "You have plenty of courage, my friend, but you are a fool. No one knows you came here, least of all The Reckoner. Didn't he tell me I would never get the envelope? How then could he have sent you here? But we waste time. Who is The Reckoner?"

"I don't know. I don't know. I was a fool to trust you. I—I—"

"You didn't trust me, Mr. Day. You expected to outwit me, that was all. You were trailed here from your apartment. I knew before you entered this room that no one came with you, that no friends of yours followed. But there! The wise man doesn't talk, he acts. Tonight, Mr. Day, I am going to be a very wise man indeed. I am going to act."

"What are you going to do?" Marty came to his feet as Rierson backed slightly from him.

"I am going to take you to Tania." Joseph Rierson turned toward the door, then swung suddenly back again. "Maybe Tania will tell you what I am going to do. For nearly nine months she has done everything to discover things in my past and my present for use in the future. Maybe she will be able to tell you what I—what I once did to a woman who crossed me." Thick lips twisted cruelly now. Rierson rubbed fat hands together. "I think that you will talk. Yes, I think that you will tell me the name of The Reckoner. Come!"

Rierson lifted the envelope from the table, glanced once toward the closed safe, hesitated a moment, then thrust it into his inside jacket pocket. The man called Hymie opened the door.

"Take this man upstairs. He wants to see the young lady. I'll precede you and— Wait!" This as Hymie stepped behind Marty and shoved his gun hard into Marty's back.

RIERSON walked to the table and lifted Marty's hat and stick, and returned, passing through the doorway to the hall.

"We mustn't leave any evidence behind, Mr. Day. Evidence that, if you don't talk, will be found with your body."

"You intend to kill me?" Marty gasped.

"Exactly, my friend. If you will not talk I intend to kill you. If I do not know The Reckoner tonight, at least I will somewhat retard the efficiency of his force of workers, and perhaps throw a touch of that fear he inspires, into him."

"You'll find there are some things you can't get away with, Rierson." Marty tried hard to make his words steady. "Murder like this is one of them."

"No?" Rierson threw the words back over his shoulder as he led the way up the dimly lit stairs. "Perhaps you're right. But right or wrong, Mr. Day, I fail to see what solace you get from that thought."

Marty, with the gun tight against his back, followed Rierson up the stairs. His eyes were riveted on the cane that Rierson clutched in his left hand. His weapon of attack—his weapon of defense! Knight was right. A gun was the thing. But he expected to be searched before he entered the house. And if he had brought a gun, what good would it have done? The villainous gunman, Hymie, had him covered from the very moment he entered that room.

No. Where he was wrong, was in not making Rierson come to him. He should have insisted that Tania be freed first. But it was too late to think of that now. Indeed, he had thought of nothing at all—nothing but of saving Tania. When he had first laid his plans the envelope had not entered into them. Then, when it did— Why, he had simply dashed madly from his apartment, jumped into his car at the curb and drove straight to Joseph Rierson's house.

And the girl, the strange woman who called herself Zee Clarke! He remembered her words now. "I am afraid," she had said, "he is going to his death."

He hadn't thought of the words then. But he thought of them now. He set his lips tightly. Well, if his thoughts had always been of caution he wouldn't be in a thing like this; wouldn't have joined forces with The Reckoner in the first place. But he got little comfort out of that thought. He wasn't afraid to die. But he didn't want to die. He'd been a fool, and Tania was to pay the price of his folly.

The third floor, a dark hall, and a door was suddenly thrown open. The single light from a brilliant floor lamp illuminated that room.

"Come in!" Rierson said. "We have brought you a visitor, Tania. Mr. Day, who may take you away from me."

And it was Tania. She was across the room, her arms around Marty's neck, crying softly on his shoulder. It was the first time she had acted like that. Tania seemed different.

"Marty. Marty!" she cried over and over. "I'm so glad you've come. Somehow, I knew you'd come. He's told me terrible things, horrible things that— Let's go. Let's go. I— I—"

Rierson laughed; Tania stopped talking. A sudden sob choked in her throat. Her hands left the back of Marty's head, her arms dropped from around his neck. Then her eyes fell from Marty's white face to his hands, to the bands of black steel about his wrists.

"You— you too." Her words were barely audible. "He's got you."

"There, there, my dear." Rierson placed a hand upon her shoulder, let his huge fingers creep along her neck. "Such is the optimism of youth. Put your arms back around him, my dear, for in him lies your safety. He has only to talk to save you."

"But he doesn't know. He doesn't know." Tania twisted herself free and backed across the room. "I told you that. I told you."

"If that is true, it would be very unfortunate for both of you. No, no Mr. Day," as Marty stepped toward the girl. "The comedy is ended; the tragedy begins. Will you talk?"

"I don't know who he is." Marty's eyes were on Tania, on those deep brown eyes that were filled with terror.

"Very well." Joseph Rierson turned quickly and threw Marty's hat and stick upon the table. He walked straight to the girl, and grabbing her by both arms thrust her into a chair. Tania screamed once, then remained silent.

Twice Marty bent forward at the hips. Once he took a step, but the gun, now between his shoulder blades, held him back.

For a moment the cane balanced on the edge of the table, then fell to the floor. It quivered like a living thing and lay still. The cane! If Marty could only reach it. Not that he saw safety in that thin length of steel with its heavy springs, but he saw action. The chance to go down fighting; the chance to be shot down as the heavy handle pounded upon Rierson's thick skull.

**MARTY** didn't speak and didn't move as Joseph Rierson swept up a coil of rope from the corner and bound the girl quickly to that chair. For all his huge bulk and clumsy-looking hands, he worked rapidly and efficiently.

"Now, Mr. Day." Rierson walked quickly to a cupboard in the corner of the room, inserted a key, and opening the little door lifted a bottle from the shelf. Plainly on the label Marty saw the warning "POISON." There was something new in Rierson's face when he turned. The beady eyes were pin points of hate; thick lips twisted back in the cruel snarl of an animal.

"I might," he faced Marty now, "resort to mediaeval history and torture the girl for hours to make you talk. Your fear of The Reckoner is perhaps much greater than your fear for the girl. You are afraid he would kill you, and while you have but one life, there are many women. Besides— Well, this is quicker." He held up the little bottle. "Vitriolic acid, my friend. A woman's trick, perhaps, but then, I never was one to deny that man may learn much from woman. I am going to toss the contents of this bottle in the young lady's face."

"No, no. You can't do that."

"No?" Rierson sneered. "For nine months she worked for me, with me. Flattering me, giving me her time even after hours. And all the time she was trying to trap me; telling The Reckoner of my friends, of those I controlled. And why was she doing it? To plan my end, to plan my death. Now, you have one minute to talk, or I'll dash the contents of this bottle straight in her pretty face. Across those soft brown eyes, over those childish lips; streak it upon the soft smooth cheeks and—"

Marty lost his head. He forgot the gun in his back, even the gangster who stood behind him. He thought only of Tania and that sneering inhuman face, and the little glass bottle held in those thick fingers. He wanted only one thing then. To fasten his fingers into that thick neck. Bullets, knives, clubs! Nothing could save Rierson then, nothing would force his fingers from that flesh.

And Marty sprang. His black eyes shone with the same cruel hatred as Rierson's. His manacled hands shot into the air. In a blurred way he knew that Rierson shoved a hand in his pocket and that those clumsy fingers produced a gun with the dexterity and speed of a stage magician. He knew that the round black hole in that gun was covering him as Rierson cried out something. But he didn't stop. He couldn't stop.

Then he did stop. His knees gave suddenly. Something burst in his head. His body half turned and he saw the gunman, Hymie, saw the gun raised in his hand to strike again. Then Marty sank to the floor, his fingers grasping at the carpet, at something upon the carpet— something cold and hard and familiar. And he knew. He was holding tightly in both his manacled hands his cane, the cane that had been no use to him tonight. No use! And Marty's dulled eyes saw a few feet before him and to his right the silk cord of the lamp wire.

"I tell you, boss," Hymie's words came distinctly to Marty, "I see a woman once who got a dose of that stuff on her map. I tell you he won't talk after. He won't want her after. No man would."

"He's built different than you—than us," Rierson corrected himself. "And even if he doesn't want her, it won't matter." And then, "No woman is going to two-time Joe Rierson."

"I thought you were all business, boss."

"I am. I am. Don't you think it'll take a jolt out of The Reckoner when they're picked up, and her face isn't so pretty to look at? It'll make him think before he crosses me again."

"Yeah, A guy would. A guy would." Hymie nodded vigorously. "Will I douse him with water?"

The room was pitched suddenly into blackness. The gangster jerked up his gun just as the light went out. Three times he sprayed lead where Marty had been. But Marty Day's body had twisted with the same quickness as his snake-like cane. It was the roll of his body as much as the jerk of his hands that tore the electric plug from its socket.

# CHAPTER EIGHT

# MASTER OF THE CANE

**M**ARTY WAS on his feet, his cane gripped tightly in his bound hands. Not such a clever weapon now, not such a hidden one. His hands couldn't grip it at either end, and with the simple release of his fingers snap it into instant action; an action so quick that the man who was struck by it could not even tell what had struck him.

No. The cane could no longer serve as a phantom weapon; that is, in the light. But it could serve as a real weapon, more dangerous and more deadly, in the dark. Held now in his two hands, it could be brought through the air with enough force to crack a man's skull. And it would be. It would be!

Blackness. Complete blackness. Feet moved, men whispered. Once Rierson called aloud.

"Come, come! Marty Day, you can do us no harm. We are both armed—" And a half-uncertain laugh as Marty sank to his knees and crawled toward that voice, his cane stretched out before him.

And the gunman's voice.

"Sh, boss! He's moving. I hear—" Then a shriek, the roar of a gun, the quick stab of yellow straight down at Hymie's feet, where he thought that a hand had clutched his leg.

But no hand had clutched Hymie's leg. It was the curved end of a cane, a curved end that twisted and caught, and jerked so quickly that Hymie struck the floor with terrific force.

Marty almost chuckled as he hurled himself forward upon that fallen body. If Tania had not been there he would have felt that his chances were pretty good. But he wanted that gun; he wanted that gun from the unconscious man upon the floor. The man whom he had brought down as he had brought many other men down before. Men who lay unconscious for many minutes after such a fall.

Almost as soon as Marty touched a limp knee and hurled himself upon the body he knew he had made a mistake. Was it the dark, his weakened condition from the blow, the nervousness of his fingers, or his manacled hands?

But Hymie was anything but unconscious. Almost before Marty threw himself on the man, fingers had sunk into his throat. Long, strong fingers were biting deeply into Marty's neck.

And there was his cane, the cane which he had dropped beside Hymie in his anxiety to tear the gun from his hand, the cane which, if he had shortened his grip upon it, he might even now have clubbed down upon the gunman's unseen forehead.

The blow on his head had weakened Marty considerably; the tightly bound wrists put him at a great disadvantage. Slowly, but just as surely, the gunman, Hymie, was turning his body—turning Marty's body with it. Another minute, perhaps seconds only, and then Marty would be underneath. Hymie's fingers seemed to be ever tightening into Marty's neck, while his own seemed to be slowly loosening, losing their power to grip the gunman tightly.

Rierson called sharply. "Hymie. Hymie!" And there was anxiety in his voice, alarm, and perhaps a touch of fear.

Wind whistled in Hymie's throat as he tried to answer, and with a final effort Marty sank his fingers deeply into the rough skin. And it was a final effort, for the next instant Marty was no longer on top of Hymie. Both were on their sides, struggling frantically to retain the upper position.

Hymie did it! His fingers shot suddenly from Marty's throat to Marty's wrists, tearing the manacled hands from his own neck.

**THAT** was the end, Marty thought. He had tried, almost succeeded, perhaps, against overwhelming odds. But truth is truth. "Almost" wasn't enough. He had failed.

As those hands went back to his throat and tightened there with a new vigor, things went black for Marty—as black inside his head as they were in that room. His hands remained upon the floor, his fingers moving spasmodically. And then he felt the cane again.

The touch of that weapon which Marty had carried so long and that had served him so faithfully, brought new life into his sluggish brain, but to his brain only. The orders came all right from his brain to his body. There was the impulse to reach up, twist that cane quickly about the gunman's neck and with a deft jerk almost tear his head from his shoulders.

Marty had done it before in almost the same circumstances and he could have done it again, if he only had the power in his hands; in his fingers that now gripped uncertainly at the stick; that lifted it slightly and swung it back and forth, perhaps a few inches from the floor.

The gunman's fingers were closing tighter, biting deeper, and things inside Marty's head began to grow black again.

The cane touched something; a man cursed. It was Rierson. And in that instant the gunman twisted Marty suddenly and flung his body on top of Marty.

There was the slightest sigh of elation on Hymie's lips, a sigh that died almost in the making. There was a dull boom in the small room, the spurt of orange-blue flame, the smell of burning powder in Marty's nostrils as the body of Hymie collapsed forward on his chest.

That sudden turn, the effort that the gunman thought would give him victory had cost him his life. Rierson, feeling that cane against his leg, had jerked down his gun and fired directly where Marty had been.

Rierson was leaning down, dragging the body of Hymie from Marty, talking as he did it. "Got him, eh? There, there, Hymie, he didn't hurt you much, did he? You'll be all right in a minute. Hell, man, I heard the struggle and knew he had the best of you. You'd have answered when I called if you could. I didn't dare fire before, but when his foot hit my leg—" Rierson talked on as Marty staggered blindly to his feet. Marty was dazed and uncertain, the cane still clasped in his hand—his two hands.

Somehow Marty knew that he swayed upon his feet, and tried to suck in great gulps of air. He knew that the cane should be held high above his head, but he didn't know just how to get it there. The directions from his brain came through, but the muscles that should carry out those directions were not working. He knew what he should do but he was unable to do it.

Marty knew, too, that Rierson was talking, that there was an hysterical laugh at the end of each sentence. And he knew that Rierson struck a match and was walking across the room, that he said something about fixing the light. And yet Marty could not move, could not act—

Marty snapped back to life, snapped back to it just as Rierson said: "It's funny Hartley didn't hear the noise and go across the street and get the four boys in. Of course I didn't—"

The lamp snapped on, flooding the room with light. Rierson,

crouched there by the base board, turned his head and let his beady eyes rest upon Marty's black ones.

**FOR A MOMENT** he just blinked his astonishment, then his hand reached for the gun he had placed beside him on the floor. Rierson fired as Marty struck. The cane came more sideways than straight down, or it would have crushed Rierson's skull. As it was, a bullet pounded into the wall above Marty's head and Joseph Rierson pitched forward on the floor, unconscious.

Marty shook his head, ran a hand across his forehead, paused, and lowering his hands looked at his wrists—the irons still upon them. He shook his head again, trying to clear the cobwebs from it, then he looked at Rierson.

"I guess I wasn't the only one who played the fool tonight," he said aloud. Then he grinned stupidly again, and was suddenly on the floor beside Rierson, fumbling clumsily at his vest, finding the key, trying desperately to unlock those cuffs.

A minute… two… three! Marty never knew how long he fumbled with that key. But he couldn't unlock those cuffs. He raised his head and tried to think. He had done it before. When? Where? And he knew. Knight had showed him the trick once in Marty's own apartment. Now—now—

Marty clamped the key firmly between his teeth. It was in the lock. The key stuck, wouldn't turn. That wasn't it, then. But it was. Marty was free; the irons upon the floor. He stood erect, smiled to himself. Then he turned sharply. Tania! What of Tania?

Tania was there, still tightly bound in the chair. But her body was no longer painfully stiff and erect. Her great brown eyes were no longer haunted things of terror. Her head had fallen on her shoulder. Her eyes were closed, her face very white. She had fainted? Or— And Marty was across the room to her, kneeling at her side, rubbing her hands, pleading with her to speak to him—then tearing at the ropes that held her.

Marty's head cleared; thoughts began again to shape themselves. Tania moved slightly, her eyes opened, closed again, and long lashes flickered.

He must get her out of there. He looked down at the silent form of Hymie upon the floor and wondered if he were dead. An ugly pool of red was slowly forming beside him.

He looked at Joseph Rierson, very still and very white. A huge hand was stretched out; fat fingers rested upon the floor, rested within a few inches of a heavy-caliber automatic.

Yes, he must get Tania out of there. Just one man downstairs. Hartley! He hadn't looked very formidable, but— What had Rierson said? Something about Hartley going for help, getting the "boys" from across the street. Did that mean that the house would be full of men in a minute, full of gunmen that Rierson kept in readiness if he should need them? Would all his effort to save Tania prove worthless?

He looked at Tania again. She was moving now; her left hand came up and brushed at her hair. Marty frowned slightly. The cane had served him well, but now— He looked again at the automatic and set his lips grimly. The cane had served its purpose, but against four men, four men with spitting guns— He walked quickly across the room and bent down to pick up that gun.

His hand rested on it, then he grasped it tightly—and jumped quickly erect.

A sharp knock had come upon that door.

**MARTY** didn't move. He just stood there, his right hand raised, the gun pointing at that door. Was this Hartley? If Marty didn't open that door, would he burst in with the others he had brought from across the street? But was the door locked? Marty didn't know. He didn't remember hearing the click, but then, he would not have heard it, he thought. He had been confused. Yes, confused and stupid ever since Rierson told him he was going to kill Tania.

Now— The knock came again, soft and very low this time.

Marty walked quickly to the door, stepped to one side. His hand grasped the knob. His breath shot back in his throat. That knob was turning, slowly moving beneath his fingers.

And Marty acted. He was himself again now. There was no key in the lock. He clutched the knob tightly, turned it in a single motion and jerked the door toward him. He hoped that whoever held that knob would be dragged quickly into the room.

The door flew in; a figure stumbled and then straightened. A gun came up and Marty's finger half tightened upon the trigger. There was a low feminine laugh. Marty's hand dropped to his side. Thin lips parted; amber eyes looked into his. The girl, the woman known as Zee Clarke stood in the doorway.

Quickly she stepped inside. With one sharp glance she took in the whole room, and nodded. "You're a wonder, Marty. A fool for luck, maybe, but a wonder just the same." She looked from Hymie to the girl. "Better take her out of here."

Tania was coming around now, her eyes opening, her breath coming in uneven gasps.

"There're others." Marty didn't even think to ask how the girl got there. "The butler, Hartley! He's to get others from across the street."

"Yes, yes. I know." Zee Clarke nodded impatiently. "Don't worry about him. Get the girl and come." And with the slightest curve to her lips as Marty lifted Tania in his arms, "You have the envelope?"

Marty reddened slightly. "It's in Rierson's inside jacket pocket. I'll—"

But Zee Clarke was kneeling at Rierson's side. A moment later she stood up, the envelope in her hand.

"What will The Reckoner say to you?" Marty asked as they went down the stairs.

"He won't know. I'll simply put it back."

At the foot of the stairs was Knight. He was holding a gun against the back of a man who stood with his face pressed hard against the wall. It was Hartley.

"That's how we got in," Zee Clarke explained, as Marty set Tania on her feet. She was able to walk now. "The man was leaving to get help. We persuaded him to come back with us. We'll take the back way out."

They took Hartley with them as far as Zee Clarke's car on the street behind. He was not very belligerent, and ran like a frightened rabbit when Knight set him free.

Before Marty's apartment Zee Clarke stopped the car. "We're leaving you," she said. "Don't worry about Rierson. He'll take care of his own dead. I'll see you again."

For a long moment Marty held Tania's hand in parting. Then he said to Zee Clarke: "Thanks for all you've done." His voice was very serious. "Tania and I won't be working for The Reckoner any more."

"Says you!"

And Marty heard Zee Clarke's laugh as the car shot ahead.

# DRAWN IN BLOOD

TO MARTY DAY THE
VOICE OF THE RECKONER
HAD COME ONCE MORE—
WHISPERING ORDERS
TO KILL. AND THOUGH
EVERY FIBRE OF DAY'S
BEING SHOUTED "NO!"
HE DARED NOT DISOBEY.
WHAT AWFUL POWER
DID THAT INVISIBLE
DEATH-MASTER WIELD
FROM BEHIND HIS STEEL
CURTAIN? HOW COULD AN
UNKNOWN VOICE FORCE
MEN TO MURDER?

# CHAPTER ONE

# THE MAN WITH THE CANE

**M**ARTY DAY stretched slightly, flexed his muscles, and continued to drum nervously on the soft grass with the curved head of his fine steel cane. For the better part of an hour he had lain there prone on the grass, hidden by a clump of Rhododendron bushes, his arms before him, his cane grasped listlessly in both his hands.

Occasionally he'd thrust out the cane and with a single deft movement clip a bit of blue stone back onto the gravel path that ran around the apparently darkened house. Marty wondered if there were a light someplace behind the tightly drawn curtains of the second-story window there to his right? Plainly in the moonlight he could see the stone balcony; the thickness of ivy twisting from the ground to its rough balustrade. But he couldn't be certain if there were a light or not.

Marty was there at the command of the metallic voice that came to him over the wire; the man that he knew only as a voice and as a name; a name that struck terror to the evil-doers of the city—The Reckoner.

Until tonight Marty had not heard from that voice in some time. Indeed, he had decided to tell the voice when it called again that he, Marty Day, was through. But the voice had called, and Marty had not told him that. He had not told him anything. The words of defiance that were rushing to his lips when The Reckoner gave his terse orders were thrust back down his throat as The Reckoner finished. For the final words of the voice had been: "You must be there from twelve o'clock on, Mr. Day. Wait outside until you are needed. The life of Tania may—in fact, probably does—depend on your presence. That is all."

Then the phone had clicked off and Marty was calling to his servant,

Knight, for his cane—frantic to obey the orders he had decided only a moment before, to ignore.

Tania! Marty wet his lips and looked up at the dark window; the window behind which he sensed that there might be a light. Was Tania there? Tania, the girl who, more than anything else, had made him work along with The Reckoner. He thought, too, of the mystery girl, Zee Clarke; the dark sinister beauty of her amber eyes, and wondered where she fitted into—

Marty jarred erect, straight to his elbows. Distant; from somewhere in that house, but distinct just the same, had come the report of a gun.

**BEFORE** Marty could rise from the ground a light flashed in that room behind the balcony, as the curtains before the window were suddenly withdrawn. Then the French windows were thrown back.

Marty saw it all clearly now. The sudden blowing of the curtains in the gentle breeze, and a figure that hurled a foot over the window ledge and now stood upon the balcony.

Then things happened in that house. There was a second roar

Day hooked the cane around his neck.

of a gun and the falling of shattered glass upon the stone of the balcony. The small, erect figure silhouetted there acted quickly. It swung over the balustrade, dropped, seemed to hang there in mid-air, then grasping the ivy jerked quickly to the ground. It crouched for a moment in the soft earth below, and straightening stood alert, listening.

A door slammed somewhere in the house; feet beat on wood, died for a moment, then came again crunching along the gravel of the path.

The figure from the balcony now stood directly in the center of the gravel path. It was small, tense. The figure of a girl. There seemed nothing of panic in the movement of the girl's head; more, a quick sizing-up of the situation. But for a split second the moon shone directly on her face, white with horror. Marty drew in a breath. It was the girl, Tania. The girl who—

But feet from the back of the house beat quickly along gravel. A huge bulk of a man came into view. The white of his face was plainly visible in the darkness, the quickening of his stride, too, as he saw the girl. Then he called out. A warning, a threat. Words that were lost somewhere back in his throat.

Almost at once the girl swung, put silk-clad legs into action and darted down the path toward the front of the house.

The man on the path increased his speed; heavy feet pounded laboriously into the gravel. He quickly saw the impossibility of over-taking those quick young legs, and slowed down. He shouted something to the girl, and as he came into the moonlight directly before Marty, raised the wicked-looking stub-nosed automatic he held in his right hand.

Marty saw his face then. It was Joseph E. Rierson, the dominant figure in the city's crookedness; the man who protected others; the unknown quantity in crime. Plainly Marty saw the soft skin with the blue veins, the snapping gray little beadlike eyes, thick lips. Even the pudgy hand with the thick fingers that held the gun; the gun that in a moment would belch lead into the night, into—

And Rierson's body started to lope past him. Marty's cane shot suddenly forward. There was no uncertainty about its movement, no silent prayer from Marty's lips that by some good fortune he might hook the curved handle above the ankle of one of those moving legs. It was with the easy assurance of long practice that he shot out his right hand, gripped the smooth steel tightly, and with a quick jerk pulled the cane toward him with a peculiar twisting motion.

Rierson didn't stagger slightly, trip and finally fall to the gravel walk. The curved handle of that cane simply wound about the leg that was settling upon the blue stone. There was the sudden intake of Rierson's breath, a curse that died almost the moment it whistled in his throat. Then his great body was in the air. His gun roared, spat fire, and Joseph E. Rierson, ex-gunman, ex-racketeer, and now a political figure in the city, crashed face downward on the walk.

**MARTY** chuckled softly. He hated the smug Rierson since that night he had threatened to throw vitriol in the face of the bound and helpless Tania unless Marty divulged the name of The Reckoner. The Reckoner! Marty laughed. As if he knew— And the laugh died. Men were calling from the front of the house, an electric flash sent a pencil of light across the grass. The girl stopped, hesitated. Marty called hoarsely to her.

She turned, saw him, started toward him—and a shot came from the front of the house. Someone had made out her figure dimly there in the shadow. But the girl was gone, diving quickly into the thickness of the shrubbery.

Men rounded the corner of the house, paused and looked toward the bushes among which the girl had disappeared. And Marty acted. He moved quickly back into the moonlight, waved his hands once, and slipping close to the side of the house sped toward the rear. His scheme to attract their attention worked. They saw him. A shout went up, guns barked, and Marty darted wildly across an open stretch, zigzagging his way to the trees beyond. Bullets whistled about him and once, as he staggered in among the trees, he heard the dull thud of lead against wood, and felt the sting of a bit of bark from the tree flicked across his cheek.

He stumbled, thought for a moment that he was hit, straightened almost at once and was making his way between the protecting, towering trees. His car was around the other side of the house far up the block. Could he make his way to it? Marty shrugged his shoulders as the stone wall loomed up before him. No, he was no longer interested in his car. He hoped that Knight would have had sense enough to drive it away when the first shots came.

Marty was safe. Crouched there atop the wall he could look down the shaded street. The little stretch of well-kept grass; the sidewalk, with its huge trees between the walk and the curb; the incongruity of the concrete street with the country setting. And across the street the high iron fence of another estate.

Behind him Marty could still hear the tramping of men, the

smashing of shrubbery, a hoarse whisper or two and an occasional voice. But out on the deserted highway it was quiet. The house behind that iron fence across the street was set far back and the roar of the guns evidently had not been heard there. Marty dropped easily to the soft grass. He'd keep close to the wall until he reached the corner, slip down the block and make his way into the night.

Marty wondered about Tania. The men hadn't gone in the direction she had taken. The shadows were heavy and the foliage thick. Certainly she must have made preparation for escape. But why had she been there, and what had happened inside that house? Marty knew whose house it was. Major Hanson's. But the major was supposed to be out of town, playing polo.

And what interest could The Reckoner have in the major anyway? It was Senator Hopewell who held The Reckoner's attention. Senator Hopewell who was investigating crime in the city. The papers had said that Joseph E. Rierson was aiding the senator in his clean-up. Marty grinned at that. And he wondered, too, if Hopewell didn't grin also. He had the feeling that Hopewell wasn't to be taken in so easily; that perhaps, after all, he was simply leading Rierson on to his downfall. Certainly if The Reckoner wished, he could supply Senator Hopewell with plenty of evidence about Rierson and his associates.

**MARTY** cut short his thoughts, shoved his back against the ivy-covered wall. Something had moved there by a tree not more than fifty feet from him. He tried to push himself further back against the hard stone; gripped his cane tightly in his right hand.

For certainly against the blackness of the tree he saw something white; thin streaks of white, as if a hand with fingers parted clutched the bark.

Marty cursed softly as he gripped his cane. Just one man. He wished he had taken a leaf from Knight's book and brought a gun with him. Not much use the cane now. And the hand on the tree moved. The white of the fingers didn't stand out so plainly now, and as Marty's eyes riveted on them he suddenly realized they were gripping not the bark of a tree but the dull heaviness of a gun; a gun the nose of which was pointing in his direction.

Had the man seen him? Marty turned and felt for the top of that wall. He was young, strong and agile. Just a jump, the tightening of fingers and he could swing over the wall, skirt along inside the estate and drop over the wall again well down the block.

Body crouched, cane across his arm, his glance darting from the top of that wall to the steady black thing held in the white hand, Marty hesitated. Plainly he heard the cracking of a twig, voices from behind that wall. He was trapped; trapped unless—

Marty started moving, slinking along the wall, back in the direction he had come; away from that menacing figure.

Apparently he hadn't been seen after all! Well, it was just as easy to disappear down a side street in one direction as another. He—

And a voice spoke; spoke from behind that tree; from behind that gun which suddenly no longer merged with the tree but stood out from it, wavering slightly, as if the man who held it were uncertain of Marty's exact position.

The voice said: "Drop your gun and step out on the grass; both hands up, Bozo. Come on, now! Drop that rod or I'll make a sieve out of you."

Drop that rod! The words of the man stirred a new hope in Marty. Evidently the man thought he was armed. Marty liked the idea and fostered it. He answered, in a voice not his own natural one but hissed through the side of his mouth.

"Easy does it, hard guy," Marty said. He thought that he saw a slouch hat edge out about where the man's head should be. And he thought too, from the position of the man's gun, that the head was no longer beneath that hat; that it was a blind to draw his fire.

Marty went on. "You stick that face of yours from behind that tree, and by next spring there'll be daisies growing on it." And in the easy indifferent voice of one who is not at all worried, "Or maybe you like flowers."

The man coughed and his gun cracked, and lead sprayed off the wall unpleasantly close to Marty. That was not so good. It would bring those from the other side of the wall. Marty thought quickly. The man would naturally expect him to return the fire and would be careful to be well behind that tree. Even as the last shot blazed in the darkness, the white hand and the flashing gun disappeared behind the tree.

For a few seconds the man would wait, silent there. For a minute perhaps. And in a minute— But Marty didn't think any longer. He was away from that wall; out in the open, running at top speed, his feet beating silently over the soft grass.

**MARTY** didn't dodge in and out among trees now. He didn't expect shots to follow him that quickly. But he knew that death—violent and certain death—was not far behind him. He knew those hirelings of Rierson; knew how badly Rierson wanted his life; knew as well as Rierson knew that if he lived—

And the shots came, much sooner than Marty had anticipated. There were no whizzing warnings past his head, just the sharp rat-tat of a spitting gun on the silent street.

But there was the corner a hundred yards away—fifty now. If he could turn that corner he'd have the whole block in which to disappear. He could make half of it before his pursuer would turn the corner. He could cross the street, or better still, go back into Major Hanson's grounds. They'd never suspect that. The last place in the world they'd look for him!

Thirty yards—twenty-five. Marty was a little proud of himself. His wind was good. Perhaps he was not as fast as he used to be when he was steadily in training, but he had kept in good trim and—

His feet skidded in the grass; he almost lost his balance as he turned suddenly and flashed out over the sidewalk, into the street. Two men had turned the corner; two men who seemed as surprised to see him as he was to see them. Men who separated quickly and reached frantically for their guns.

They did not shoot at once but called hoarsely to him to halt. There was a decisive note in their voices, authority; but uncertainty too, and Marty suddenly understood. These men were not Rierson thugs. They were of the police. Plainly, as he half turned his head, he saw the flash of brass buttons. One, at least, was in uniform.

Marty had no desire to meet the police, but they were better than being shot to death by hired assassins. Already, as he slowed down, he was thinking what he'd say. He had been attacked by hold-up men; was fleeing for his life!

"Take it easy there," one of the men was saying as Marty's feet scraped along the cement. "What's this shooting and what's— Geez! The lousy bum intends to run us down." The man who spoke jumped frantically back to the curb he had just left.

There was a flash of lights, the roar of a motor, the grinding of brakes, followed by the screech of protesting tires as Marty, too, leaped for his life and a big black car swept between him and the law. The back of the car swung sharply. Marty clutched at the handle of the side door, felt his feet slipping beneath the hurtling car, pulled himself to safety and clutched for his cane. The next instant he had thrust his body through the open window above the door and was on his hands and knees on the whirling, pitching, floor of the car.

"The devil, Knight!" Marty said sharply. "Those were police. And we have nothing to fear from the police tonight." Then Marty climbed over and dropped into the seat beside Knight. "Will they spot the car?"

"Not them!" said Knight, with emphasis. "They'll have trouble locating the owner of the numbers on this car. As for fearing the police—" and Knight swung a corner suddenly, jarred the rear wheels against the curb and straightened out again. "Hear that!"

And Marty did hear it. The screech of a police siren on the block they had just left. They were off again, straight toward the city.

"I don't know what happened in that house, Mr. Day, but I left the car and sneaked down the street and saw that bit of vermin, Rierson. He was talking to Lieutenant Frank Bradley. I got under the hedge and listened, and got part of the conversation. I heard Bradley say that it was the second time Rierson had tried to implicate you in something. And I heard Rierson tell him to cover your apartment and the house of Frederick Strome, the banker, and trip you on an alibi."

Marty drew in a deep breath. "What did Lieutenant Bradley say?"

"He said something about Strome having an unimpeachable character. Then some shots came, and he ordered those two men around the block. And I picked you up just in time."

"But what happened in Major Hanson's house?"

"I don't know." Knight shook his head. "But whatever it was, it was enough." And suddenly, "That lad behind drives like a lunatic. It's a cinch they've picked up our trail again. Will I try losing them up and down blocks?"

Marty shook his head. "No, Knight, no—" he said slowly. "If Strome is to be any good as an alibi I must be there at once."

"Right!" said Knight, as he pushed the accelerator down to the floor. "You'll have to hop fast. Then I'll drive the car to the garage. The garage is covered, of course."

And Marty laughed. "The Reckoner owns the garage. Go home and go to bed. You never sleep. The car's alibi and yours will be perfect."

"Quite right," said Knight. "But after all, Mr. Day, it's you, and not the car or me, this Rierson skunk wants."

Marty nodded. "And I want him. By God! Knight, they're right on our tail. You'd better slow down for the corner. I'll get into Strome's from the block behind, of course. I wonder just what happened at Hanson's tonight, and I wonder about Tania."

"If she had a coupe—gray, and was sporting a Connecticut license," said Knight, "you don't have to worry about her. That car passed me just after I left the hedge. And it was traveling like a bat out of hell."

## CHAPTER TWO

## THE LAW'S LONG ARM

**S**ILENCE AFTER that. Knight drove with a grim determination to outdistance the police car behind, and the police car hung on. Back in the city streets, things were not so good. Twice Knight skipped through a red light, and the second time Marty felt the dull thud and heard, too, the crash of metal as they tore off the front bumper of a taxi.

"Careful!" Marty's hand rested for a moment on Knight's tense right arm as the car swerved dangerously, righted itself and sped on.

Knight grinned and said: "Always wanted to give a taxi driver a thrill; they've given me plenty. Slowed up the pursuing car, eh?"

Marty looked back, nodded his satisfaction, and seeing Knight's eyes glued to the road ahead, said: "You gained a couple of blocks on them."

Grimly Marty watched their progress. Not far to go now. They had swung a corner and for a moment the police car was not in sight. But Marty knew the chase could not go on much longer. The screeching siren behind would bring others into it. Quick word would be flashed along the line; a message to headquarters, and then the short wave radio alarm and— He looked at the flying street numbers. It would be much easier to duck in and out of streets, change the license tags and— Marty shook his head. He wanted an alibi; an alibi he couldn't get unless he reached Frederick Strome's house before the police. From what Knight had told him, Marty knew that Lieutenant Bradley would go straight to the banker's residence. Marty must be there first.

Frank Bradley was an honest, efficient officer. Rierson knew that, and Rierson made use of him for that very reason. Now—

And Knight spoke. "Clear ahead and clear behind," he said, and the car slowed down a bit.

Marty Day looked at the stone fronts of the houses, flung open the door of the car and was in the air even as Knight stepped on the gas again. The team work was perfect.

Marty's moving feet struck the hard pavement and kept going. So accurate was his timing that he did not even lose his stride. His speed took him by the first brown-stone front, up on the sidewalk and almost beyond the second house before he swung quickly and disappeared in the dimness of the alley between two houses.

Even then Marty's speed did not slacken. Running lightly on his toes he passed the length of that alley, sped across the open stone court in the rear, and hooking his cane to the tab sewed under his arm lightly vaulted the fence. He was breathing easily when he jumped to the barrel and let himself in the open window that gave on Frederick Strome's little conservatory.

Passing gingerly down the lines of potted plants Marty opened a glass door, and hanging his coat, hat and cane on the hooks in the small hall stepped to the door beyond.

A moment later he flung open that door and was brushing back his hair with a pocket comb and flicking the dust and dirt from his trouser legs.

**FREDERICK STROME** leaned against the mantelpiece. He was breathing hard and little beads of perspiration stood out on his forehead. He said, without preliminaries: "A police car just went down the block and turned the corner. I tell you, Mr. Day, if I thought for one moment that I was entering into a conspiracy to—"

"Yes, yes. I know," Marty said impatiently. "That's where you and I are different. I'm in this thing for what's in it for me. You're in it, no doubt, because you have to be in it. We have nothing in common except perhaps we both take orders. But," and Marty pointed to the small table with the half-played game of chess upon it, the bottle of Scotch and silver pail of ice and the two partly filled glasses, "if that police car had stopped here directly, you'd find it hard to explain this little layout."

"You think they'll come back?" The banker rubbed a handkerchief across his forehead.

"Sit down!" Marty said sharply. "They'll come back. Probably they're just around the corner. That smacks of Rierson's suggestion. Now, now," as Strome started to talk again, "I know. Don't tell me again. Your motives are highly altruistic. I am not interested in your reasons; only the results. You'll excuse me if I attend to my nails while we discuss the game. Rhododendron plants evidently thrive best in thick black soil."

Frederick Strome coughed once, leaned ever and placed a bit of ice in Marty's glass, watched Marty light the partly smoked cigar and tried not to frown as Marty talked.

"Let me see." Marty thought aloud. "We had exchanged bishops just after I checked your king and prevented your castleing. Now, damn it! Strome, my memory's gone back on me, or you actually copped a rook on me while I was gone. Even if these little games don't—"

"I hope," Strome cut in as he drummed on the table, "that nothing untoward happened tonight."

"Not yet." Marty grinned as he puffed on the cigar. "But it will if you don't take that frown of disapproval off your face and stop perspiring all over the board." And jerking suddenly erect and pushing his king's bishop far down the board, "That's the doorbell. Your butler? Has he been in the room tonight?"

"Only once." The words stuck in Strome's throat. "I kept him by the door, where he couldn't see the chess board. But he heard me talking to you—er—apparently talking to you."

"Good!" Marty nodded. "We'll make a first-rate criminal out of you some day, Strome. Perhaps a step up from being a banker, eh?"

Strome puffed out like a pouter pigeon. "The suggestion of carrying on such a conversation came from you. I—" And turning as the door opened, "What is it, Collins? I told you—" And coming to his feet as two men pushed by the servant and entering the room. "To whom am I indebted for this—this intrusion?"

Marty nodded his satisfaction. He didn't know just what The Reckoner had done for, or held over the head of Strome. But he certainly had picked a good man. For all Strome's nervousness and apologies and explanations he was a wonder when the pinch came.

**LIEUTENANT FRANK BRADLEY** stood in the doorway. Behind him and pushing his way forward was Joseph E. Rierson. He glared from behind the police officer at Marty. Bradley didn't like the situation and showed it. He looked at Strome. Strome was not a big man as big men go in a large city, but he was president of a bank, had influence in his district and could make things distinctly unpleasant down at headquarters.

Bradley's steady, unemotional eyes took in Marty Day. "I'm sorry," he said. "I came to see Mr. Day. It's rather important."

"Yes, yes. Of course." Frederick Strome played with the chain across his vest, and looked at Marty. "You wish to talk with him alone?"

"We wish," Rierson cut in quickly and with some heat, "to know how long Mr. Day has been here, what you did, and if—"

"Before you bother to answer this man, Mr. Strome," Marty said, "we'll hear what the lieutenant has to say. I've never met Lieutenant Bradley; that is, formally. But I know of him by reputation. This other person has no authority whatsoever."

The doubt in Bradley's eyes was turning slightly to suspicion, Marty thought, so he hurried to start the seeds of a new one in Bradley's mind. An officer of Bradley's record, Bradley's efficiency, could not be unfamiliar with the unpleasant gossip concerning Joseph E. Rierson—big political influence or not.

"If," Marty said to the officer, "in the performance of your duty, you wish me to establish an alibi, very well. Mr. Strome will answer any questions you wish, and I too—and his man, of course."

"Alibi?" Bradley's eyebrows went up. "What put that word into your head?"

"Rierson," said Marty promptly. "This is not his first attempt. You recall the other, though you very wisely took no part in it. There is, of course, an unpleasantness between Mr. Rierson and myself."

"An unpleasantness!" Bradley looked at Rierson. "Personal?"

"Very personal." Marty nodded gravely. "So personal that neither one of us, I'm sure, would care to discuss it."

"That's a lie." Rierson shot his face forward, and for the first time Marty got a good look at it. It was hard for him not to smile. The blue stone of the pathway had dug and scraped. Now the veins of Rierson's face were crossed with red lines. It looked as though some animal had clawed it.

Marty moved closer to Rierson; squinted his eyes. "It is Rierson, isn't it?" he said in mock doubt. And then, "You shave too close or don't pay enough attention to the radio advice on—"

"This man's a crook and he works for—for—" Rierson bit his lip. Although he killed the hasty words, the anger still remained in his little eyes and the pudgy fingers at his side clasped and unclasped.

"Max Arnold is my lawyer," Marty started, but Bradley stopped him.

"No cause for unpleasantness now, gentlemen. You've been kind enough to give us full swing here, Mr. Day." And to Frederick Strome, "Form, sir. Police routine. What time did Mr. Day arrive here?"

And Lieutenant Bradley did ask questions. But Marty's alibi was perfect. Collins, the servant, all unconscious of the perjury committed, let his imagination stretch a bit and told of hearing the voice of "both Strome and Mr. Day, sir."

The interview concluded, Rierson and Bradley left, and despite Strome's objections Marty insisted upon finishing the game.

**IT WAS** only a short walk from the banker's residence to Marty's exclusive apartment house. Marty went slowly down the banker's steps, paused to light a cigarette and was quite conscious of the figure that moved along the sidewalk toward him before the hand was placed on his shoulder.

"I was wondering if you'd let me walk with you, Mr. Day," Lieutenant Bradley said.

"More questions?" asked Marty.

"No." Bradley shook his head. "I may have some answers for you though." And after a rather long pause, "And a warning."

Together the two men walked down the block. Bradley talked. Nothing, at first, that interested Marty. Mostly what Bradley knew about his past, and it was rather a thorough knowledge.

"You had money, Mr. Day; ran around the world a bit. Then you lost it in the crash. And now—you're up again. Not that I mean you were ever down, but you're getting money some place that isn't on the books. There's no doubt you're right and Rierson is trying to put the finger on you. And Rierson is talking about that myth of the underworld; that righter of wrongs, The Reckoner. Yes, Mr. Day, I'm beginning to believe in him myself."

Marty laughed. "Sounds fantastic to me," he said. "But Rierson does think I know something about it." And with a shrug of his shoulders, "But it's nothing for the police to worry about. A doer of good deeds, as I understand the mythical Reckoner."

"No—" Bradley stretched the word out. "Righting wrongs with vengeance is not the law's idea of justice. Fighting crime with crime. Did you ever think, Mr. Day, that perhaps this Reckoner is working for his own profit. The good of The Reckoner rather than the good of humanity."

"Really," said Marty, "I never thought much about it, for I never took much stock in it."

"Well, think about it." In the darkness Bradley nodded very seriously. "You're a young man who likes excitement, and you can use money. But remember that crime is crime, no matter if you smear it with the honey of righting wrongs. You've got a police department to dispense justice."

Marty laughed. "What about Joseph E. Rierson? Former gangster, racketeer, murderer. Now a political leader. You're not going to stand there and tell me you know he's straight."

"You're a citizen," said Bradley slowly. "It's your vote that makes our laws, elects our officials. Make a charge against him; don't talk generalities or his past environment. Give me something I can stick on Joseph E. Rierson or any other man, and I'll put the finger on him. After all, he was in the confidence of Senator Hopewell." And very slowly with those steady eyes on Marty, "He was with me at Major Hanson's tonight."

"And what," said Marty, "was Joseph Rierson doing at Major Hanson's tonight, and how does it interest me?"

"He went there with me," Lieutenant Bradley said very slowly. "He has an alibi as good as yours, if that's what you're thinking about. We had dinner together."

"Something—something happened at Major Hanson's?"

Bradley looked at Marty long and fixedly. "No," he said slowly, "you couldn't know. You're the kind that would show it. But someone left the house by a window who did know."

"And how am I and The—this Reckoner connected with that, if you do believe in The Reckoner because Rierson does?"

"Not because Rierson does. Senator Hopewell called to see me today—or rather, yesterday, now. He had a message that The Reckoner would put valuable information into his hands tonight. Suggestive, that? But here we are at your apartment. Sorry I can't come in."

Marty shook hands with Bradley there on the curb. Queer man, Bradley. What good had the walk done him? Was he studying Marty? And if he were, what had he found out?"

"Good night!" said Bradley.

But Marty held his hand. "You promised me some answers." He smiled. "Changed your mind?"

"Well, I don't know." Bradley shook his head. "There'll be an awful smell in the papers about it in the morning. Senator Hopewell was shot to death tonight. The servants say he let in the expected visitor himself; the messenger from The Reckoner. You see, Major Claude Hanson, the sportsman, had turned over his home to Senator Hopewell."

Marty stood there on the sidewalk as Lieutenant Bradley turned slowly and walked down the street. Marty was stunned. But chaos or not, in his mind, he thought that he knew the truth. Rierson had planned things; planned things to strike directly at The Reckoner, at him, at Tania. Yes, Frederick Strome had served a good purpose that night.

Marty stood silently before the massive doors of his apartment house, trying to figure things out. Rierson had the confidence of Senator Hopewell. What was more likely than that Hopewell had told him of this message from The Reckoner? Yes, Rierson was going to stamp out the activities of The Reckoner with crime and blood—and murder.

## CHAPTER THREE

## TORTURE

**TANIA! THAT** was Marty's single thought as he walked through the palm-lined hall of his pretentious apartment house. Ignoring the attended elevators he walked to the automatic lifts in the rear, and ascending to his own floor passed slowly over the smooth tile.

Tania! Had Rierson planned to trap her at the Hanson estate; bring Bradley and the police, perhaps at the very moment Hopewell was murdered? And Marty too? Joseph Rierson knew that they both worked for The Reckoner. He couldn't prove it of course, but he knew it just the same. And he knew also, or at least made a very good guess at it, that Marty was there; there in the Rhododendron bushes when Tania let herself out of that lighted room. Perhaps the room of death; the room where the murdered body of Senator Hopewell still lay.

Marty nodded. That was it. That was the horror he had seen on the girl's face for that brief second in the moonlight. Then another thought. Perhaps Tania had seen the murderer, gotten clean away and— But why such thoughts? Tania knew that he was there; knew that he thought of her all the time. She would get in touch with him; let him know that she was safe. Even now her message might be inside, there on the little pad by the telephone.

Gingerly Marty stuck his key in the lock, hesitated after the first long click and thought of Knight. Fine servant, Knight. And fine friend, too. He mustn't disturb his sleep now. He was selfish about that. Knight never seemed to get much sleep.

So it was that Marty slowly turned the knob of that door and softly let himself into the apartment. He tossed off his hat and coat and placed them on the costumer in the hall, half started to drape his cane over a hook, grinned and thought better of it. That cane was anything but the simple adornment of a gentleman. That is, in the hands of Marty. He flexed it now, watched the steel glimmer even in the dull hall light. Yes, a good weapon; a terrible, deadly weapon too when properly used. Marty could feel the heavy steel spring beneath that fine outer covering vibrate as the cane arched between his strong hands. Just a single snap, and that handle—Marty hung the cane in the crook of his arm, entered the living room and went straight to the phone on the little table beneath the single light.

It was there—the message he had hoped for; more than he had hoped for. Tania was not only safe but she was coming to see him. Coming at once; due almost any minute. There it was, in Knight's methodical, round, school-boy hand.

> Miss T. called. She is all right but wishes to see you. I suggested different under the circumstances, but she is coming here at once.

There was nothing more. The handwriting was Knight's all right. There could be no mistake about that. Yet something was missing. That great "K" that Knight had the habit of smearing at the bottom of such memoranda.

Marty leaned forward and read the note again; looked at it closely. There was the beginning of the "K," he thought. As if Knight had started it and stopped—stopped suddenly, interrupted in the very act of making it. The telephone again perhaps? Marty frowned. No—it wouldn't take a second to mark down the two quick lines. It—

And Marty knew just what had interrupted Knight; felt the presence even before he heard the voice and straightened, tense and alert.

The voice spoke behind him. "Make a move for that gun, wise guy, and I'll blow the top of your head off."

MARTY turned slowly, mechanically, and faced the man. That hard, cruel, flat face seemed out of place above the well-tailored gray tweed suit. In a single glance Marty took in the man from the tip of his bright yellow shoes with the brown spats to the gray fedora that was shoved far back on well-oiled black hair. Marty didn't speak. He just stared at the man; at the heavy black automatic held in unwavering fingers, and was glad he had decided to leave the cane hanging over his left arm. This man looked as if he were used to carrying guns—and worse, Marty thought with a little gulp, accustomed to using them.

"Sit down!" The man jerked his gun in the direction of the couch, and when Marty dropped onto it, "We're waiting for a visitor; you and me, eh?"

"Where's Knight?" The words came tonelessly from Marty's throat. The dead silence of the apartment; the evil glint in those narrow eyes; the menacing gun and the cursing, cruel lips all jerked those words from Marty.

"The skinny guy with stooped shoulders?" The man laughed. "The punk that left the note about Miss T? Don't worry about him. He rather fancied himself as a gunman." A shrug of broad shoulders. "He's taking a nap now. It's Miss T. I'm interested in."

"Why?" Marty gasped.

"Well," the man stroked his chin with his free left hand, "for one thing, I was thinking of building a fire on her face." He laughed hollowly. "An old Indian custom!"

Marty shuddered, moved his left arm slightly so that the cane draped across his knee. Tania might come any minute, and he couldn't stop her. Just soft feet across the tile outside, and the key in the lock. How glad he had been when she had first taken that key and promised to use his apartment as a place of refuge in time of danger. Now, if she only didn't have the key! She would have to ring the bell, or tap. That would be enough to give Marty a chance to bring his cane into action, dive from the couch toward the man. The chances were that he would be shot of course. But what of that? The very sound of the shot that killed him would warn her of the danger—but now—just a turn of a key.

Marty measured the distance between him and the man with the gun. "What have you got against Miss—Miss T?" Marty asked finally.

"Nothing. Nothing personal. It's just a job to do, and I'm the guy to do it."

And Marty saw it. A shadow beyond the man; a shadow that came from the hall which led to the bedrooms, to Knight's room. Marty stiffened on the couch. Someone was in that hallway; the shadow was plainly visible. Long legs that folded at the knees, and climbing up a chair stretched into a grotesque body along the wall; a bobbing body.

Knight! Good old Knight had not then been as unconscious as this gunman thought. Knight who, if tied, had now— And a board creaked under feet in that hallway. Marty looked quickly into the rat-like eyes. The man grinned. Evidently he had not heard. Would Knight have a gun, or would he have to pounce on the man from behind? Marty spoke quickly, sparring for time; to drown out those moving feet.

He said: "What job?"

"Just the name of a certain party. A guy that hitches the fancy moniker, The Reckoner, onto himself."

"Rierson sent you?" Marty shot in the words.

**THE MAN** shrugged. "Maybe you know all the answers, buddy. That's what I've got to find out. I've been told you're one of those noble birds that lives like a movie hero. Death before dishonor, and such baloney. That's why they sent me to work on you. I've got ways of putting heroes on their knees, screaming for mercy. But since the little lady is making a midnight call—well, I always take the easiest way."

"She doesn't know." Marty shook his head.

"No?" The man laughed. "Well, I ain't a guy to ask ladies questions they can't answer. I'll let you do the talking."

"But I don't know either."

Again the board creaked. What had happened to Knight? Why didn't he act? The man wouldn't see him enter the room. Just a sudden lunge; just get the gunman's attention even, and Marty would go into action. What was Knight waiting for? Was he waiting for the coming of Tania; to catch the gunman by surprise then; to shoot maybe as the man stepped back to watch both Tania and Marty? Marty nodded. Yes, that movement would put the man in the line of fire from the little hall there to the right. Perhaps that was best. Knight would be shooting from darkness into light.

But the gunman was speaking, leaning far forward; just a few feet between him and Marty. And Marty was grasping his cane firmly in both his hands. If that evil face would come just a bit closer! Marty's eyes shifted to the shadow; the bobbing, weaving shadow which should any moment turn into a man. No—the distance was too great. He would have to throw out both his hands before the cane went into action. He wouldn't chance it. Not with Knight so close.

"Listen, feller." Thick, sensuous lips curved up, disclosing stained, uneven teeth. "I'm paid plenty for this job. I'm paid because I get results. I—" He straightened, half turned so that his back was to the wall and he could cover both the entrance hall to the living room and Marty there on the couch.

There was the slightest click of steel against steel, then the more pronounced snap of a lock. A moment of silence and a door closing softly. Marty did not cry out. He sat there stiff and straight, his hands gripping his cane, his eyes staring down the room where the girl would enter. In that moment, which must be as tense for the gunman as it was for Marty, Knight would act.

Tania came. Running feet now along the hall, and her voice just before she turned into the living room. "Marty, Marty!" she called out. "It's been terrible. I saw him murdered. I saw the man who—"

And the words died, choked in the girl's throat. The sudden red of eagerness to reach Marty drained from her cheeks as her feet scraped along the polished floor and she drew up sharp, to stare straight into the grinning face of the man who held the gun.

"You!" she jarred out in a hoarse whisper. "The man who murdered Senator Hopewell."

And in that single sentence, Marty saw death for Tania; death for both of them.

"Knight!" he cried out, and half rose to his feet.

And the shadow in the doorway moved back quickly and merged with the figure that entered the room. The figure was tall and the shoulders were slightly stooped and the hand it thrust forward carried a gun; a gun that was— Marty gasped almost in the moment he was going to let fly his cane at the head of the gunman who was staring so steadily, and moving his gun so steadily toward Tania.

And the gun the shadow held; the shadow that had become a man, was not directed toward the gunman who now watched Tania, but toward him—toward Marty. Marty cursed inwardly as he dropped his hand. The shadow was not Knight. Marty knew it, of course, before the man spoke. But he didn't fully digest the shock until the words reached him.

"No, no." The man leaned forward and sharp eyes centered on Marty. "Don't you worry none about a certain Mr. Knight. He's safe and sound. What do you say, boss? Will I give this bloat a bellyful of lead?" He jammed his gun into Marty's stomach, dragged the cane from his hand and tossed it across the room. Marty's last hope; his last weapon of defense! He had been a fool. But then, he was so sure that Knight had been there. Why had the man stayed there out of the light, waiting? And a minute later Marty was to know the answer to that question.

MARTY'S hands were tied behind his back by the new arrival. A quick, sure, workmanlike job, because the flat-faced man had grabbed Tania roughly, swung her around and kept his gun trained on Marty while his partner worked.

"Is it true—what the girl said, boss?" The man who came from the hall spoke as he jerked the last bit of rope tight into a knot, drawing Marty's arms so far up that he had to bend forward. "Did she—can she put the finger on you for that—the bit of business at Major Hanson's tonight?"

"Shut up!" the boss snapped back, and all the humor, gruesome or otherwise, had gone out of his voice. "We've got a personal interest in things from now on. Sort of knocking over two birds with one stone."

"Or one razor." The other nodded. "Will I fix up the dame?" He jerked a thumb toward Tania, who stood silent, staring at the flat-faced man.

Things moved swiftly after that and with a mechanical precision that not only surprised Marty but sent terror surging through his body like an electric shock. These men were no novices at this business of—Marty gulped—of torture.

Marty wasn't sure after that if he tried to attack the man who had bound his hands. He did know that he had refused to leave the room despite the prodding gun that the flat-faced one dug into his back. And the man who had bound him walked straight across the room to Tania and without a word closed his right hand and struck her violently on the chin. Marty saw her great brown eyes open wide, and he thought that her lips framed his name as her knees gave and she sank to the floor.

He knew that a sort of insane anger possessed him for the moment. He knew that he tried to do something but couldn't. And the flat-faced man behind him raised his gun and struck him on the head. Marty's knees wavered and a hand came out and steadied him slightly, thrust him forward toward the hall that led to the bedrooms.

Stumbling, staggering, half supported by the man behind, Marty was shoved into that hall. In a dazed way he saw Knight, bound and gagged there, against the wall. "That was it then," something inside his head kept saying. The bobbing shadow, the slightly squeaking boards was the man binding Knight. Things must have happened just before Marty entered the apartment. Things must have happened—

But things were happening now. Things Marty was doing nothing to prevent; things he could do nothing to prevent.

Hands behind his back, feet uncertainly lifting and falling, body careening from one wall of the narrow hall to the other, Marty was forced along; knocked sideways through an open door by the nose of the gun and into his bedroom. There was a buzzing in his head from the blows of the gun, a mist before his eyes, and an uncertainty to his thoughts.

One thought Marty did get and keep. His head would have to be clear. He would have to be able to think if he was going to help Tania. Instinctively this thought dominated his every action. He must obey the instructions of the leader behind him. There must be no more blows on the head—

A hand stretched out and gripped at his throat, jerked him backward with such force that his head jarred against the top of the straight-back chair. In a dim way, as he sat there, he could see his bed, and beyond it the open door to the hall. He shook his head and tried to clear the fog from before his eyes.

"That's the stuff," the man behind him said grimly. "You'll want to see the whole show; see it before things get so far you won't have the guts to stand it."

**MARTY** heard footsteps pass up and down the hall. He had been a fool. Why hadn't he fought it out before? Why hadn't he made the man shoot him? What did it matter if he died? They would hardly have waited for the girl with Marty dead there on the floor. He half turned his head to look at the man behind him, and felt the cold nose of the gun knock his head forward again.

"What are you going to do? What are you going to do?" a voice asked over and over before Marty realized it was his own.

The man behind him didn't answer. Marty sat straight in the chair. Footsteps again in the hall. Slow, even, labored steps that hesitated, then came on. And Marty saw the other man, the stooped shoulders more bent now under the burden he carried. It was Tania; feet and arms tightly bound. Marty could not see her face.

Fascinated, Marty saw the man turn sideways so as to ease the girl's feet through the door. There was a dull thud, a choked scream from Tania and a laugh from the man as her head struck brutally against the side of the doorway.

A hand grasped Marty's throat as he half jumped from the chair. "Easy does it, brother," the voice behind him said. "You haven't seen anything yet."

Marty's vision was clear now; too clear. He saw Tania's face; the whiteness of it. The set lips and the brown eyes, open, staring—terror in them.

"No trouble here, 'Razor.'" The tall man threw the girl on the bed. "They built this place for it. You could almost rattle off a Tommy-gun without it being heard." He looked down at the girl as she lay there on her back. "Will I stuff up her mouth or will I let her sing?"

The man behind Marty hesitated before he spoke, then he said: "Let her squeal a bit. After all, it's Mr. Day's show. He's entitled to a thrill or two. Here, Fritz, take this bozo. Keep your hand on his throat. Crown him if he gets clowning around. But don't shoot him."

The lanky man, Fritz, moved quickly behind Marty. A gun dug into the back of his neck; strong fingers came around and encircled his throat. The other man, called Razor, moved quickly to the bed, tossed his gun upon it, dug a hand in his pocket and swept it out again. With a single jerk the shining black curved object it held snapped open. And Marty knew where the man got his name. He was holding a wicked-looking razor beneath the light by the bed. He looked down at the girl, grinned and nodded, then lifting a few strands of hair from beneath her hat he held them a moment in his left hand. The keen edge of the razor hardly moved. The man turned and tossed the bits of hair away. They separated and floated easily to the floor.

**MARTY'S** mouth opened and closed. A dry tongue licked at drier lips but no words came.

The man by the bed spoke. "I won't kid you along, Mr. Day," he said slowly. "I want to know who The Reckoner is. I've been called fiendish. I've been called The Devil. Doctors cut up people for their own good. I'm going to cut up this little lady for someone else's good. You give me the name. I'll buzz a certain party on the phone, and if he's satisfied you didn't lie, you can have the dame in undamaged condition."

"You'd kill her anyway. She saw you tonight, and—"

Razor scowled. "We won't discuss that. She's not in a position to squawk to the cops—not her, nor you neither. You heard my proposition. One of you talks, or—" He flourished the razor above the girl and turned directly to Marty. "I'm not one to describe the details of my methods of getting conversation. I'm a man of action, not words; and I work fast and don't drag things out. Now—the name of this man; the real identity of The Reckoner!"

Should Marty lie to him; make up a name? Would he know, or would Rierson know? Marty saw the man's eyes, the evil mouth. If he lied to him and the man knew it—well, Marty felt that he was looking inside the man and what he saw there filled him with loathing, horror. Here was a man who would find pleasure in torturing a helpless girl. Who would— But if Marty could convince him that neither he nor Tania knew the identity of The Reckoner, then—

And Marty said: "But we don't know. No more than you know or Rierson know. We—"

The man's face changed. Eyes narrowed, lips slipped back like the snarl of an animal. He gripped the razor tightly in his hand as he moved toward Marty. His words were low and forced through his teeth with a whistling sound.

"You think I'm going to give it to you and the dame anyway, talk or no talk. Well, have it that way. Now, do you want me to drag the blade across her throat and be done with it, or—" His face was very close to Marty's. Marty could feel his hot breath across his cheek. "Look at me. Do I look like a guy who talks just to hear his own voice? All right. You've got ten seconds to tell me what I want to know."

The man swung back, reached the side of the bed and stood there above the girl, the razor extended. "Do you know what I'm going to do, Mr. Day? Count just ten, then gouge an eye out for you. One—two—"

The man was counting; he had reached seven. There was a Satanic expression to his lips, and gloating in the way he called off the numbers. Tania tried to move now, but the man swept down his left hand and fastened the fingers on her white throat. It wasn't bluff. Things went black to Marty for a moment. Fear, terror, horror all turned to one thing now. Blazing, insane rage.

Marty Day jerked forward, felt the fingers tighten upon his throat, put all his strength into the effort to break free. What would he do then? He didn't know exactly. He only knew that, hands bound behind him or not, he'd dive straight for the man called Razor; use his head, his feet, his teeth even. Anything, to—

Nails were biting into his neck; nails that tore at his skin and gave slightly. The man who held him cursed, mouthed something about cracking his skull wide open, and just as those nails seemed to be tearing loose from his neck Marty stopped in his effort, gave slightly and jerked back into the chair again.

In the struggle his head was turned, his eyes torn from the helpless girl upon the bed. Now Marty was looking straight toward the hall door; the door that was open and that now framed a figure. A figure that Marty recognized at once. It was the sinister, uncertain quantity in this game with crime that he played. It was Zee Clarke, the girl with the amber eyes.

## CHAPTER FOUR

## THE BODY IN THE BAG

**A**MBER EYES. Steady, piercing eyes that held no fear or terror; just a deadly earnestness, a purpose. A purpose which the man behind Marty must have seen and recognized, even as Marty did. For Zee Clarke held in a small white hand a gun. No tiny automatic this, that girls of the night and girls in fiction carry, but a heavy forty-five police automatic.

The man behind Marty called out a warning. The razor in the other's hand paused almost at it started down toward the girl. Then

Marty saw the gun that was jammed over his shoulder. He moved his head quickly against that arm. There was a roar close to his ear, a streak of yellow-blue flame before his eyes. Two streaks, as the weapon in Zee Clarke's hand flashed fire.

Zee Clarke still stood in the doorway; close to her head was torn white wood. And the man behind Marty, what of him? Marty jerked his head. The chair shook; there was a slight thump as the man sank to his knees, a heavier thump as he fell forward on his face.

Hardly thirty seconds had passed since Zee Clarke was first framed in that doorway. But in those seconds Razor had turned his head, taken in the situation, stood perhaps stunned for the moment when his friend fell. Now, as Marty looked toward him, Razor sprang for the gun on the foot of the bed.

But for Tania he would have had it. Consciously or unconsciously now that no hand held her, the girl twisted and kicked out with both feet. The gun slid across the bed, hung for a moment on the edge, then crashed to the floor. And Marty acted. He threw himself forward and butted Razor just as he reached for the gun.

Zee Clarke called out. "Don't do it, Razor Burke. I'll put a bullet in your back."

And Razor Burke held Marty between himself and the girl's gun. Marty fought desperately, his bound hands useless. But he could not break that grip. Zee Clarke cried out something and came into the room. And Burke hurled Marty from him, across the room against the woman. Then the light by the bed was smacked out with a single movement of Razor Burke's arm.

Marty didn't stop to think at the time that Zee Clarke knew this man; called him by name. Things were happening too fast for that. He knew that he rolled aside after knocking against the girl and falling to his knees, and he knew that there was a thump; the sound of something falling—a body crashing to the floor.

Then he was on his feet, staggering toward the hall. There was light there. Plainly he saw Burke, just for an instant, before he passed into the living room.

Marty knew that he called out for him to stop; that he dashed down the hall by the silent form of Knight, and was through the living room in time to hear the front door close and the lock click. Razor Burke had gone. But before he left, had he— There was a lump in

Marty's throat. He remembered the thump he had heard, as if the girl had been dragged from the bed.

There was a light in the bedroom when Marty returned, and Zee Clarke was standing there with the razor in her hand. Marty stared at the shimmering keen blade, and the queer feeling in his stomach departed and the lump dropped back from his throat. The razor was clean and bright, with no red on it.

"Where is Tania; how is—" Marty started and stopped. Zee Clarke was pointing beneath the bed.

"You always think of her; even now, when I saved your life," she said as Marty got Tania from beneath the bed and cut her bonds. Then, slightly bitter, "After you look at Knight, you might find out how I feel since you knocked me about the room."

"The man!" Marty had placed Tania on the bed now, her eyes wide, staring, uncertain. "Is he dead?"

Zee Clarke shrugged her shoulders. "It's a forty-five, and the bullet went into his head. What do you think? It seems I've always got to save her for you. You might say 'Thank you.'"

But she stopped Marty when he was profuse in his appreciation of her courage and daring. And smiled—just a bit sadly. "I'll stay with Tania," she said. "Take care of Knight. They gagged him; he looked rather white when I came in. Hurry. There's lots to be done."

**IT WAS** some five minutes before Knight was able to explain what had happened. He was at the telephone, writing down Tania's message, when the man came in. He had just stood there behind Knight and struck him as he turned.

"I don't know how he got in, sir—but he was there... No, no. I'm all right; just found it hard breathing." Knight staggered to his feet. "I'll run a bit of water on my head and—" he paused, leaned against the wall. "I don't know what happened, Mr. Day, but I heard the shots, and it must have been plenty."

"Do you think others heard?"

"No." Knight shook his head. "If anyone below or above was awake, they might. But your rooms are farthest from the main hall and the windows were closed, and the apartment above is unoccupied, you know. But, Mr. Day, you'll have to notify the police, and—and here's a chance for you and Miss Tania to clear out of—of this Reckoner thing. No good will ever come of it."

"That's right." Marty nodded. "We're through now. Go and fix your head. I'll call the police."

Zee Clarke entered the room so quietly that Marty did not know of her presence until her hand stretched out and pushed the telephone he was lifting back in its cradle.

"What are you going to do?" she asked.

"Call the police," Marty told her.

"And tell them you killed a man here?" Amber eyes watched him closely.

"I killed him?" Marty turned fully and faced her.

"Certainly." Her eyes remained on his. "You wouldn't let me take the blame for that." And with the slightest curve to her lips, "Since it saved Tania from more than just death. You killed him, of course. My record wouldn't stand an investigation."

"Of course." Marty nodded. "I shot him. The police will hardly object to that."

"No?" She shrugged her shoulders. "And what story will you tell them that won't involve me or Tania. Anyway, I did it for you; to save you, and I can't stand the gaff of a police quiz. The moment they knew I was here, they'd—"

"But they won't know. You can go, and—"

The phone rang. Marty hesitated, and picked it up. Zee Clarke bent forward, listening. The superintendent of the apartment was talking.

"Everything all right, Mr. Day? The people below; that is, Mr. Jordan's wife, thought that she had heard a shot, but— What did you say?"

Zee Clarke whispered in his ear. Marty gulped and said: "I came in a short while ago, and nothing has happened. Oh, yes, I was at the front window a few minutes ago and did hear a car back-fire."

The superintendent thanked him in the tired voice of a man who is used to receiving imaginary complaints, and Marty turned to Zee Clarke.

"I'm into it now." He spoke the thought that came to him the moment he had told the superintendent that lie. "I'll never be able to explain that to the police."

"But the police won't be brought into it at all." She held Marty's arm. Those amber eyes were soft and alluring now. "Oh, Marty, you'll have to see this through for me. I killed a man that you might live."

"But the body."

Zee Clarke shook her head. "The Reckoner will attend to that. I already told Tania how you grabbed the gun in your bound hands and shot him." She hesitated a long moment. "We'll have to change that story for The Reckoner. It won't wash. You'll say you worked your hands loose then grabbed the gun from Fritz when I entered."

"You want The Reckoner to believe I— I killed him."

"Everyone must believe that." She nodded vigorously and lifted the phone. "He'll send Max Arnold, the criminal lawyer. But you know him. There! You go and comfort Tania. Death sickens her. I put her in the guest room."

MARTY sat beside Tania on the low couch in the guest room while she told him of her experience of that night.

"I went to Major Hanson's place to see Senator Hopewell. The Reckoner sent me to tell him the things we had learned about Rierson, and suggest to the senator a way to trap him. You see, I had known the senator since I was a little girl. My family are—" she smiled slightly, "well-connected. Of course they have no idea that I work for The Reckoner."

"And why do you, Tania? Why must you?" Marty just blurted the words out. "Let us give it up. Let us—"

She came to her feet and stood looking down at him. Her brown eyes were big and troubled. There was a nasty bruise below her mouth where the man had struck her. Somehow, for the moment Marty was glad that the man was dead.

"You mustn't question me. You promised you wouldn't. Some day, perhaps—" And with a sudden shudder, "It was terrible tonight. That man, Razor Burke— But I was up in the study with Senator Hopewell. I told him all about Rierson; the evidence The Reckoner had about his influential friends and the method The Reckoner suggested for trapping Rierson. Footsteps came down the hall. Senator Hopewell laughed and said, 'Don't worry. That will be Lieutenant Bradley. I told him of the message from The Reckoner and gave him a key. He seemed to think I might need protection.' He smiled so nicely then, Marty, when he finished. 'You see, my dear, I didn't know that you'd be the messenger.'

"There was an alcove, with curtains. The senator told me to wait behind them and he'd see Bradley and send him below, and arrange for me to leave later unrecognized. I was watching through the curtains when the senator opened the door, Marty. And it was that man, Burke. He had a gun in his hand." She placed both her hands over her face. "It was horrible, Marty. So brutal. He didn't speak; just raised the gun and fired, and I ran out. Don't ask me why I did it. I couldn't help it. And Burke saw me; smiled too, if it was a smile. Just like he looked when I lay there on the bed. He lifted the gun again as the senator stood there clutching at his chest.

"There was blood on his hands, Marty, and he was dying then. I know he was dying. His head sort of swung, and he must have seen me. The papers have praised him, Marty, as a courageous man. But they didn't know. No one could know how brave he really was." She placed both her hands on Marty's shoulder and shook him as she sobbed. "He was dying then, Marty. I tell you he was dying then. And he threw himself forward and took the shot that was meant for me. Took it as I flung open those French windows and fled."

And Marty took her in his arms and held her head close against his shoulder as Knight came in.

"They came from above, Mr. Day," Knight told him. "The rope is still there by the kitchen window. The apartment upstairs is empty and— Did you notify the police?"

Marty shook his head as he led Tania to the living room. The police weren't to be in it now. Marty had taken the blame, or the honor, for killing a man. Well, he couldn't do less than that for Zee Clarke. But he knew that, later, it might prove very hard to explain to the police. But the body. What of the body?

Zee Clarke was apparently the least disturbed of any of the four in that living room. She emptied her second highball as she walked about the room remarking on Marty's fine collection of books.

"It really is the first time I've had a chance to study your diggin's, Marty," she said easily. "I'm not fortunate, like Tania here. You might present me with a key."

"A key!" Marty jarred erect. "You must have one. That lock is—"

"Yes, I had one," she said. "But not presented to me by you. Tania lent it to me." And as Marty looked at Tania, "I didn't mean voluntarily. I took an impression from the one in her bag. I've had a duplicate for several weeks. I didn't approve of her coming tonight, so I followed her."

Marty shrugged his shoulders and paced the room. There was still the body. And Zee Clarke answered his unspoken question.

"Max Arnold is coming. There is nothing to worry about."

TEN MINUTES later Max Arnold came. He was tall and slim, with a jerky wiry movement to his body. His face was sharp, his eyes were set far back and very close together. They seemed to look off the end of that beaklike nose.

He gave each one of them a cold damp hand, then took Zee Clarke over in one corner of the room and whispered to her long and earnestly. She seemed to be denying something.

Finally he came back and stood in the middle of the room, his long thin legs far apart, his hands rubbing together.

"Bad business," he said at length. "Very bad business for a criminal lawyer." Then looking from one to the other of the four, his eyes finally rested on Knight. "The servants' entrance, downstairs!" he said suddenly. "It's bolted on the inside. You go below. Let in two men and bolt the door again. Bring them upstairs—unseen." As Knight left, he walked to the window and looked out. "No outside fire-escape, of course. You say the rope is by the kitchen window. We shouldn't have much trouble." He stroked his chin, knitted his eyes and looked at Marty. "It will be better if all our activities take place from the floor above. No, no. There is nothing to discuss, Mr. Day. If you will just show me the—er—specimen."

Knight brought in the two men. Both carried bags. Neither spoke a word. One was huge and muscular, one slim and small. Marty accompanied Max Arnold and the two men to the room of death. The others remained in the living room.

"At least," Max Arnold took Marty by the arm, "we shall have conflicting stories as to the departure of the body if anything untoward should happen later. But have no fear. The girls are not in a position to talk. Knight, I understand, is an ex-convict, over whom you hold a threat, and—"

"I need hold no threat over Knight," Marty said as he watched the two men unceremoniously dump the body into a black canvas sack they took from a bag.

"Of course not. But as I was saying, Knight might talk. That leaves only you." Shoulders shrugged. "And you, Mr. Day, having produced the corpse, will hardly later claim credit for it."

**MARTY** looked at the tall, slim criminal lawyer. His name was known from one end of the city to the other. If not the most brilliant lawyer in the city, he was certainly the most successful in his own line—the defending of the city's greatest public enemies. And yet there was something about the man that Marty liked; something that fascinated him; something that also repelled him and—

Max Arnold was talking. "The little man," he said, "was a performer in a circus. The rope by the kitchen window will get him into the apartment above. It is very dark there by the kitchen window, and a brick wall is opposite. The body will be lifted from the outside, since it is so convenient. The hall seems simpler, of course. But a tenant returning late or one who slept lightly might just duck into the hall in time to embarrass us. Not likely, I admit. A coincidence, perhaps. And where coincidences are not permitted in fiction, they unfortunately do happen in life—and in death."

"But won't the same coincidence be apt to happen when the—the dead man is taken from the apartment above?"

"Certainly," said Max Arnold. "But it would be more difficult to hold you responsible for something that happened in the apartment above than in your own apartment. The boys, of course, will bend every effort to remove the corpse to such a distance that it's demise can not even be connected with you."

"Can you get away with it?"

"My dear boy," Max Arnold permitted his thin lips to part slightly, "I have defended many high-class criminals and few of them ever permit the—shall we say 'corpus delicti' to remain at the scene of the crime."

Certainly Marty knew that the two men worked quickly and efficiently. He saw the smaller man crawl out the kitchen window, disappear like a monkey up the rope. Marty had lived close to death, but it was with a feeling of nausea that he helped carry that canvas sack to the kitchen and hold the body while the bigger man secured it to the rope that dangled from the window. All this, of course, was done in the dark. Then, just before the big man left him, the fellow spoke for the first time.

"Jake will let me in the door upstairs," he said. "When I jerk the rope, ease it out the window. If the cops should rush me in the hall, jerk the rope. Jake will be wise and you can let it ride. But I think things will be O.K. It looks like a good lay."

"But how will you finally get rid of it—altogether?"

"Don't you worry about that," laughed the big man. "It'll be lowered from some place in the back in jig time." And he smirked and jabbed a finger into Marty's ribs. "You got a break; evidence all gone. That stiff wasn't a bleeder."

Marty breathed easier when the black canvas, with the thing it held, left his hands, hung for a moment in the air and disappeared above the window. These men thought of everything. Even the color of the canvas blended with the night.

## CHAPTER FIVE

## THE RECKONER SPEAKS

**M**AX ARNOLD was smoking and sipping a highball Knight had mixed him when Marty entered the living room. Tania and Zee Clarke were not in the room.

"Where's Tania?" he asked abruptly.

Max Arnold put down his drink, removed his nose glasses, polished them carefully and said: "They have left. I thought it better." And with a shake of his head, "Bad business, tonight, Mr. Day. Very bad business."

"I had to kill him," Marty said grimly.

"I wasn't thinking of that man. I was thinking of Senator Hopewell. Yes, yes. Tania reported to my client and I heard about it. You understand that it was because of The Reckoner that Hopewell died. You shot the wrong man, Mr. Day."

"He struck Tania," said Marty. "He deserved to die."

"To be sure—to be sure." Max Arnold nodded vigorously as he slowly replaced his glasses and came to his feet. "I am not questioning the ethics of your act." He looked at Marty shrewdly, grasped his hand as he moved toward the door. It was a cold hand; damp and clammy. "A good man was murdered tonight. The murderer still lives. Call it justice or vengeance, as you please. But The Reckoner will demand a reckoning."

"Tania saw the man; saw Burke murder Senator Hopewell. A conviction should be easy."

Max Arnold laughed. "A single witness, with the power of Rierson against her. Politics, money, bribery and threats." Max Arnold shook his head. "And if she did stand up in court and accuse him, what then? Her usefulness to The Reckoner gone; a hundred eyes watching and knowing that perhaps some day she would serve them the same, and a hundred hands ready to press a single finger that would— But enough of that, Tania will not be alive to testify if Razor Burke lives."

"What do you mean by that?" Marty demanded.

Max Arnold ignored the question. He took out his watch; looked down at it. "It's after two," he said. "The Reckoner wishes to see you at once. Same place, same methods of entrance." But he turned as he reached the door. "What did I mean by that?" He repeated Marty's question. "Perhaps it might be clearer to say that Tania dies if—if you permit Burke to live."

"You—you suggest that I—I kill this man?" Marty gasped.

"My dear Mr. Day, I suggest nothing. The Reckoner will give you orders and you will obey them."

"I'll obey them no longer," Marty said. "I'm through—tonight."

Max Arnold smiled. "You will obey The Reckoner. You would have hard work explaining that corpse here tonight without—well, it's too late for you to explain now. Good night!"

"Good night!" Marty stood by the door and watched the long, bent form walk slowly to the automatic lift. He nodded. Deeper and deeper he was in the grip of The Reckoner. He looked at his watch, lifted his stick from the costumer where Knight had placed it, called to Knight once, and taking his hat left the apartment. He was going to see—well, at least he was going to talk with The Reckoner; hear the rasping voice of the man he had never seen.

**MARTY** found a cruising taxi and drove downtown. He jumped out a block and a half from his destination, passed the front of the little pawnshop, and going around the side street slipped into a dark musty vestibule, and closing and bolting the door behind him tapped lightly, upon the inner door.

A moment of waiting, shuffling feet, the clank of a chain, and the door opened slightly. Sunken eyes stared out of a parchmentlike face; corrugated hands rubbed ingratiatingly. A dull light snapped on and off. The door closed, steel clanked, the door opened again and Marty entered.

A moment, as the chain clicked into its lock, and Marty followed the shuffling figure down a narrow hall. The old man opened a door and stood aside for Marty to enter; then the door closed behind him and a key turned. Marty was alone in that room beneath the single light from the ceiling.

The room was sparsely furnished. A chair was drawn up to a counter that stretched the width of the room. An ordinary counter, for people who wished to do business privately with the owner of the shop. But now no keen-eyed money lender leaned over to bargain. Instead, stretching from the top of that counter to the ceiling above was a curtain of steel. On the edge of the counter was a high-powered electric bulb with a brass reflector. Marty took the chair before this light and waited, his fingers twisting in a nervousness he could not control; never could control when he waited in that room.

A minute passed; two, then the ceiling light went out. A moment of darkness and the creak of steel. Marty knew that a small section of that steel curtain was moving. A dull click and the sudden stab of light, directly in Marty's face. The brass reflector throwing it full in Marty's eyes—blinding him.

A soft cough, and a voice spoke. Marty jarred erect. It was the voice of The Reckoner. And that voice was always a surprise to Marty. It was metallic; like the scraping of a phonograph needle over a worn record. There was no attempt to make it sound natural.

"Mr. Day," that voice ground out, "you killed a man tonight; a man who was not fit to live, and I am not at all displeased. We can only better life through death. Now, there is another man who must die. He brutally murdered Senator Hopewell. Joseph Ellison Rierson stands behind him. A conviction would be impossible. Burke must die before daylight. You may be proud. I have selected you for this act. Twenty-five thousand dollars will be your reward. There! Do not thank me."

"You want me to kill a man," Marty stammered. "Murder a man. Why—" Then he laughed. "The thing's preposterous. Besides, I wouldn't know where to look for him."

The Reckoner said very slowly: "I shall tell you where he is. So— you are ready?"

"No," said Marty, "I am not ready. Burke brutally murdered a man. Tania saw him. Her evidence should—"

"Enough!" The Reckoner cut it, and for the moment there was

almost a natural, human note in his voice. "I must make you understand the situation. I am giving you an order to kill this man tonight."

"And," said Marty, "I am not taking that order. You think because I accepted your help tonight; because I killed a man you can hold that over my head. But you can't. Disclose it if you want to. I'll face the gaff, and I'll disclose things too. I'll—"

"Don't threaten me, Mr. Day." And the laugh was like a shovel on a cellar floor. "I am not threatening you. I shall tell you a few facts, and you will do as I say. I have built up a fear in the evildoer; the common gangster of the city streets, the racketeer, crooked officials. Even have I built up that fear in Rierson. I have evidence that will strike at those he controls, and so bounce back on him. Now, tonight Rierson arranged to have Senator Hopewell killed. Even had Lieutenant Bradley with him as an alibi when the foul murder took place. And he arranged, also, to have it look like the work of The Reckoner. My work; to put the blame on me! He knew that Senator Hopewell expected information from me. Bradley knew it. And I—I was laying a foundation to suppress crime in the city. Suppress Rierson through Senator Hopewell, who could use in the open all the vast knowledge that I have gathered.

"Now—" and The Reckoner's voice rang with passion, "Rierson has struck at my power as I struck at his. Hopewell was murdered. And if I do not strike back, all the fear I have been to such pains to build up will be dissipated. You will be next; perhaps Tania. Rierson knows you work for me; fear of me has kept a thousand murderers whom he might control from wiping you out. Now, go. You have half an hour to kill this man. There! Take this."

A HAND moved along the counter, fingers that were pinkish-red held a slip of white envelope. The skin of the hand shone for a few seconds in that light; skin that was so tightly drawn over the bones that no wrinkle showed on its smooth surface. It was eery—strange. An illusion perhaps. Then the hand was gone, and Marty held the envelope.

The Reckoner said: "Razor Burke will be at that place in half an hour. Send me word that he is dead."

Marty bit his lip, but he did not hesitate. "I won't do it," he said. "I can't do it. But how do you know where he'll be?" The Reckoner's voice was very low. "I set a trap for him. Razor Burke will fear that Tania may talk. Rierson will fear that Tania's talk may cause Burke to talk and accuse him of instigating the murder of Senator Hopewell. Where Rierson's influence and corruption might save Burke, it is a much simpler matter to dispose of Tania. Eliminate at once all danger of a living witness; strike at my power again. Also remember, Mr. Day, that Tania once worked as secretary for Rierson. He must wonder just how much she knows."

"I don't quite understand this trap." Marty was puzzled.

"Simple," said The Reckoner. "I had no way of knowing just where Burke went tonight. But I knew that he would get in touch with Rierson. So I had word sent to Rierson by someone who has sold him information before that Tania will be alone in that penthouse apartment tonight. Naturally he will tell Burke and—"

"And Burke will go there to kill her. That's it, eh?"

"That is human nature," said The Reckoner.

"And Burke won't suspect a trap?"

"No. For Rierson will tell him. And Rierson won't suspect a trap, or if he does he won't care. If Burke kills Tania, that fear is eliminated. If Burke is killed—well, Rierson can find others to take his place. So—you will be there to kill this Burke."

"That is not justice." Marty shook his head. "It's murder, and I'll have no part in it."

"We don't want justice tonight. The criminal doesn't understand justice. It is the criminal that we must impress with the power of the unknown man, who strikes quickly. The Reckoner. We want simply vengeance."

Marty set his lips tightly. Burke deserved to die all right. But to go hunting for a man with murder in your heart! He wouldn't do it. He'd find Tania. They could go away together. Go some place where The Reckoner could not reach her. Go— And he asked: "Where is Tania now?"

A chuckle came from behind the curtain of steel. The Reckoner spoke. "Tania is in that penthouse now, alone, as Burke was told she would be. She does not know that Burke is coming or she would hardly stay there. She is waiting there now, Mr. Day. Bait for Burke; human bait."

Marty Day jarred to his feet. "It's not true," he cried. "It couldn't be true. If Burke believed in the message, why have her there at all? It's unnecessary."

"Burke might make inquiries, though perhaps it is unnecessary in the trap I laid for Burke. But it is necessary to the death of Burke. Necessary for you, Marty Day; necessary to make you go there."

"I can't believe it. I won't believe it." The words choked in Marty's throat. "It's fiendish. She might be killed."

"There is always that danger, of course." The Reckoner's voice was very low now. "It is for you to prevent it."

**ANGRY,** bitter words rushed to Marty's lips. He killed them with an effort; clutched his cane tightly in his hand. The temptation to bring it into action; just a quick movement toward where the voice came from, was strong. And Marty remembered another time when he had stretched out a hand quickly, and his fingers had met steel; a thin grating of steel. And he stood there.

The Reckoner went on. "You have the address." Marty heard the fingers tapping impatiently on wood. "You will enter the apartment house by the servants' entrance, which will be unlocked. Go to the twenty-third floor and enter the penthouse with the key you will find in that envelope. You are young; you are strong. You should be there before Burke. There are French windows before Tania's bedroom. You might watch for Burke there. Tonight you will carry a gun. You will find it on the counter when I leave you."

"How will Burke get in?"

"He will enter as you will enter, by the servants' entrance. A key to the penthouse was sent with the message to Rierson. Remember he would have brutally tortured Tania tonight."

"And you want me to murder him?"

"There can be no such thing as murder in our fight against crime. You are the law tonight; the law of The Reckoner; the law of vengeance. Dispensing justice which corruption denies the honest citizen. Afterwards you and Tania will simply leave; everything will be taken care of when I get your report. Simply telephone the number I have given you."

"If—if I get a confession from him—from Burke that Rierson instigated the killing of Senator Hopewell, how will that be?"

The Reckoner hesitated a long moment. Marty thought that he heard his lips smack. "Burke," he finally said, "will not talk, and he will not be taken alive."

"But," said Marty, "if I should—should—"

"Fail?" The Reckoner supplied the word. "I have arranged things so that you cannot fail. Don't misunderstand me, Mr. Day. Hesitation on your part, and Tania may die. You too may die. But I will not fail. Burke's life is forfeited tonight."

Marty would have talked longer perhaps. But the dull click of steel told him that the grating had closed. Then the bright light died. For a moment Marty was in darkness. Then the ceiling light snapped on and Marty stood alone in the room, clutching a small white envelope in his hand. Beneath the light on the counter was a gun. Marty hesitated, then thrust it into a hip pocket. He blinked several times, tore open the envelope, and unfolding the single sheet of paper removed the key and studied the address. Then shoving both paper and key into his pocket he swung his cane across his arm and faced the door. Three full minutes must pass before that door would open. It was always that way.

As for The Reckoner. He was gone. More than once he had told Marty that he had many means of exit from that building.

The lock clicked as a key turned, and the bent old figure preceded Marty to the street door.

## CHAPTER SIX

## WHAT OF TANIA?

**M**ARTY'S THOUGHTS were jumbled as he stood on the dark side street and sucked in great mouthfuls of the pleasant summer air. The Reckoner! How thrilled he had been; how proud he had been when he first started on the mad adventure of working for this unknown man! Now— And as Marty reached the corner he set his lips grimly. He'd get a taxi, rush to Tania and have her out of there before Razor Burke arrived. Then—

Marty swung quickly and half raised his cane. But he dropped it to his side almost at once. Something round was digging into his side. Then, as he recognized the man, the man laughed.

"Mr. Day, eh?" Lieutenant Bradley looked long and searchingly into Marty's face.

"That's right," said Marty. "What can I do for you?"

"You can tell me," said Lieutenant Bradley, "just who you called on behind that pawnshop at three o'clock in the morning?"

"There's no law against that, is there?" Marty laughed.

"No," said Bradley. "And there's no law against arresting you as a suspicious character, or holding you for the murder of Senator Hopewell." A hand ran quickly down Marty's side, jerked into a rear pocket and drew out the gun The Reckoner had given him. "Sporting fire-arms, eh?"

"I have a license for that." Marty dug a hand into his jacket pocket. "And I have a very important engagement."

"Have you a license to keep that very important engagement?" Lieutenant Bradley blinked down at Marty's gun permit. Then, as a cruising taxi slid to the curb and the driver called to them, "Come on, Mr. Day. You and I are going bye-bye. I want to know who you met in that pawnshop."

Marty entered the taxi and Lieutenant Bradley snapped out an order to drive to the precinct station.

Marty threatened, pleaded, promised to come in to see Bradley the first thing in the morning.

"No." Bradley shook his head. "You're nervous enough to be a good subject tonight. I was watching the front of your apartment house from across the street. You had a visitor, Mr. Day; at least someone in that house did. A man who left in a hurry. A bad character—Razor Burke. I was tempted to tail him, but waited for you instead and followed you downtown. I was thinking of coming up and paying you a visit when Burke came out."

And if he had, Marty thought with a little gulp. The dead man there on the floor, and— Marty sat erect in the cab. Even that would have been better. Tania at least would have been safe from Razor Burke. Now—she was there in that penthouse, sleeping no doubt. A sleep she might never wake from unless—unless Razor Burke decided to go through with the torture he had planned.

Marty looked at Lieutenant Bradley. If only that gun wasn't still jabbed against his side! If only— And he thought of The Reckoner, and of his reason for using him, Marty, because his brain was active, his body alert. Well, he needed that active brain now. He spoke quick, hurried words.

"Listen, Lieutenant. You've got to let me go. The life of someone; a woman, a girl, depends on my being—being at a certain place at once. By God! Don't you see, death will be on your head if you arrest me now."

"Why, I'm not arresting you." Lieutenant Bradley laughed. "I'm taking you around for a little chat, and—"

"Won't anything make you change your mind—anything?"

Bradley studied him in the dull darkness. " 'Anything' is a big word, Mr. Day. But if you mean money— No."

MARTY hesitated. The green lights of the police precinct showed up down the block ahead of him. He said quickly: "For my freedom now—for a few hours' freedom, I'll tell you the name of the man who killed—who murdered Senator Hopewell."

Lieutenant Bradley whistled softly, leaned forward and shouted through the glass, to the chauffeur. "Drive around a bit," he said.

And Marty added: "Drive uptown."

Bradley made no objection, but grinned in the dark. "So the business of the woman is uptown." He nodded. "Now, who killed the senator?"

"And can I go free, to keep my engagement?"

"We'll see," said Bradley as the taxi jogged easily uptown.

"No. Your word! I give you my word of honor I'll tell you the truth."

Lieutenant Bradley stroked his chin and tried to study Marty in the darkness. He smiled to himself as he recognized the sincerity in Marty's words; the brightness of his eyes, that stood out even in the dark. "Shoot!" he said at length. "And if you tell me the truth you can run along to the lady."

"Good enough," said Marty. "Razor Burke shot the senator to death. Now let me out."

"Not so fast." Lieutenant Bradley half pulled Marty back on the seat as he leaned forward. "You've got to give me the proof. And, besides—"

"You're not going to let me go? I'll give you the proof in the morning. I'll—" And Marty clutched his cane in both hands; flexing it slightly.

"Oh, I'll keep my promise." Lieutenant Bradley laughed. "But we'll have to have a signed statement before a witness. We'll just run down to the precinct and get a stenographer."

Lieutenant Bradley leaned forward, raised a hand to tap on the glass. His mouth was opened to call out. But his gun was lowered, and for the fraction of a second his eyes were off Marty. And Marty acted.

Strong fingers tightened for a moment on that cane. There was a whirring sound as the curved handle left Marty's hand and shot upward with the speed of a striking cobra.

The words of instruction to the chauffeur never left Bradley's lips. He sank slowly forward. Marty stretched out a hand and prevented the unconscious lieutenant of police from slipping to the floor. Then Marty eased the man back in a corner of the cab.

The blow from the cane had not been an especially hard one. Nor was it a light one either. Marty grinned. Bradley had it coming to him. Marty realized, of course, that his action would prove embarrassing later, but he couldn't think of that now. Max Arnold would have to attend to that. Tania's life depended upon his actions now.

They passed a taxi that was slowly making its way up the broad thoroughfare. Marty ordered his chauffeur to the curb, jumped from the car and flagged the cab that passed. To the driver of Bradley's car he simply said: "My friend is going home," and he gave him the name of a hotel. Then he was in the other cab, ordering the chauffeur to make all speed to the apartment house further uptown.

That the driver of the first car looked at him quizzically and started to say something did not interest Marty. Just one thing now. To reach Tania; reach her before Burke reached her. Even now—even now—And Marty shuddered. But he could not dismiss from his mind the horrible picture of what might be taking place in that penthouse apartment twenty-three stories above the street.

**THERE** was a sleepy-looking elevator boy sitting on a lounge in the foyer when Marty dashed through the doors. He jumped to his feet, said something, and Marty clutched him by the arm.

"Twenty-third floor," Marty said. "Quick! I'm expected."

The boy started to remonstrate and Marty clutched him by the throat. For the first time he realized he didn't have any gun. And now—he didn't care what happened. The servants' entrance was forgotten; The Reckoner's orders were forgotten. Just one thought. To reach Tania in time. To save Tania!

The boy, paralyzed with fear, finally started the elevator. His eyes bulged; great breaths of air sucked into his throat as he watched Marty. Mad! That was it, the boy thought. Well, he'd take him where he wanted to go, get safely away himself, then call the police.

But Marty didn't care what the boy was thinking. He reached the twenty-third floor, saw that the elevator left him in a private hall and that the door before him was a heavy, steel-lined affair.

Marty knew that the bell buzzed in the elevator and that the elevator door clanked closed as the thoroughly terror-stricken boy slammed it. But such things only registered distantly in his mind. He was fumbling to insert the key in the lock when he suddenly realized that the door was open; that the catch had not clicked closed when— when— And a great fear gripped Marty. He was too late. Razor Burke had already been there. Razor Burke had—

He cautiously opened the door and stepped into the apartment. A dim light burned in the hall. He listened. Quiet, a dead quiet. Dead. Dead. Dead! The word kept ringing in Marty's ears. He cursed The Reckoner; he cursed Bradley. And then he heard a sound. Was it the steady movement of feet; quiet, careful feet that crossed wood?

Someone was still in that apartment. Some living thing moved. Was it Razor Burke, who— And Marty did not even let his frantic thoughts finish that question.

The Reckoner wanted Marty to kill a man. Well, he would. But he had no gun. What a fool he had been not to take back his gun from the limp hand of Lieutenant Bradley. But he hadn't. And now he had only his cane. It had served its purpose twice in the last few hours. There, when Rierson would have shot Tania, and again in the taxi with Bradley.

Now he gripped it tightly and passed through the hall into the living room. Quiet there, and no light. He stepped back and listened. Again the tread of feet; careful, slow feet, as if their owner took a few steps and stopped to listen.

Then there was the sound of a softly closing door. And Marty pushed quickly through the living room, down a narrow hall. A bedroom to the right; a light in it. A bed that had been slept in but was now unoccupied. Sheets thrown back; chair turned upon its side, as if someone had gotten hurriedly from that bed. Marty sucked in a deep breath. There on the edge of the pillow was red; just a tiny bit of red. Blood! And Marty's eyes flashed from the red to the overturned chair; to the French windows. One full-length window was wide open, and there was glass on the floor.

Fear, horror, gripped Marty. The bed that had been slept in; the blood on the pillow; the overturned chair; the broken glass! No, it didn't seem as if someone had gotten hurriedly from that bed now, more as if someone had been dragged from it; dragged across the room and through those open doors to the terrace, and then—Marty crossed to the window, his cane gripped tightly by the ferrule in his right hand. The Reckoner wanted Burke dead, eh? He'd get what he wanted, and then— Marty's lips set grimly.

Then he'd tear that thin steel mesh away and—

Footsteps—soft, but clearer this time. The tread of feet upon stone; upon the terrace outside. Steps that were approaching that window; steps that were—

A shadow crossed the light; then the figure. A flat nose, evil ratlike eyes, cruel sensuous lips. Marty Day and Razor Burke looked straight into each other's eyes.

## CHAPTER SEVEN

## MURDER ABOVE

A MOMENT of tenseness then; a moment when two bodies stood rigid. Marty's right hand half raised, with the cane in it. Razor Burke's right hand half raised, with sharp steel in it. Steel that glittered in the light from the open French window; steel that was red—red! And Razor Burke acted first.

The blood-stained razor dropped from his right hand and rang loudly as it hit stone. Burke's hand shot beneath his left armpit; flashed out of sight even as Marty drew back his hand and whipped his fine steel cane forward.

Marty had never seen a gun appear so quickly before. Just a single movement of that white empty hand, gone for a split second beneath a coat, to appear again almost at once. And now Burke's white fingers gripped black steel; square black steel. Black steel that belched orange-blue flame almost the very moment it showed in the white hand.

There was no time for Razor Burke to aim; just time, fast as he was, to draw and fire. He ducked his head too as his finger tightened upon that trigger. For as the roar of the gun split the stillness, tempered steel purred like a jungle cat.

There was a smell of powder in Marty's nostrils as the jar of the bullet drove him back. Funny that! He wouldn't have known he was hit except for that backward movement. More like a push. And then

Marty set his lips grimly. Even as his body twisted from the impact of lead he heard the thud of steel against bone; saw the sudden cut above Burke's right eye, the tiny trickle of blood that ran down the man's face.

Burke's hand had lowered; dropped to his side as Marty staggered forward. Tania was dead. He knew it now; knew it from the red on the razor. Burke had killed her, and— Grimly Marty raised his cane and beat down the arm; the hand that Burke was raising again. Back across the stone terrace Marty drove the torturer and murderer.

Narrow, cruel, ratlike eyes were wide now; wide with fear as that whistling cane pursued him. Back, back Razor Burke went. His right arm, which held the gun, had been raised to protect his head now. And still Marty came on. He wasn't striking wildly now; he was striking with a deadly accuracy that long experience with this strange weapon had given him. Just the soft purr of quickly moving steel; the crack as the bone split in Burke's arm, as if a surgeon had snapped it. Then the cry of pain.

The gun crashed to the hard stone; the right hand fell to Burke's side. He raised his left one above his face as he bent his body before the advancing man.

"You killed her!" Marty said over and over. "You tortured her, and now you're going to die."

Murder; justice; vengeance. Call it anything you like. Marty didn't care. Tania was dead. Here was the man who had killed her; brutally murdered her while—

And Burke was back against the stone parapet. Just a low wall at that section, with two iron railings atop it. Burke's back struck the railing as the cane beat down his left arm.

"Don't—don't!" Burke screamed as that flaying cane forced his body back over the iron railing.

Then, as the cane rose again, Burke turned his head, looked far down in the darkness; the darkness just beginning to be broken by the summer dawn. He screamed out in fear as he looked into the yawning pit twenty-three stories below. His feet slipped, caught frantically at the iron railing, and his body started over.

SOMETHING snapped in Marty's head then. The desire to kill was gone almost at the moment Burke's body started toward the pavement below.

Burke was almost head downward now. One foot, caught beneath the lower rail, held him for a moment—and Marty acted. His cane, which would have knocked Burke unconscious and sent him to his death far below, turned in Marty's hand. With a deft movement, that curved handle passed Burke's head, and as his foot began to give from the weight of his body that steel handle snapped upward behind his neck, breaking the weight and drawing him slowly up into a half-sitting position.

"Are you trying to kill him or save his life?" said a voice behind Marty. "There! Don't turn; tend to your business. I'm not a ghost; I'm Bradley. The thick dick you knocked out. But the taxi driver was clever enough to follow you, and having a hard chin I came around in time."

"Don't touch him," Marty warned, and Bradley was surprised at the passion in Marty's voice. "He's just murdered—the girl you caused to be murdered. Well, you want him for the murder of Senator Hopewell." And suddenly, to Burke: "You killed Hopewell, didn't you, Burke?" And when Burke did not answer, but tried frantically and unsuccessfully with the hand of his broken arm to clutch the railing, "You did, didn't you?" The cane loosened slightly from the support of Burke's neck, and Burke's body sagged.

Lieutenant Bradley cried: "He's going."

But Razor Burke's shriek cut in. "Yes—yes! I killed him. Don't let me go!"

"You heard that," Marty said grimly to the lieutenant of police, and to Burke, as his left hand now clutched at the lower rail, "Who made you do it?"

There on the terrace far above the city below, both Bradley and Marty heard Burke suck in his breath; heard his dry lips smack as a tongue tried to moisten them. And Marty brought him up straight, so he could talk more easily. But he did not speak at once.

Marty said very slowly and distinctly: "Tell the truth, Burke, or I'll send you to your death over the rail. Keep out of it, Bradley." He nudged Bradley with his shoulder and for the first time felt the pain there. "Now, Burke, Joseph Ellison Rierson paid you to kill Senator Hopewell. He also sent you to torture Tania and me, to find out the name of—"

Marty Day jarred erect. The cane almost jerked from his hand at the sudden spasmodic jar of Razor Burke's body. In the dim dawn he was looking straight into the ratlike eyes of Razor Burke. Fearful, terror-stricken eyes, that had blinked continually. And now the fear had suddenly snapped out of them; snapped out of them almost before Marty realized that a shot had been fired.

Burke's eyes were glassy now. There was a dull blue hole in the center of his forehead; a hole that was widening and— The body of Burke folded up like a jack-knife, twisted free from the clutching cane, and turning grotesquely over disappeared in the semi-blackness of the coming dawn.

Marty knew that he grabbed frantically at the rail. He knew also that Lieutenant Bradley had turned and was running across the terrace, firing as he ran. And he thought too that a door slammed someplace in the apartment.

Marty staggered to the rail and looked over, then he dropped to his knees. He had wanted Burke dead, he had even for a time wanted to kill him. But now that it happened—like that, it seemed so terrible, so ghastly. Eyes that were alive; staring, frightened eyes, had suddenly—

And Marty turned from the rail. Someone had come along the terrace and fired that single shot that had killed Burke just before he went hurtling into space. Before— Yes, before he was able to tell that Rierson had hired him or ordered him to kill Senator Hopewell. Now, who would wish to still his mouth enough to shoot him there while Marty held him above the street and Lieutenant Bradley looked on? Who knew that Razor Burke would be there? Rierson, of course, since he had sent him. No one else! Marty frowned. The Reckoner knew, of course. But The Reckoner—

**MARTY** shook his head. What did it matter who killed him? What did anything matter? Tania was dead. And how did she die? Had Razor Burke dragged her from bed, across the terrace, and thrown her into the street? That would be like Burke. And what a yellow cur he had turned out to be when the time came for him to die!

Bradley had gone, in pursuit of the one who had fired the shot, Marty guessed.

Marty turned and walked across the terrace, toward those broken French windows, the light beyond them, and—and— The figure that stood framed there in the doorway! A woman's figure; a girl's figure. Brown eyes that shone. Live eyes; a living body—that—that— And the next moment she was out on the terrace and Marty held her in his arms.

"I heard a voice and switched on the light," Tania told him. "And he was there, Marty; almost at the foot of the bed. I guess working for The Reckoner has taught me to move quickly in times of danger, and I did move. I threw myself from the bed as he struck. Look!" She bared her shoulder slightly and Marty saw the sharp gash. "Then I tore at the partly open French windows and was on the terrace. He passed me as I hid there by the giant ferns. I reached the hall through the other door and I heard you. But I didn't know it was you then, and I was waiting in a closet for a chance to escape. Now he's— he's—"

"He's dead," said Marty.

"You killed him?"

"No," said Marty, "I didn't kill him. I've got proof of that." And he thought of Lieutenant Bradley who stood by his side when the fatal shot was fired. "It's—"

And Marty stopped dead. Lieutenant Bradley was standing between those open French windows.

"That's right." He nodded. "You've got an alibi that can't be shaken."

"But how did you know where to come; what floor?"

Lieutenant Bradley laughed. "The elevator boy wanted to shout it to the whole city," he said. "I've got the block watched." He shook his head. "But the lad who pulled that stunt was either desperate or—or certain. I think he got clean away."

"Got an idea?" Marty asked.

"Yes," said Bradley. "And you?"

"It was Rierson." Marty was emphatic.

"Maybe." Bradley stroked his chin. "Or another, who was anxious to show—well, the criminal how sure is his vengeance."

"You mean—"

"That's right," Bradley said when Marty did not finish. "I mean The Reckoner." He turned abruptly as feet beat across the bedroom. "That'll be Captain Madison."

But it was not Captain Madison. It was Max Arnold.

"Mr. Day," said Max Arnold slowly, as he smiled pleasantly, "is now represented by counsel. And he won't talk."

"That's fine." Lieutenant Bradley grinned back. "He put a feather in my cap this morning. He don't need to talk." And as he walked toward the outer hall, "It's of more importance to your client, Mr. Arnold, that I won't talk—not even about what happened in a public cab. Good night—or rather, good morning, gentlemen. And, madame." He bowed with a grin to Tania. "If I were young and had the world before me, I'd drop The Reckoner. I understand that Razor Burke is somewhat of a mess."

# BLOOD ON THE CURTAIN

"BE SUCCESSFUL." THAT
WAS THE RECKONER'S
ONLY ORDER AS HE
SENT DAY OUT WITH
EVIDENCE TO BREAK
THE CROOKED JUDGE
WHOSE GREEDY HANDS
HAD BATTENED ON THE
UNDERWORLD. LITTLE
DID HE KNOW THAT
BEFORE THE NIGHT WAS
OVER HE'D BE HUNTED
FOR THE MURDER OF
THE MAGISTRATE—FIND
HIMSELF ON A SPOT FROM
WHICH THERE WAS ONLY
ONE OUT. DEATH FOR
TWO—SIGNED WITH A K.

# CHAPTER ONE

# THE RECKONER'S DUDE

**M**ARTY DAY sat in the bright light and listened to the monotoned, metallic voice of The Reckoner. Finally the voice died away; the thin sheet of steel slid closed, and the bright glare of the light that always prevented Marty from seeing the face of the unknown man who gave him orders snapped out.

A moment of waiting, and the ceiling light showed dully and Marty faced, as he had so often faced, the curtain of steel. It shut off completely the front of that room from the back. A pawn shop by day; a place where The Reckoner met and talked to those who obeyed his orders, at night.

There would be three full minutes now, anyway, before the key would turn in the lock of the door behind him and Marty would be free to go—go on the errand that The Reckoner had commanded. Those three minutes Marty spent in thought.

He thought of The Reckoner, whom he had first met through the girl, Tania; whose orders he took because of the girl and the spirit of adventure, for The Reckoner's business was the righting of wrong—Marty smiled. There was money too; The Reckoner paid well for service and his resources seemed unlimited. Besides, once rich, Marty's funds, like the funds of countless others, had been swept away in the great depression.

There were times, of course, when Marty Day thought of quitting The Reckoner; when the good The Reckoner was doing was overshadowed, far overshadowed, by his method of accomplishing that good. There was that time for instance, when he had been willing to sacrifice Tania's life rather than meet the demands of the crooked politician, Joseph T. Rierson. There was that time when he used Tania as bait, human bait, in his trap to snare "Razor" Burke, the murderer

"You'd better come in
out of that window."

of Senator Hopewell. Marty had saved her then; Marty had thought then to throw up the whole business and leave the city; leave The Reckoner, taking Tania with him of course.

But Tania would not go, and now Marty too was more deeply enmeshed in the net of The Reckoner. Marty nodded. Yes, if facts were known; if The Reckoner wanted to, he could disclose to the

police the dead man in Marty's apartment. Oh, Marty hadn't killed the man; and even if he had, the man deserved to die—had to die.

Zee Clarke, the mystery woman who feared nothing, perhaps not even The Reckoner, had shot that man to death to save Marty; to save Tania. And Marty could do no less than take the blame; or rather the responsibility for that killing. Zee Clarke had asked him to do that; to admit the killing to The Reckoner; to Max Arnold, the criminal lawyer who had seen to the removing of the body. But it was too late to think of that now. The woman had saved his life. But who was this Zee Clarke? What—

And Marty was through thinking. He came to his feet. The lock had clicked in the door. From the little ledge below the thin curtain of steel he lifted the envelope The Reckoner had given him to deliver and walked toward the door. His steps were quick, even eager. Not because he had just been paid well for taking that envelope, but because his reward was—well, he was to see Tania again.

**THE LITTLE** pawnbroker, who must have tended the shop by day, though Marty didn't know, for he never visited it except at night, bowed ingratiatingly as he led Marty down the narrow hall, around the bend to the side entrance and onto the street.

Marty, whistling now as he turned across town, hesitated as he spotted a cruising taxi—and decided he had time to walk. He felt pretty good about The Reckoner this time. He felt pretty good about the message he was to deliver to Judge Ramdelfia. Indeed, it was he—Marty, who had been instrumental in that message to the judge. It was he who had raided Joseph T. Rierson's house; almost lost his life as well as his freedom, and taken from Rierson the written information that should—that would make Judge Ramdelfia an honest man; at least, on this occasion.

Marty tapped his pocket where the envelope was, thought of the money he had received, wondered where The Reckoner's unlimited resources came from. Was he just a wealthy man who abhorred crime? But that didn't seem possible. The Reckoner knew the under-world; knew its workings; knew almost to a certainty who committed crimes, who was behind them, where evidence could be obtained. But mostly Marty thought of Tania. The Reckoner's last words to Marty had been—"Tania will have a late supper with you at your apartment tonight. No—no, Mr. Day, there is no reason for you to telephone your servant, Knight. I have arranged that. Be successful!"

No wish that Marty would be successful; no hope, even, that he might succeed with his mission. Just the command, "Be successful!" Nothing more.

**MARTY** swung his cane easily over his arm, started around the corner—and threw himself flat on the sidewalk.

The car must have been waiting and jumped from the curb. Black curtains flashed open, white faces showed, and almost at the moment Marty crashed to the sidewalk orange-blue flame spat suddenly from that car. There was no doubting the steady *rat-tat* of the machine gun; no doubting the whining death that sped over the spot where he had stood a few seconds before; leaden death that was flashing down toward the walk on which he lay; on which he lay for a stunned moment only. Then, twisting his body, he rolled quickly toward the areaway.

But he had little hope of saving his life. For the moment only would he dodge that spraying death. For a time only it had ceased. The men in the car had spotted the twisting body. What good would the sunken areaway do him? A minute or two, maybe, of protection; a few seconds even. Then men would jump from that car and a Tommy gun would play its tune of death into his body.

A moment of silence. At least, silence after the steady *rat-tat* of lead. Then the grinding of brakes, the screech of protesting tires, and Marty felt that the end had come. Funny that, as he waited for death. His past life didn't flash before him, his misdeeds, or even his childhood. Just one thing; one clear picture. He would not eat that supper with Tania! He would—

And the lead came; he heard the sharp report of it. One, two, three shots. Close together, those shots? Certainly. But not with the staccato notes of a machine gun.

Running feet now, a hoarse voice calling. More pounding feet, the shrill blast of a police whistle. Then again the steady, deadly notes of a machine gun; and far distant, the shrill cry of a siren.

The machine gun stopped, a car door slammed, a motor raced, and there was the grinding of badly meshed gears. More shots after that, the dying of a distant motor—and a light straight down on Marty's face.

A voice spoke. "Did you make it? If you can come up out of there and—" a whistle from the man above him! "God! Marty Day—Mr. Day, eh? So you're the one they wanted."

Slowly Marty mounted the steps to the sidewalk. Mechanically he brushed at his clothes, draped his cane over his arm, straightened out his crushed hat. But the light words of banter that heroes are supposed to use did not come from his lips; indeed, his mouth just hung open.

"Detective Frank Bradley!" he gasped at last, then added inanely, "Lieutenant Bradley, of the police." Marty was looking into a hard, grim, unemotional and honest face.

"That's right." Bradley took his arm. "Didn't get you, eh? Damn it! I might have known who they were after when the stoolie told me he heard one of them say, 'That dude gets it tonight.'"

"Dude!" Marty adjusted the carnation in his lapel. "Then it can't be me they were after."

"Well now," Bradley rubbed his chin, "you don't look much like a dude at present. But you act like one of them lads in books that go around straightening out other peoples' affairs or become gentlemen crooks; Robin Hoods of crime. Personally—in twenty-two years I never came across one face to face." He nodded vigorously. "But I like them in books"—and pushing a finger into Marty's chest—"and only in books."

"I suppose I owe my life to you, Bradley," Marty said, "and I'm grateful indeed." And with a shake of his head, "But I don't understand your allusions to my—er—activities. I can assure you I never stepped out of a book and I don't know who—

"Well, I suppose these men took me for someone else."

"Sure. Sure!" he said. "But they'd have buried you as Mr. Marty Day. As far as your record goes—and you know I've got a line on you since you first slipped the strap off your go-cart and went places—it's honest enough. But now you're in dangerous company, and you're getting ready to go places that will surprise you."

"You're not threatening me, Bradley, with—with—"

"Threatening you!"

**BRADLEY'S** eyebrows went up.

"Threatening you! I'd do you a favor if I locked you up. I'd do it too if you didn't have such a smart lawyer—Max Arnold. That's another thing, Mr. Day. Honest men, walking the streets with honest purposes, don't have lawyers like Max Arnold sitting around with *habeas corpus* writs in their hands." And suddenly, "Why don't you talk while you can talk? You're not a crook. You're just kidding yourself into the belief that you're having adventure; romance, when you're really just—just—"

"Just a fool, eh?" Marty finished the sentence. "So you still believe in this newspaper myth, The Reckoner!"

"Sure!" Bradley agreed. "That's my weakness. Yours is that Rierson, the big-shot politician, is for some reason after your hide." And with steady gray eyes on Marty's black ones, "I suppose you figure he had a hand in this one."

"If it wasn't a mistake in identity, that guess might be as good as another. I wish you wouldn't keep such an eye on me."

"There's a lot who wish that." Bradley shook his head, and as a police car turned the corner, "I'll explain to the boys how the intended victim got away."

"Thanks!" Marty started to move down the street, then turned back. "I suppose you're doing this because I gave you the name of the murderer in the Senator Hopewell case."

"Yeah—sure." Bradley smiled crookedly. "After you pasted me on the chin with your fist and left me cold in a cab! No! Mr. Day; it's because I think you'll lead me some place." And grabbing Marty's arm as he would have left, "Here's another tip. Go home and go to sleep. I sort of like you, Mr. Day; yet I'm a police officer and I'm letting you walk away tonight so I can arrest you later—on a real charge."

"Later—on a real charge!"

"That's it," nodded Bradley. "Remember that people are safest in bed. But move along! I'll talk to the boys." This last as the police car drew up down the block and two men, seeing the couple close to the areaway, stepped out with drawn guns.

Marty turned and walked back down the street. Things were happening now. Windows were up; voices were calling; half-dressed people were visible far back in doorways.

Marty knew that Frank Bradley was explaining to the men who arrived in that car. He knew too that other cars were arriving. But he turned the corner at the far end of the street, entered a hotel, went immediately to the wash room, where an eager attendant who could not reconcile the condition of Marty's clothes with the absence of alcoholic breath carefully cleaned and brushed him.

Time was passing now. The hour of his meeting was eleven o'clock. When Marty left the hotel he climbed into a taxi and drove directly to Judge Ramdelfia's house.

## CHAPTER TWO

## A QUESTION OF BAIL

**T**  **HE OLD** brick house was still much the same as it had been many years before. Judge Ramdelfia had been raised in the lower city; he stuck to it. Not because he loved the old place or even liked it. He had always planned to move; always hoped to move. But when the time came that he could afford an elegant apartment on Park Avenue the time also came when he had become "the man of the common people." Somehow, when he couldn't move he gave that as his reason; now that he could afford the most pretentious quarters, that "reason" had back-fired on him. Politics and politicians—one politician in particular—kept him there. Joseph T. Rierson thought that his "man of the common people" was a good line. And since Rierson's nostrils did not have to be assailed by the odor of peddlers' fish nor his eyes offended by the dirty children of the poor, who played in the street, he kept Judge Ramdelfia "the man of the common people."

Marty Day nodded his satisfaction as he climbed the steps and pushed the door bell. It was exactly eleven o'clock. He liked that. Psychology played an important part in the business of The Reckoner. A man inside expected that ring, yet in a way he hoped it would never come; believed, perhaps, that it would never come.

The door opened almost at once; Judge Ramdelfia stood in the doorway. He wore a long dressing gown that went well with the interior of the house; it being done in the Park Avenue fashion that the judge felt himself denied. He was a tall thin man with his hair cut far back, so as to make a small forehead appear a high and scholarly one. He carried a book in his hand and a black ribbon hung from his glasses.

Marty thought that he stared overly long at him through narrowed judicial eyes, making no attempt to close the door. Then he spoke as Marty stepped into the hall.

"You are," he said, removing his glasses, rubbing them on his robe and replacing them again, "Mr. Marty Day, the man who made an appointment with me for tonight, or at least had an appointment arranged."

"I am," said Marty very slowly and solemnly, "the messenger from The Reckoner." It was part of his stock in trade to put feeling into his voice. But if the intention was to awe, as it very often did awe those The Reckoner threatened, it failed miserably this time.

"Yes, yes; to be sure." The judge closed the door slowly and said: "Come this way."

He led Marty into a well equipped and comfortable library, indicated a chair and dropped into another behind a flat desk.

"So"—the judge held his glasses in his hand now and tapped them on the palm of his other hand—"there is such a person then; such a personality as The Reckoner. How quaint! That envelope you are holding in your hand I presume is for me."

"It is," said Marty. "Later."

"So you are to talk first, Mr. Day. Let me warn you that the papers and gossip have informed me somewhat of this strange character. I have been on the bench a good many years. Before that I worked my way up from the streets; the very street, indeed, that I now live on. Those that know me can tell you without fear of contradiction that I cannot be intimidated, coerced or threatened. As for bribery"—he spread his hands apart—"my tastes are simple ones."

Marty Day nodded. "We are quite alone?" he asked.

"Quite. My single servant sleeps out." And after a moment's pause, "I am willing to listen."

AND MARTY talked. Some of it he knew; some of it was what The Reckoner had told him.

"Joseph T. Rierson," he said, "was a gangster, murderer and racketeer some years ago. Prohibition swelled his pocket book; political influence bought by that pocket book swelled his head. He is now the big frog in the big puddle—a particularly dirty, filthy puddle. Big men take orders from him. Some simply for money and advancement; some through personal fear, which so often follows money and advancement." Marty slightly raised his hand but the judge was not going to talk; he had just leaned forward upon the desk. "There have been a number of times when, in your court, justice has miscarried, witnesses have disappeared. And on occasions murderers, without sufficient evidence against them at the moment, have been admitted to bail just before that promised evidence has been produced."

"You are," said Judge Ramdelfia very slowly, "accusing me of these things?"

"I am," said Marty Day just as slowly, "stating facts. Shall I go on?"

"Certainly. It is all quite interesting—and quite damaging." Judge Ramdelfia smiled.

Marty continued. "Rierson is in a fair way to control the entire city. That, at least, is his ambition, his hope. He wishes to be the secret power that guides a great government; he is laying the foundation for that control. Not so long ago Joseph Rierson gave a dinner. You were one of the many men in the city who attended it. That dinner was for the purpose of letting each of you understand just how large and how terrifying was the big stick that Rierson wields over your heads. Separately, each of you were taken privately aside and shown the evidence that Rierson had collected against you. He was ready to strike and strike hard, and he wanted each of you to know the danger to yourselves in disobeying his orders. And you, Judge Ramdelfia, were shown evidence against you; evidence that would, if made public, put you away in a place where you would never more dispense 'injustice' to the people."

"That is all?" Judge Ramdelfia's eyes narrowed, his thin lips set tightly.

"No," said Marty, "that is not all." And though his voice was still confident, beneath he was worried. The judge did not seem alarmed, struck with panic—even fear. But Marty went on. "The envelope that contained each one's misdeeds was stolen." He threw that suddenly at Judge Ramdelfia and waited for the blow to take effect.

But there was no blow—no apparent blow. The judge said quietly: "Yes, I know. You, Mr. Day, are the man who stole that envelope."

**MARTY** stared at the man. This was the point where terror was to strike the color from the judge's cheeks. This was the point— Could it be possible that The Reckoner was wrong for once, or was it simply that the judge had made up his mind to obey The Reckoner's orders even before Marty came? Marty went on, stumbling slightly now; not so sure of himself; uncertain in his speech. But he carried out The Reckoner's orders.

"Senator Hopewell," he said, "was shot to death by a man called Razor Burke. We believed that Razor Burke got his orders to kill straight from Joseph T. Rierson, but he didn't. He got his orders from someone else. He got them from Don Parks, Rierson's official killer.

Lieutenant Bradley discovered this. He will have the evidence complete tomorrow noon. You are going to release this Parks tomorrow morning; that is, you were going to release him tomorrow morning—set free a man you have never even seen."

"And the point?" said the judge, rapping the desk with one hand and stifling a yawn with the other.

"The point is—that Parks is like most of his kind. He can give it but he can't take it. He has let Rierson know that if he isn't set free by tomorrow he'll talk and talk plenty. He'll talk Rierson right out of the control of the city and into Sing Sing Prison. Big men, for personal reasons, do not wish this. You are one of those big men. You have your orders to release Parks on bail."

"But my dear man"—the judge seemed bored—"there is really no evidence against Parks. Promised evidence is not sufficient to warrant my holding him further. In most cases we have such promises. Parks has now been held"—he looked toward the ceiling—"two—no, three weeks. Your plea may be very honest, very unbiased and very sincere. But it comes in a strange—"

"It is not a plea." Marty leaned forward on his cane.

"A threat?" said the judge.

"An order," said Marty. "If Parks is released on bail tomorrow"—Marty tapped the envelope he held in his hand—"the original of this document goes to the district attorney; copies to the press."

"So—" The glasses went onto Judge Ramdelfia's nose, his hand stretched out for the envelope. And as he took it and tore it open he kept his eyes on Marty and talked.

"You are very naive, Mr. Day." His voice was still quiet, but an ominous note had crept in. "You threaten me with blackmail in an effort to corrupt justice." He had torn the envelope open now and was taking out the several sheets of paper; smaller legal papers clipped to the back of a single larger sheet. "If you took these papers from Mr. Rierson and examined them you would see that they are not proof of any wrong doing. They may have cited a few cases which, on the face of them, seemed peculiar. But—"

The judge was reading the long sheet now and Marty, watching his face, saw it drain to a dull white. Then there were quick flashes of red in his cheeks that were gone almost at once as he turned the long sheet of paper over and with trembling fingers examined the oblong bits of legal forms. He spoke, and his voice was thick; his words hardly audible.

"But he couldn't know that. Only Rierson knew that. It was not on that stolen sheet." And dropping the papers upon the desk he looked straight up at Marty Day. Gray eyes were wide and frightened. He said, and licked at his lips between the words: "Well, what am I to do; what can I do? Either way—The Reckoner or Rierson, it means prison for me."

Marty said slowly: "Do your duty. If this man, Parks, is not released tomorrow he will talk about Rierson, and then Rierson will have other things to occupy his mind than you."

"But this Reckoner! How did he know; how could he find out?"

Marty shrugged his shoulders. "He has had that notation about you for several months. He knew what to look for, evidently found it. Those papers are but copies of the originals he can and will produce." And eagerly, for above all he wanted Rierson and wanted the crooked officials he controlled; wanted the murderers he directed, "Rierson won't turn you up; at least, yet. He'll need your influence; he'll need your friends. He won't go against you until he's certain all hope for him is gone. Like Parks, he'll hope and wait."

"And then," Judge Ramdelfia hardly breathed the words, "like Parks, he'll strike."

"Then," Marty said, "you will leave the city—the country. You will have time to collect your resources and escape."

"Yes, yes." The judge was nodding now, mentally picking up his house of cards that had so suddenly collapsed; like a child trying his best with pudgy fingers to save the few bent wobbling, cards that still remained. "But the fifty thousand dollars! Couldn't it be less? I'm not a rich man."

"What fifty thousand dollars?" Marty was surprised into the question.

The judge tapped the paper on the desk. "That The Reckoner demands." He jerked up, straight in his chair. His face went ashen; his hand fell upon the desk, crushing the papers beneath it as he came slowly to his feet. The door bell had rung—long, demanding. Then it was ringing again.

"Detective Frank Bradley," whispered the judge, and before Marty could voice the question, "I thought it would only be—be what was taken from Rierson. Nothing wrong on the face of it, and I sent for Bradley to—to—" He looked at Marty.

"To have me arrested for blackmail, eh? So that was it!"

"That," said Judge Ramdelfia as he moved toward the door, "was it. I'll tell him—to go away." And he started slowly toward the hall, suddenly an old man.

Marty looked at the documents upon the desk. Even his untrained legal mind could see at once the completeness of the case against the judge; the thoroughness with which The Reckoner had gathered his evidence, even to the affidavits clipped to the back of the main sheet. That was why The Reckoner was slow to strike with the evidence Marty had furnished him. He waited until he was sure.

Marty gasped as the papers fell back on the desk and the long single sheet, with its closely typewritten letters, stared up at him. It was a P.S. at the bottom that made Marty's mouth hang open. It explained the final words of the judge; also, perhaps, explained the source of The Reckoner's income. The last few lines read simply.

> P.S. The expenses and fee for this service which I render the citizen is fifty thousand dollars. Arrange to have the money in cash, by twelve o'clock tomorrow morning. By this time you will have refused Parks's bail, and a telephone message to your chambers will inform you as to the method of IMMEDIATE payment.
>
> The Reckoner.

## CHAPTER THREE

## THE COBRA CANE

**T**HE OUTSIDE door slammed, feet were coming down the hall. Marty quickly gathered the envelope and its contents from the desk and shoved them into his jacket pocket. Then he looked for a place to hide. There was the door he had entered; another door, probably to a front room of the house; and behind him heavy tightly drawn curtains, which must lead to the dining room. But whether a door was behind those curtains or not Marty didn't know.

Marty started toward those curtains, and listened. Feet were crossing the hall without, coming to the library. Marty straightened. Just a single pair of feet; uncertain, tottering feet. Perhaps not as uncertain as the feet that had staggered from that room, yet the same feet. The door to the hall opened and Judge Ramdelfia came into the room. His face was still white; there were beads of perspiration upon his forehead.

"It was Bradley?" Marty whispered hoarsely.

"Yes, yes. I had told him you were coming tonight. I didn't know, didn't understand." The judge ran a hand across his forehead, his moist forehead. "I told him you hadn't come; that the attempted intimidation did not materialize; that I had been mistaken, and for him to go."

Marty looked at those filmy eyes; the pale, dry, quivering lips, and the little beads of perspiration which had formed again on his forehead. He said: "Did Bradley believe you?"

"I don't know, I don't know." The judge crossed the room, stood between Marty and the curtained doorway.

"Did he go?" Marty took the judge by the shoulders, backed him across the room, almost to those curtains. "Come, man—pull yourself together. Did Bradley go?"

"He— I don't know. At least, he's outside. I closed the door, bolted it. He looked strangely at me—smiled."

"Did he say anything? Did he—" Marty half shook the dazed man.

"*Shs!*" Dim eyes grew bright with fear. "There's a man above; a man I had wait upstairs, if—if you— I don't know. I feared violence."

"So—" Marty half curled his lips—"you intended to double cross The Reckoner—me—Bradley, if possible. A man to kill me, perhaps. Just self-defense. That was it, wasn't it?"

"No, no!" the judge moaned. "Rierson suggested that; the—the killing of you. But—no. I wouldn't have tolerated it." And gripping Marty suddenly by the shoulders, "Rierson! If he were dead now, nothing could harm me. The Reckoner wants him dead. Then I might stay on the bench, serve justice, serve The Reckoner."

"Serve him—how? Do as he told you, justice or no justice?"

"Yes, yes. That's it." The judge's voice was ingratiating. "Only Rierson knows the truth about me. People admire me, respect me. I might go far—far, if Rierson were dead. The Reckoner could order. I could do things cleverly; I have done things cleverly. No one would suspect. I— Yes, I have even— Well, for him I could clear men even of murder."

"God!" Marty pushed the man from him. "What a filthy swine you are."

"Not so loud—so loud." The judge looked toward the closed hall door. "Better go—go. The window there in the dining room, and into the alley. Why do you stay? Why don't you go?" And gripping Marty's arms tightly, "Tell The Reckoner what I offered for Rierson's—" and perhaps seeing Marty's eyes, "If Rierson shouldn't talk—couldn't talk. Go! Why don't you go?"

"Just one thing." Marty looked coldly down at the crouching, trembling little figure. "About tomorrow? You will deny the man bail?"

"Of course. Of course. I'll let Rierson think differently, then I'll make a speech from the bench against freeing public enemies. I'll— I'll see that Parks is convicted too; that he talks about Rierson, if Rierson can't—can't talk back."

MARTY turned his eyes away. He couldn't look at the whining, cringing figure. The man of the people! The rottenness of politics and crime. Only a month before the judge had been given a dinner. Marty recalled reading about it in the papers. The judge's speech; his public hatred for all that was criminal! The big official who had said Judge Ramdelfia was doing more to wipe out crime than any other single man in the great city! The judge—

Marty jumped back. There was a single crack of a gun; a shot that seemed to be in that very room itself, yet slightly muffled. And Marty lowered his eyes and looked straight into the eyes of the judge. There was nothing bright in them now; nothing quivering about the lips.

Things happened quickly after that. Marty heard the glass of a window crash, yet couldn't locate the direction of the noise. But he was watching the man before him.

Judge Ramdelfia's eyes held a pained, hurt, childlike look. He seemed to shake his head—as he stared at Marty, half questioning, half pleading with Marty to—well to help him, or was it to spare him? Spare him what?

Then Judge Ramdelfia's hands dropped to his sides; his eyes took on a glassy, uncertain look. Words that never came rattled far back in his throat. He bent slowly at the knees, half tried to raise his hands; then his chin dropped forward on his chest and he sank slowly to the floor.

"God!" Marty's breath whistled back in his throat. But he knew the truth even before the judge's body crumpled there upon the library rug. Someone had shot the judge; shot him directly through the back;

shot him from behind those curtains. And that crash of glass? The man had escaped through the dining room window then.

Marty gripped his cane, tore through those curtains, found the old-fashioned folding doors partly open. He forced them wider, mostly with his body. He was in the dining room; across to the window. The window was open, curtains waved gently in the breeze. That was how the killer had escaped. One foot over the window sill, Marty paused. There was no glass on the floor. Still, it might have fallen outside in the alley. Might have, but it hadn't. Marty felt carefully of the window. No glass broken there; he had covered both the upper and lower sections.

Yet he had heard glass. The killer, then, had gone another way. Through the front hall, into the front room—

Should he follow him? It was almost certain he was out of the house; the breaking glass told him that. He had run in panic then. Panic? Strange, that, in a man who so calmly raised a gun and from between tightly drawn curtains had shot a man straight through the back. Who was he? The man who waited above, of course; the man whom Rierson had sent. He had sneaked below, heard the judge plan to hold Parks; to even betray Rierson; to work for The Reckoner. But the man was gone; and he was fool enough to sit there like that astride the window sill.

And then, abruptly, Marty's indecision was gone and his course of action was suddenly decided for him. For the second time that night, within the hour, a bright light flashed upon his face. And a familiar voice said: "Come in out of that window." Light showed in an old chandelier above a round table, the flash dropped from Marty's face and the voice went on. "Not so pleasant this time, Mr. Day. I told you to go to bed, but I didn't think it would be murder."

**MARTY** climbed back into that room. The eyes of Lieutenant Bradley, still unemotional, were cold and hard. There was an unfriendliness in his voice that Marty had never noticed before. But Marty only said what was on his mind. He was still confused, puzzled.

"The man—the man who shot him got away. I thought—" He looked toward the window behind him, suddenly back to Bradley; and the jumbled, odd pieces in his mind snapped quickly into place. "It was you, Bradley, who crashed the front window. Then the murderer escaped by this one."

"Not yet he didn't." Bradley was very serious. He waved a gun toward the library. "Get in there, Day. Judge Ramdelfia wants to talk."

"My God!" The words just shot from Marty. "You don't think I did it?"

"No?" said Bradley as he prodded Marty through the curtains with the nose of his heavy police gun, with his other hand fanned him expertly for weapons. "If the judge doesn't talk and talk your way, they'll fry you sure. That sitting-on-the-window-sill act doesn't look so good, nor does the judge's message he sent me that he expected a blackmailer tonight."

Bradley was right of course. Marty knew that. He saw himself now in court, facing a jury; telling of his meeting with Judge Ramdelfia; of the man the judge said lurked in the house; that Rierson had sent the man to— Rierson, one of the biggest political influences in the city, and to be still bigger unless— Marty looked down at the figure gasping for breath. Well, there was still that evidence in his pocket. When Bradley found that on Marty, would it help him or hurt him? He turned his head from the gasping, dying man and spoke to Bradley.

"He was a crook; not fit to live, and—"

Bradley, kneeling by the body, his gun directed toward Marty, said: "You can't go around killing all men not fit to live."

"But he isn't dead yet." Marty gripped his cane tightly in tense fingers. "He wants to talk. Look! Lift up his head. He— Let me go to the kitchen for water."

"No!" said Bradley. "I couldn't do that." He lifted the gasping man's head and let it rest on his left arm, but the gun he held in his right hand was still pointed straight at Marty.

"But my life may depend on it," Marty gasped. "You know me, Bradley. You don't think, can't believe that I'd shoot a man in the back."

"So that's how he got it." Bradley nodded. "People do strange things when they're pushed; swept into the stream of crime they thought they'd just drift along on the edge of." And with a shrug of his shoulders, "After all, it's what twelve men will think and believe that will count."

"But I couldn't do it." Marty was alarmed at the strange gurgling sound in the dying man's throat. "You felt me for weapons. I haven't got a gun."

"Just a quick frisk," explained Bradley. "You might have dropped it from the window. We'll find that out later. But since you remind me of it—keep both your hands in front of you, gripping either end of that stick like you are now."

"If I could get him water! If he'd talk, he'd tell the truth. The curtains just parted from behind and—"

"No!" snapped Bradley; and sharply, "Shut up. This lad's going to talk now—talk real words."

**JUDGE RAMDELFIA** raised his head slightly; his glassy eyes turned brilliant—feverishly brilliant. Little bubbles of saliva formed on his lips. He looked long at Lieutenant Bradley, turned his eyes but not his head and stared at Marty Day. And Marty saw fear in his eyes; then hatred.

Twice Judge Ramdelfia opened his mouth to speak and twice closed it again. At least, tried to close it; for his lower lip hung down, preventing his mouth from closing tightly.

Then his right hand began to move. Very slowly it raised. There was agony in his face; he was forcing himself with his last ounce of strength to raise that arm.

Marty didn't speak, Bradley didn't speak. Both men knew that the moment was coming. The lump went out of Marty's throat. The judge would clear him! Might accuse him of something, or The Reckoner of something. But certainly free him of any charge of—of murder.

The arm ceased to rise, the fingers of the judge's hand closed one by one, until only the index finger remained extended. And this finger pointed directly at Marty Day.

The judge seemed to suck in a great breath. His chest expanded, his head came up, and his burning eyes followed that finger—that accusing finger as he spoke very slowly and very, very clearly.

"That man is the one who shot me. His name is Day." Lips opened, snapped back; then again, just as clear, "He called me a filthy swine, then shot me."

Bradley laid the dying man's head down on the rug and looked up at Marty Day. "God!" he said, "I didn't believe it; couldn't make myself believe it until he spoke. But we live and learn."

For the moment Marty was stunned, stunned into silence. Then he fairly shouted the words as he moved forward. "It's a lie; a lie! Make him deny it. Make him—"

And Marty stopped. He didn't know what was on his mind; if he intended to shake the truth from the dying man—dying as he lied. But why did he lie?

Marty knew why he stopped if he didn't know why he had started forward. Bradley had come to his feet and stepped across the body. His right hand held the gun pointing almost directly at Marty's stomach, his left hand dug into a rear pocket. He said, and there was no friendliness in his voice: "Keep your hands just so, gripping that cane. No—no, Mr. Marty Day. Dying men don't lie like that, or if they do you'll have your day in court. There!"

Gun in his outstretched right hand, handcuffs dangling now in his left, Detective Bradley walked toward Marty Day. His eyes were riveted on Marty's eyes.

"What are you going to do?" The words were spoken before Marty knew that the voice that spoke them was his voice.

"Put the irons on you and call headquarters. Keep your hands on that cane a moment now." The gun was held close to his own body, covering Marty but still a good foot or more away. His mouth was tightly set, his chin thrust forward.

"Keep your hands on that cane!" The words echoed in Marty's ears. He didn't have to think now. The thing was a natural. Detective Bradley had made his own trap and then stepped into it. Marty's cane; his cobra cane! The heavy steel already arched in his hands for that swift, unseen attack. No, Marty didn't think then; he wished afterward that he had thought. Or if he did think, it was just one thought. It was the time to strike, the very second to strike. That gun coming an inch nearer, that forward chin straightening and—Marty knew.

There was no danger that he'd miss, not with that deadly weapon in the expert hands of Marty Day. It was all mechanical this time; no maneuvering for position. No—

Just for the flash of a single second the accusing voice of Judge Ramdelfia rang in his ears. "Day. He shot me." Then Marty did it. Mechanically certainly, if not actually unconsciously, Marty's right hand tightened close to the ferrule of that cane. His left hand pressed downward sharply, then released the curved head of the cane entirely. There was a sudden whining, almost inaudible sound as the hidden springs jumped into life. Bradley's eyes widened slightly. Then a dull thud as steel hit bone, and Marty Day was easing the unconscious body of the detective to the floor. No prize-fighter could have struck a cleaner blow nor put such power behind it. But the beauty of that cane to Marty Day was that, unlike a knife, a gun, a blackjack or even a human fist, the victim seldom if ever knew what had struck him. It could be used over and over and the trick was always a new one.

Yet, the satisfaction that Marty always felt at his deftness after years of practice with his strange weapon was absent this time. He had done it of course to—well, to save his life. But he hadn't wanted to strike Bradley. He hadn't—

Marty whirled quickly and faced the curtains. A voice had spoken.

"Good work, Marty Day. In another moment I would have shot him to death through the curtains."

## CHAPTER FOUR

## AMBER EYES

THE TALL, dark, willowy form of the mystery girl, Zee Clarke, stood between the curtains. In her hand she held a revolver. Those amber eyes, generally so cold and sinister, were now alive with admiration.

"I knew about that cane, but never— It was glorious." She jerked her head down toward the judge. "Has—" And listening to his gasping breath, "He won't last much longer. I'm glad you got Bradley yourself. I know men. Men like you would much rather do their own life-saving than have a woman do it."

"You know what—what happened?" Marty half stammered.

"Yes." She nodded. "I have a car around the corner. It was for you, if things went wrong. You were a long time, so I came to investigate, found the window open, heard the voices and climbed in. I listened to the accusation; the judge's dying statement, but I won't talk." She smiled—yes, smiled beautifully there in the presence of death. "I would have shot Bradley sooner, only you stood between the curtain and him."

"Then, by striking Bradley—" Marty looked down at the unconscious form of the detective—"I really saved his life."

"Saved his life?" The girl's eyebrows went up. Then, "Well, yes—for the moment. Let him have it now and we'll get going."

"Yes." Marty nodded. "Get going. But—'Let him have it.' What do you mean?"

"What do you think I mean?" she flashed suddenly at him. "Don't be a child, or worse—a fool. Oh, it's not a pleasant job. But he has to die. Bradley knows the truth. He heard the *ante mortem* statement, as Max Arnold would say. Bradley's got to die that you may live."

"And you—you expect me to kill him? Kill a defenseless man!"

"You killed the other, didn't you? Murder follows murder. Or death follows death, if you can't stomach it the other way."

"But I didn't kill the—the judge," Marty stammered.

"Stop the play-acting." The amber-eyed girl fairly snapped the words. "Of course you killed him. Do you think I'm a fool?"

"You—you believe that?"

She looked at Marty a long moment.

"Of course I won't believe it if you don't wish me to, Marty." And the smile broadening, "At any event, I'll go on the stand and swear you spent the evening with—with me. With me! I have never loved a man, Marty, but once. I find men hard to love." A long pause. "I would find it very easy to love you."

"Well—yeah. Thanks." Marty was thrown completely. "We'd better get going."

"You can't leave that man, Bradley, here." She stood by the curtains and blocked Marty's passage, and when he went to push her aside, "Why, it's suicide. You're well known; distinguished-looking. God in heaven! Would you spare a cop; a cop who will stand up in court and point you out?" She placed her hands upon his shoulders, hair brushing his cheeks, hard eyes were closely knit. "He didn't have time to use the phone. There's his gun. Just the nose to his head; the slightest pressure of a finger. No one will ever know about him; about the judge. At least—" she was very close now—"I only know. Maybe I'll drive a bargain with you for my silence; a bargain you'll like."

**MARTY** pushed her from him. "No, no." She was mad, he thought or maybe he was. She— But she was talking.

"It's his life or yours. You'll be a hunted man; a man who can't avoid the law. The time to act is now, not regret it a few months from now when Bradley puts the finger on you; when the twelve men come back, and one—"

"But I didn't do it," Marty told her.

"Who'd believe that, even if it were true. Not the judge who sentences you to death. Not the man who switches on the juice—yes, the juice. Picture that now; not later, when it isn't a picture but a ghastly fact—a terrible dream of truth."

"Come!" Marty thrust her roughly between the curtains. "We're different people, Zee Clarke; from different worlds. I can't understand you. You must be mad. A helpless man—a man who saved my life tonight!"

"Saved it to take it. That's the law. They hire skilled surgeons; the finest specialists, to drag some poor soul back to life so that the State may have the pleasure of frying him. Well—" She twisted suddenly, broke from Marty's grasp, crossed back into the room, knelt by the silent form of Lieutenant Bradley.

"All right." She spoke as she came to her feet and stood over the detective. "If you haven't got the stomach for it, I'll do it."

Marty turned; his eyes widened, his mouth hung open. Zee Clarke was standing above Bradley; Bradley's gun was in her hand. Her finger was on the trigger, the stub nose pointing down at the side of the man's head; pointing, and, yes— Paralyzed, Marty saw the knuckle of her index finger whiten; whiten as the finger started to close upon that trigger.

Then he was paralyzed no longer. The girl was very close to him. He reached out, grasped her arm, swung her around so that she faced him, his hand slipping to her wrist—to the gun it held, twisting it from her grasp. The girl stared blankly at him.

"I might—might have shot you," she said as she watched Marty take his handkerchief, and after wiping the gun free of fingerprints toss it beside the unconscious detective. Confusion was gone now. Marty was the man of action again, whom The Reckoner found so useful; paid so well.

Marty, his cane hooked over his arm, grabbed the girl, almost rushing her off her feet as he half carried, half hurled her through those curtains and across the dining room to the open window. For a moment only she fought; then, as he lifted her to the sill and dropped her to the stone alley below and jumped down beside her she stopped her struggles; even laughed lightly.

"You can work fast when you want to, Mr. Day. You could go far with The Reckoner if—if you'd stop being the moving-picture hero. You're just too noble." Her shoulders shrugged and she took his hand and started leading him down the alley. "It's too late now. A murderer should never return to the scene of his crime. Have you still got the gun?"

"His gun—now?" And seeing her eyes, even in the darkness, "I didn't have any gun. I tell you—I didn't shoot the judge."

"All right." She sighed. "That's your story and you're going to stick to it." She stuck her head out of the alley and looked up and down the street. "Not a soul in sight. The car is around the corner, but there's still time; still time to go back and finish the job. God, Marty—" she clutched at the lapels of his coat—"I'm superstitious as hell about returning, but I'll do it for you. Let's—"

Marty tried to smile down at her; tried to speak, but didn't. Amber eyes, soft and shining in the darkness, became hard and narrow; thin slits of animal-like brightness.

And the shots came!

**MARTY** never knew if they were out of that alley and speeding up the street when the first shot came, or even the second for that matter. But, anyway, they did reach the street, did run up it, did turn the corner and climb into the long low roadster. And they were away, jumping from the curb, as the car picked up speed under skilful driving. They were around the corner, dashing uptown—ducking down one side street, to turn up another before he spoke.

"Someone else was in the house then, or came through the alley in back," he said to the girl. "A cop, who—"

"No one else was in the house, no one came through the back." She was very emphatic. "I looked directly past you. Remember, in your hurry to throw me out that window you left the dining-room lights burning. I was looking directly from the darkness into light. I saw the white face plainly at the window, recognized it before he even raised the gun and fired. It was Lieutenant Bradley. The hunt has started."

Marty gasped. "He saw us, recognized us! He came around quickly."

"He might have seen us—just shadows in the darkness. But he could not have recognized us." She swung another corner, straightened and sped uptown again.

"Where are we going?" Marty clutched her arm. "My apartment is—"

"Good God!" Zee Clarke said. "You wouldn't be fool enough to go there."

"But—" Marty stopped, with the name of Tania on his lips. "I guess I'll have to hide out for a while. But I can go there a minute, before—"

"I know. I know," she cut in before he could interrupt again. "It's Tania Cordet. You were to have had supper with her. I'll bring her to you."

Marty looked at her as they turned up the pretentious street and swung suddenly into the driveway of one of New York's famous old mansions.

"You—you live here?" Marty could not keep the surprise out of his voice as the car jerked to a stop beside wide stone steps. "This place belonged to the—" He mentioned one of New York's best known social and former financial names; and suddenly as he followed her from the car, "Why, this place was bought by Colonel Jacob Clarke, the eccentric millionaire. You're not his widow?"

The woman laughed. "I am, perhaps, the most noted of his eccentricities."

"And The Reckoner forced you into this—this fight on crime?"

"No one forced me into anything. I like it. I like the excitement and danger of it. You all fear and tremble before the words of The Reckoner, but not I." She opened the outer door, ignored the great double entrance doors before her, turned to the left and opened another door; one which Marty had not seen, could not see. They entered a small room.

"You—you must have many servants," Marty warned. "Some of them will see me and talk, and—"

"They will not see you and they would not talk if they did. When I enter by that side door it is indicated by a light in each servant's room. They all know that I have returned and do not wish their services. This is not a secret room; only the entrance to it by the vestibule is hidden. The door there gives off on a small hall which leads to the entrance hall as well as to my rooms above." She walked across the room, pressed against a large picture which swung back at once. There was a small wall safe behind it.

Her fingers were on the dial when Marty asked: "Why that? I don't need money." He felt in his pocket. "At least, not yet. But, Tania. She—"

"Right!" The woman turned from the safe, sought a small telephone on the low table and quickly dialed a number—Marty's number. She said, over her shoulder to Marty: "Tania had better be informed at once, before the police get there. If she is followed and— Hello, Knight, Mrs. Clarke speaking. Have Tania come and see me at once. Yes, I know that she is waiting for Mr. Day, but tell her to come to me at my home. Now Mr. Day will speak to you."

**MARTY** lifted the phone, spoke quickly. "Trouble, Knight. Have the police been…. They haven't! Very well. Have Miss Tania leave at once. Then leave yourself. Explain downstairs that I have gone on a hunting trip and you are joining me. Leave no address. Then register at a quiet hotel; say, the Dolphin, on Fifty-fourth Street. Use the name—" and without any reason for it but seeing that Zee Clarke was quite interested—"the same name as last time. I'll get in touch with you when I need you." The phone snapped back in the cradle.

Zee Clarke spoke. "You are to stay here. I have rooms; rooms that have waited for you."

She went back to the wall safe again, manipulated the dial, then stood back. A large section of the paneled wall swung open, the small safe almost in the center of it, the steel back sticking out behind. Marty saw a flight of narrow stairs, leading above.

"It's very sensible." Zee Clarke nodded. "A careful search by a clever man or even by one educated in such devices would locate the spring which releases the picture. Once the safe came into view the picture is satisfactorily explained. One would not look further. Come!"

She led Marty onto the small flight of stairs, left him there a moment in the sudden darkness as she manipulated the mechanism that returned the door and picture to their former position; then she snapped on a light.

At the top of those stairs was a small door and beyond that door a room of almost Oriental grandeur; luxurious ease amidst that grandeur.

"My weakness." She tapped a bear skin with her foot. "Beyond, through the bath, is a bedroom; modern, serviceable—comfortable even for a man." Soft lights shone from many lamps as she looked at Marty, held him with those amber eyes; very soft now, even moist.

She came close and looked up at him. "I want you to like this room, Marty."

"I do like it." Marty saw for the first time how deep the amber eyes were; almost a bronze, far back in those hidden—well, perhaps not entirely hidden depths. He was startled, partly worried.

Then with a swiftness—somewhat like his cane, Marty thought—
her arms were about his neck. Her face below his, eyes alive, staring
up; searching, wondering eyes, a new light in them, a brightness that
meant—well, Marty was not a conceited man but he knew what they
meant; what those lips meant. And he knew something else. Certainly here was a woman of great passion. Not simply a great love,
but capable of a great hate—that might be visited on him, but mostly
might be visited on Tania.

**MARTY** was human too. That body so close to his was— He lifted
his eyes from those burning bronze balls. Her chin was raised, her
lips were very close; warm breath swept his face. There was a second
of indecision—and Marty raised his hands, took her wrists, lifted her
arms gently from his shoulders, forcing the hands from the back of
his head; hands that had begun to draw his head forward—downward.
Then, holding those wrists, he spoke.

"You have done a lot for me, Zee," he said, and his voice was husky.
"I can't understand you but you've been a friend. You saved Tania's
life and mine; you would have saved it again tonight. Would have—"
His breath caught far back in his throat as he thought of the unconscious Bradley. His hands went to her shoulders. "I love Tania," he
said simply, thrust her roughly from him and turned and crossed the
room.

He had done it. Given her the truth. Now what? Had he unleashed
a fury; a hatred toward him and Tania? And he waited for the tirade
of words; the abuse that she would hurl at him.

But no angry, threatening words came. No abuse. Just a moment
of silence. Then a laugh; a low, musical laugh.

"You're afraid of me, Marty," she said. "But mostly you're afraid of
what I may do; how I may strike Tania; the influence I may have with
The Reckoner; the truths that I might tell the law; the trap that I
might lay for Tania, whom Rierson would so willingly destroy. But
all that is for a woman of weakness, who lets hate take the place of
love. No, what I want, I get." She was across the room now, had gripped
him by the shoulders and swung him around. "Look at me, Marty. I
fear no woman; recognize danger in no woman. Tania, who works for
The Reckoner through fear of a past wrong being exposed! Were I in
her position I would have killed him long ago. A woman whose blood
is water, whose stomach is a lump of fear in her throat. And I—" Her

arms were about his neck again, her chin was on his chest, her bronze eyes searching, calling—demanding. And—

A buzzer, low and soft; yet, like the screech of a great siren to Marty, sent him staggering back.

Zee Clarke looked at him a long moment. Then her eyes turned from Marty to the tiny red light on the wall above the bathroom door.

"Tania," Zee Clarke said, but there was no malice in her voice. "It's a break for her, eh, Marty? But we won't begrudge her that. She'll need all the breaks she can get." She turned suddenly and walked toward the door. "Wait here."

## CHAPTER FIVE

## TANIA

**Z**EE CLARKE passed out onto the stairs. The door closed; there was the decided click of a key. Marty grinned. He was a prisoner in that room. And the grin turned to a perplexed expression, more than an actual scowl. He was a prisoner to Zee Clarke. He thought that over a moment. Was he a prisoner in more ways than one? He shook his head and looked the room over.

The air was clear and fresh but there were no windows. While he wasn't looking for or especially interested in the ventilating system, he was interested in windows. And Marty suddenly realized he hadn't seen the other rooms.

He walked through the bathroom. No windows here either. Then a bedroom beyond. Surely there must be another method of entrance; or rather, exit! It wouldn't do to be hemmed up here with escape only by those stairs. Surely— And he was in the bedroom. The same method of ventilation existed in both the bath and bedroom, and there were no windows.

Then Marty saw it. The door close to the bed. No secrecy about that. Nicely paneled, hinges exposed top and bottom, and a knob to grip. Also a key in the lock. Quickly Marty crossed the room, placed a hand on the knob and found the door locked. With a little grimace he tried the key, turned it and pulled the door toward him. It came slowly. But as he pulled the harder the door swung fully open. It was heavily weighted down. From the top to the very bottom of the other side of that door were shelves, and those shelves were neatly packed with freshly ironed linen.

Marty nodded his understanding as he stepped into that closet and pulled the door partly closed behind him. By the light of the bedroom he saw that the closing door fitted in with other shelves above it, making the whole appear the back of a linen closet. There was another door that almost met the shelves. It yielded beneath his grip. Marty turned and went quickly back into the bedroom.

When a few seconds later he again entered that closet the light in the bedroom was out and there was a small pocket flash in his hand. He tried that outer door now and found that it gave on darkness; darkness that, after a moment's listening, he pierced with his flash.

There was a long narrow hall, a door at the end to the right, a window to the left. Marty moved rapidly to this window, looked out into the rear of the grounds and was surprised at the garden in that spacious yard. Surprised too, to find a grassy terrace almost directly beneath the window, a luxury seldom found in that section of the great city. But what Marty looked at mostly was the distance to the ground, and what gave him considerable satisfaction was the fact that the window was not barred.

All his movements were quick and alert. It was a matter of seconds rather than minutes, and Marty was back in that bedroom, the closet door that led to the hall closed tightly; the other door, with its shelves of linen, swung back and locked. Just one thing missing; just one difference. The key was missing from that closet door. The key was safely in Marty's pocket.

So, with a cigarette aglow, Marty was examining the shelves of books along the wall of the living room when the door from the stairs opened and Zee Clarke stepped back into the room.

**HE SWUNG** quickly, his eyes eager, his face boyish; but that was gone in an instant. Tania was not with her.

"Tania!" he said. "It wasn't she, then?"

"But it was, Marty." Zee Clarke nodded. "You'll see her in a few moments." And reading the question in his eyes, "No, I won't bring her here. That's one thing I can't do for you. I'll take you to her but first I must make you familiar with these quarters."

"But I've seen them. I've been through them while you were downstairs."

"Nevertheless—" amber eyes never left his dark ones—"you will not deny me the simple pleasure of showing you this retreat, while Tania waits."

Marty followed her through the bathroom and into the bedroom, half listened as she explained the system of ventilation. But he nodded as he heard her say: "So, because of lack of windows and the air conditioning, these rooms are pleasantly cool even on the hottest summer days."

She was standing looking at the door to the linen closet while she talked. Then, pausing in the middle of a sentence, she turned and stretched out her hand to Marty.

"The key to that door please." And when he tried to look at her blankly, "I'm not going to speak of the possibility of the outer door being locked. The key!"

Marty dug into his pocket and handed it to her without a word.

She stood looking at him. "Trapped." Her voice was melodramatic but her eyes and lips smiled. "A man trap." And in a soft, low voice, "I hope you like it."

She dug the key suddenly into the palm of his hand and folded his fingers tightly over it. "You're wanted for murder, Marty Day," she said very seriously. "I wouldn't trap you here like that, and I don't think you'd be a coward enough or fool enough to run out on me. There's a linen closet beyond the door, a hall, and— Come, I'd better show you, in the event that the police should come."

Marty grinned. "And a window," he said. "I've been over the ground. Seems rather discourteous, after what you— You don't mind?"

"Mind!" she said. "Why, it's nice to feel that you're not altogether dumb, seeing that I'm going to marry you."

"Zee," Marty grasped her by the arm as they passed into the living room and reached the door to the stairs, "I'm very grateful and—Tania is grateful, but you must understand that I—we—"

She swung and faced him. Her eyes were brilliant bronze. They burnt into his. Mechanically, perhaps unconsciously, he raised his hand and brushed it across his eyes. She said: "Don't be a fool, Marty; and don't talk like a book. When I saved Tania's life I did that for you, and for myself. I told you that I did not want the dead between us. The moment I want you I'll take you."

And when he just stared at her, "Conceit? Perhaps. But truth just the same. I know!" Her head came up. "The moment I fear Tania you will know it, but she will not. For a few minutes, perhaps, tonight you will hold her in your arms; for the last time. I will not deny her that. Come!"

**THE CONCEIT** of the woman. The assurance, the confidence in her personal powers. Marty could have laughed; except, perhaps, that it was so tragic. He could have laughed; except, perhaps, that for the first time in his life he experienced a new sensation. A sinking feeling, that he tried not to recognize as fear; a new and terrible kind of fear. For a moment and a moment only he held a mental picture of this same woman standing over Lieutenant Bradley with a gun in her hand and—murder in her heart. And in this mental picture the face of Bradley seemed to change and become the face of Tania.

Then the picture was gone. Dazed and with uneven steps Marty followed Zee Clarke down those narrow stairs. When he reached the bottom, the fear was gone. His head was clear, his eyes were bright. After all, he was young, and he was going to see Tania.

Tania came! But she was not there in the living room below waiting for him. Zee Clarke had carefully closed the panel in the wall and pushed back the picture. She didn't insist that Marty bind himself to silence about those hidden quarters. She simply said: "I'll trust you, Marty, not to divulge to anyone my hideout; your hideout." Then she was gone.

Tania had come through that open doorway. She stood there a moment, frightened eyes searching that room. Then her firm mouth curved suddenly at the edges and she was across the room to him.

"What has happened?" Her breath came in quick sharp jerks, as if she had run a great distance. "I was sure there were two detectives outside the apartment. They saw me, of course, but they didn't know me. At least, I wasn't followed. Oh, Marty, something terrible has hap-happened." And then, "Why are you here at Zee Clarke's; in this—this woman's home?"

"Shs—" Marty whispered, for Zee Clarke stood in the doorway.

"I'll leave you two alone for a bit," Zee Clarke said. "You will want to talk." And with a touch of sarcasm in her voice, "Tania, in her vast experience, will give you advice. But—" she turned in the doorway and flung the final words over her shoulder—"the man to advise you will be here in five or ten minutes. You see, Marty, I am practical as well as romantic." And she was gone, closing the door behind her.

"Who has she sent for—The Reckoner?" Marty placed his voice somewhere between Tania and the closed door.

Tania wasn't interested in who was coming but in what had happened. Not instinct alone told her something terrible was wrong. Marty here at Zee Clarke's was enough. But he told her all that had happened that night.

He felt better, too, as he talked. There was no doubt in Tania's eyes; not even when he reached the part of the judge accusing him and Bradley believing it. But he didn't tell her about Zee Clarke and her threat to kill; just said that she had been waiting for him and had brought him here.

"How terrible. How terrible. To know that he was dying and to lie like that."

"I'll have to find the man." Marty clenched his hands tightly. "I know Rierson sent him. He will return to Rierson. If—"

"But you can't—you can't. The police will be looking for you, Marty. You must hide. You must stay—" She paused, looked toward the door. "I'm jealous, of course, Marty; but it isn't that. I know Zee Clarke better than you do. She's hateful and vicious and— Don't you see, Marty; don't you understand? The woman loves you. I'm afraid."

Marty held her tightly then. "You needn't be afraid, Tania. I—"

"It isn't that." She read quickly what was in his eyes. "At least, not only that, for she's a beautiful and charming woman. But she's also a dangerous one. She might— Marty, if she thought that you—we—she might—"

They both turned. Zee Clarke had opened the door and was holding it so, pressing her tall, slender body against it to let a man pass; a man who was taller than she was; as tall as Marty but who gave the appearance of still greater height because of the looseness and slimness of his body. His steps were quick and jerky, his shoulders slightly bent as he crossed the room. It was Max Arnold, the famous—or perhaps better described as the most notorious criminal lawyer in the city.

He bowed deeply to Tania and seemed to keep those eyes that were rather too closely set together on her for a long time. Then he crossed to Marty, put a corrugated damp hand into his, snapped his thin lips and said: "You seem to have gotten into a mess." He jerked a thumb toward Zee Clarke. "She told me, but I want to hear it all from you."

## CHAPTER SIX

## WANTED FOR MURDER

**M**ARTY TOLD the story again. Everything that had happened, straight up to the time he struck Bradley. But he made it his fist then, not his cane. He stopped there and looked at Zee Clarke. She smiled behind the lawyer's back, nodded and spoke.

"It's all right, Marty. I told him I was there. Max has to know everything."

"Everything!" Marty's eyes went wide.

"That's right," said Max. "She told me of her suggestion to you. It is not for me to discuss the ethics of such an act, but her legal reasoning was perfect."

"And with Bradley dead, you— After that, you would have defended me?"

"My dear man—" Max Arnold coughed behind his hand—"I am not saying you should have acted on the young lady's advice. In fact, I deplore such a suggestion. As for my defending you then!" Narrow shoulders moved. "If you had taken her advice you would have no need of my defending you. There would have been no witness, hence no accusation and no necessity of a lawyer."

"I did the best I could," Marty told him. "I knocked out Bradley and made my escape."

"The act of a guilty man. I understand you wish to deny the killing."

"Certainly. You, too, believe that I—"

"I'm your legal adviser and not your religious one. It is not what I believe that matters. It is my duty to make twelve men believe you are not guilty. If you had stayed on the ground and faced the music, could they have found the weapon on you or in the alley?"

"I had no weapon; no gun," Marty said sullenly.

"I take that as an answer to my question—that they would not have found any. That would have been a point in your favor."

"But the judge accused me of—"

"I know, I know. You were carrying papers that would have shown any jury that the judge was hand in glove with crooked politics. We would have produced those at the trial; will yet, of course—if we deem it advisable for you to stand trial. The judge's action might have been one of simple hatred; vengeance, in accusing you of his death. We would have claimed that, of course."

"And Parks— Don Parks?" asked Marty. "Wasn't he to turn on Rierson if he wasn't released by morning? He'll be a double menace to Rierson now, and—"

Max Arnold smiled, but it was not a pleasant smile. "Rierson put over what is known as a fast one on us; yes, on The Reckoner." He set thin lips grimly. "Rierson was afraid Judge Ramdelfia would weaken and hold Parks. Parks was simply being detained at present as a material witness. By tomorrow—or rather, this afternoon—Lieutenant Bradley would have had the proof that Parks was actually guilty of murder, and he would have found no difficulty in taking him before a grand jury and obtaining an indictment. That's not guess work; that's knowledge. For The Reckoner would have furnished that proof through me.

"Somehow Rierson knew that our pressure on Judge Ramdelfia would be severe. He could not be sure the judge would break it, but Rierson has friends, has influence, has power. While we thought that by waiting until the last moment we'd catch Rierson sleeping, he caught us sleeping; caught The Reckoner sleeping. Yes, he went before another judge with a writ of *habeas corpus*. A few hours before you went to Judge Ramdelfia, Don Parks was released on bail. I have just discovered that."

"Then it was he—Don Parks—who went to Judge Ramdelfia's house and killed him."

"Why?" demanded Arnold.

"Someone shot the judge from behind that curtain," said Marty. "If it wasn't Parks it was another. But whoever it was, was greatly interested and very close to Rierson. So much so that he realized that if the judge betrayed Rierson he betrayed him also, or—" and Marty paused. "Parks was behind that curtain and realized that the judge was—was—" He looked suddenly up at Max Arnold. "Why do you look at me like that? I know! You don't believe the judge told me there was someone upstairs. You don't believe my story that a man hid behind that curtain."

**MAX ARNOLD** did not speak. He looked straight at Marty.

"Well—" Marty demanded. "You don't believe Parks shot him?

You don't believe that that was the price of Parks's freedom; something else for Rierson to hang over his head? You don't believe that?"

"No," said Max Arnold, "I don't believe that."

"You don't," Marty talked rapidly, "because you believe I shot him. You think me guilty. Can you name a reason for my killing the judge?"

"He might have threatened you; secured a gun. You took it from him, and in the struggle shot him."

"My God!" said Marty. "Why, when I carried disgrace; a prison term for him in my hand? The Reckoner knows that; you know that. Does that make sense?"

"No, it doesn't," Max Arnold said grimly. "I'm trying to be easy on you, boy; I'm going to do everything to free you, or keep you free."

"Easy on me! You believe me guilty. You—" Marty stretched out both his hands, grasped the hawked-faced lawyer by the lapels of his coat. "Well—tell me, then. What makes me guilty, to you? Can you name one sensible, or half-sensible reason for my killing the judge?"

Max Arnold pulled the hands from his coat with a strength that would have surprised Marty had he been aware of it at the time. Then he looked over at Zee Clarke. She turned her head from his steady eyes. After a bit she said: "It's up to you, Max. Tell him if you want to; you've got to save him."

"It's my duty then," Max Arnold said very slowly. "So here it is. Judge Ramdelfia told you that he had evidence which would send a certain party to jail; maybe burn that party." And when Marty would have cut in, he raised his hand. "You asked him for the evidence and he said it was personal; only in his head. Maybe he explained it. Maybe you lost your head. Oh, I dare say you have a hundred excuses, but not one legal one. Then he turned, and you shot him."

"And who," said Marty very stiffly, his lips curling as he looked at Zee Clarke, "could so influence me, when I refused to kill a man to save my own life? Who—?"

"Tania Cordet," said Max Arnold simply. And certainly, with his shrewd brain, his long experience with crime and criminals, he would have seen the stunned innocence in Marty's face if the telephone had not rung just at that moment.

Max Arnold turned and lifted the phone, muttering something to Zee Clarke about expecting the call, as she crossed the room toward Marty.

"Cheer up, Marty," Zee Clarke said. "I suspected something like that all along. Half a man would have done the same thing. Max doesn't understand that. You thought you were in love with the girl, anyway, and—"

But Tania was between them, sobbing bitterly. Marty looked into her eyes. Did she believe it, too? Did she—?

MAX ARNOLD turned away from the telephone, and said: "Judge Ramdelfia died five minutes ago, at the hospital."

"Did—did he talk again?" said Marty.

"He never regained consciousness after being taken from the house." And as Zee Clarke asked if there was more news, "They are evidently keeping things quiet down at headquarters. The late morning editions will carry the story."

"And Marty's name in the headlines! The man-hunt has begun?"

"The man-hunt, maybe." Max Arnold stroked his chin. "But Mr. Day's name will not be mentioned. The police say they have learned the identity of the murderer but they are not divulging it. Of course there are always police leaks—" he smiled knowingly—"and I get them quickly. My agent at headquarters informs me that several of the shrewdest and most capable men have been told to bring in Mr. Marty Day and to do it quietly. That's Lieutenant Bradley's work, of course."

"Why the silence?" Marty demanded.

"Well, Lieutenant Bradley is a clever man, a shrewd man. It is quite possible, Mr. Day, that he wants you alone; wants to offer you a proposition. He wants to know who The Reckoner is."

"Hell!" said Marty, "I couldn't help him much on that."

"But you could help him on the names of The Reckoner's friends."

"He'd be wasting his time on that." Marty jerked his shoulders. "The last thing I'll do is talk."

Max Arnold looked at him a long moment before he said: "Many men have thought that, until the constant reminder of burning flesh in the warm chair up the river makes them change their minds."

"But they haven't got me yet. Not by a long shot they haven't!"

"No, not yet. And that's what I want to talk to you about. Hiding you away some place. If you stay here you would involve Mrs. Clarke; make her an accessory after the fact. It's very serious, and—"

Zee Clarke cut in. "Marty won't talk, if that's what you're figuring." Her amber eyes blazed now as she swung on Max Arnold. "And don't hand him that high-minded act. He puts on enough of his own. He'll be safe here, and I couldn't be involved if I don't know; if the papers don't tell me that—"

Max Arnold's eyes were very narrow; seemed very close together now.

Tania spoke. "Mr. Arnold,"—she tried to make her voice calm, but it was high-pitched, somewhat like Max Arnold's—"you're not—not afraid that Marty may—that he—that there is danger; a personal danger to you or The Reckoner—that he might talk?"

"No, no. Of course not, my dear." And again Max put his eyes long and steadily on the girl. "I am thinking of his safety. That's why I am taking him along with me. That's what The Reckoner will want."

**TANIA** looked at those narrow eyes, and mechanically her left arm came up and crooked through Marty's right. For a moment there was fear in her eyes. Fear for Marty or herself? She hadn't liked the way Max Arnold looked at her.

It was Zee Clarke who spoke. "Marty Day is staying here," she said coldly. "We haven't been followed or we'd know it now. You weren't followed, for they didn't have the time even if the police did check you up as Marty's lawyer. Later— Well you're my lawyer and come here often, day or night. You can visit Marty when necessary." And somewhat softening, "Besides, there has been no such order from The Reckoner." And with a smile, "If there should be I'll be needing another lawyer."

Max Arnold smiled; at least, his lips parted. "It was simply a suggestion, my dear," he said. And then abruptly, "I'll want Mr. Day's telephone number—a private phone he can answer. You have many here, I know." And when Zee Clarke gave it to him, "And you, Tania, I'll drive you home."

"But—" Marty stopped.

"I'm afraid," said Max Arnold very seriously, "that this time I must insist." He held open the door from the living room. Tania looked once at Marty, hesitated, then moving quickly across the room passed out the door. It wasn't exactly that she feared Max Arnold then, but she didn't wish to further—yes "further" she thought was the word—antagonize him against Marty.

## CHAPTER SEVEN

## CRIMINALS ALL

**F**OR SOME time Marty stood there, stunned. Tania! Judge Ramdelfia knew something about Tania? But he hadn't told him. The girl's name had not been mentioned; had not— And he thought of the words of Max Arnold; the chair at Sing Sing. Was there suspicion in Max Arnold's voice? Did he, like Rierson, fear a man who, to protect himself, might talk? Was Arnold classing him with Parks; Don Parks, thief, murderer? Would The Reckoner want him out of the way? Would—Marty shuddered. He had gone into this thing for adventure; then stayed in it for romance—for Tania.

And then Zee Clarke was in the room, facing him. Marty spoke quickly; exactly what was on his mind. "Max Arnold, Zee. He suspected me, feared me maybe; feared that I might divulge his connections with The Reckoner. Are we then; am I then to be classed as a common thug, like Don Parks; like—?"

Zee Clarke smiled at him. "You can't just look at it through your own eyes, Marty. You've got to look at it through the eyes of others. To the law we're all criminals—common criminals. The law can't see the good behind robbing a man's house; the law can't see the glorious adventure in shooting a man to death. Yes, I think Max feared you tonight—or—" She shrugged her shoulders. "Men are queer. It is possible that you both love the same woman."

"You"—and Marty's eyes widened—"Mean—mean Tania?"

"Yes—" she nodded. "I mean Tania. But don't worry. Nothing can happen to you here, through Max Arnold or anyone else. Not while I protect you." Was there a special emphasis on those words; a significance in their meaning?

"Zee"—he went closer to the woman and looked down at her—"this reason for my shooting the judge. You believe that?" And when she didn't answer, because Marty didn't need an answer, "What could the judge know of Tania?"

"He could know what The Reckoner knows, for Rierson knows, too. And he could know what Rierson told him; what Rierson might have told him to protect the judge from you."

"But if Rierson knows anything against Tania—Tania, whom he

must hate since she fooled him, posed as his secretary and gave me the opportunity of robbing his safe—why hasn't he acted?"

Zee Clarke raised her shoulders. "Rierson threatened The Reckoner; threatened to expose Tania to the police unless he returned those stolen documents and quit hounding him."

"And The Reckoner wouldn't do it, of course." Marty remembered The Reckoner's refusal once before to meet Rierson's demand, to save Tania's life. "The why didn't Rierson strike?"

Zee Clarke said, and her voice was either tired or disinterested: "The Reckoner would not save the one to sacrifice the many. At least, he wouldn't then. Rierson didn't expose her for several reasons. One, that he might use Tania to influence you, if not The Reckoner. Two, because the knowledge that he has about Tania may be simply knowledge; not evidence. He is waiting until the truth he carries in his head can be placed on paper and become legal evidence. When Max heard the judge was shot and his naming of you as the guilty party he believed it." She looked at him steadily now. "It was natural."

**MARTY'S** attempted smile was not much of a success. "I didn't know," he said simply. "Tania's name was not mentioned by the judge. It doesn't matter much if you believe it or not."

"No." Zee Clarke looked at him. And then, "Would you have done it for her, Marty?"

"Murder! Shoot a defenseless man? Why—"

She was watching him very sharply. Then she took two quick steps. "You could have if you really love her. I—" She hesitated, her whole attitude changed. She walked quickly to the hidden door, manipulated picture and panel. "There is much to be done; you need rest. You will not be disturbed."

"Knight!" Marty said, as he moved onto the flight of stairs. "Can I—?"

"There is a phone in your rooms—a private number. Entirely separate from all other phones in the house. Good night!"

Marty hesitated a long time on those stairs, facing her. She was very beautiful, very— But the amber eyes now were cold and—yes, perhaps sinister. There was something hard and cruel to those narrow lips; something in the eyes that— And Marty realized that whatever it was it was not for him. Although she faced him she was not watching him; those eyes were not looking into his.

"Good night, Zee," he said very low.

And for a long moment his black eyes looked straight into those amber balls that did not see him. Then Marty went slowly up the steps. Twice he turned. Zee Clarke was still there, still watching— watching what? Then the panel closed noiselessly behind him. He was in the oddly furnished room, alone. He closed the door and locked it. He felt very much alone—and he was wanted for murder!

Thoughts! Many of them; none encouraging. He saw again the eyes of Max Arnold; searching, speculative, suspicious. Arnold didn't believe him, and now feared him; feared his capture. Zee Clarke didn't believe him, and she, too, feared his capture.

And, Tania! She believed him. Marty knew that. But, Tania—Tania and Arnold!

The bedroom. No use to go in there, Marty thought. He'd never sleep that night. The thing was impossible. He would get in touch with Knight. He dialed the hotel. Knight was not there, had not even registered at the hotel. There was a curtain close to the bed, a little recess behind it. There was a dressing gown there, pajamas—slippers even.

Marty undressed slowly, then stretched out on the bed.

Five—ten minutes, perhaps, while wild chaotic thoughts raced through his mind. Then sleep Marty thought impossible came.

WHEN Marty awoke, light was blazing down in his eyes. The sun? He rubbed a hand across his eyes, suddenly remembered where he was and that there could be no sun, and sat bolt upright in bed. The little lamp on the table beside his bed was shining in his eyes; directly in his eyes. The shade was tilted, too. Someone had been in his room then. And a voice spoke from the living room beyond.

"You'll find everything in the bathroom; razor, shaving cream— everything you can need. Then breakfast out here with me." A door closed, and Marty jumped out of bed. It was Zee Clarke.

A shave, a shower, a good rub-down could not and did not drive the thoughts from Marty's head. They were still there, unpleasant and disturbing as the night before, when he walked into the living room.

A card table was set up in the middle of the room. Grape fruit, plates and— That was all Marty saw as he grabbed up a morning paper.

The story was there all right. Fearfully, yet eagerly Marty scanned the headlines for his name. Then he ran his eyes quickly over the fine print; turned the pages. His name was not there. He went through the columns, then sat down and read every word carefully.

"Forget it, Marty." Zee Clarke came in, took the paper from him and tossed it over on the couch. "Somehow we'll straighten things out. If you have to skip, you have to skip. At least, you're safe here for the time being."

"What do you hear—besides the papers; anything?" he demanded.

"Nothing. No leak has come out that you are wanted for murder. At least, Max hasn't found any—and Max is good."

"But The Reckoner?"

"He hasn't—" She stopped suddenly. "I haven't seen him yet. I will later. Don't you worry. I'm rich, Marty. Money will do anything, and The Reckoner has many channels open for your escape. Just forget it." She smiled. "We'll spend our time getting acquainted."

"But, Knight—"

Zee Clarke shook her head, pushed him into the chair by the table. "It's the first time I ever waited on a man, Marty," she said as she poured the coffee. "And, do you know—I rather like it."

**ALL THAT** day Marty spent alone. Not a word from Knight, Zee Clarke did not visit him; and worst of all, he did not see Tania. It was just before seven o'clock that Zee Clarke barged in on Marty, took him quickly to the room below and left him as Max Arnold came. Marty wanted to ask him about Tania, but he didn't.

Max Arnold was not encouraging and not overly friendly, Marty thought.

"No leaks on this case," he told Marty. "The fact that your name has not appeared startles and alarms me. They must be pretty sure of your arrest very shortly for the police to keep the news from the papers; from certain trusted officials even."

"But I am wanted?" said Marty.

"Yes, you're wanted all right. Wanted badly." And after a long moment, "Lieutenant Bradley spent some time with the commissioner. It is quite possible that you are wanted quietly; to be brought in secretly. It is quite possible that you may even be offered—offered— " Beady eyes set straight on Marty; hard eyes. There was more than suspicion in them. Speculation.

"You needn't be afraid I'll talk. What does The Reckoner say—think?"

"He must think as I think," said Max suddenly. "That from now on, certainly you can be of no further use to him; only a danger."

Marty wet his lips. "And what does he intend to do about that?" Marty didn't like the look in those eyes; the hardness of Arnold's voice as he said, "You need have no fear. You will be removed to a place of safety."

Max Arnold stepped back. He walked around behind Marty, toward the door. But in the glass that hung on the wall Marty saw his face, the cold sternness of it—a sudden sort of determination. But mostly he saw that corrugated right hand; saw it raise slowly and slip beneath his jacket; beneath his left—

Marty whirled, started forward—and stopped. The door opened; Max Arnold's hand dropped to his side. Zee Clarke spoke.

"We haven't had dinner yet. Marty must be starving," she said. And those amber eyes settling on Max Arnold, "I have arranged things with The Reckoner. Marty leaves the country tomorrow night."

"He doesn't. He can't. Why, you—"

"You—what?" Amber eyes shot fire.

Max Arnold hesitated, and then, "Your life may depend upon his silence; his assured silence." There was a threatening note in his voice, a deadliness to his eyes, and the hand again was moving slowly beneath his jacket.

Queer, Marty thought. Was it possible that this man was going to kill him? This lawyer, whose cleverness Marty had to admire despite his unsavory reputation. A man who had cleared more men of crime than any other, perhaps any other ten lawyers in the city. Now did Max Arnold see the same danger to himself that he had seen so often to others? But Zee Clarke was talking.

"I am going with Marty," she said, and Max Arnold turned and looked at her. His eyes widened. And then very slowly and very carefully Zee Clarke finished. "And Tania remains behind."

That was all. The woman had grasped Max Arnold's arm and led him from the room.

Marty took three quick steps forward and then stopped. What had been in Max Arnold's eyes when Zee Clarke finished her sentence?

## CHAPTER EIGHT

## " K "

**Z**EE CLARKE had dinner with him. That was two hours later. And in that two hours Marty had decided to play a different game—a waiting game. He'd pretend to agree to anything Zee Clarke suggested; at least, until the moment came to act upon that suggestion.

"Passports and everything will be arranged, Marty," she told him when she left him. "I'll have a lot to do—a lot of packing."

"But The Reckoner! Won't he— Max Arnold distrusts me. He'd rather see me dead. He'll suggest that to The Reckoner if he doesn't carry it out himself, or get—"

"No," she broke in. "The Reckoner, Max and myself agree that the thing to do is to get you out of the country. It's the thing for you, too, Marty. If the real murderer can be found, then we can return. Max agrees that you shall go; he's arranging things."

"But are you certain?" Marty followed her to the door. "He seemed so—so sure I was a danger. What made him change his mind?"

"Don't you know?" Zee Clarke laughed, stretched both her hands up and placed them on his shoulders, to drop them again almost at once. "It was when I told him that Tania remained behind."

"Oh," said Marty. "Max Arnold must have great influence with The Reckoner."

"More than anyone in the world."

"He fears—fears Arnold then."

"He fears him far less than—than he fears me. Indeed, I know of no man that The Reckoner probably counts on more and fears less. Till tomorrow then. We leave early in the morning." And she turned and left him.

Marty paced his rooms. Of course he should get out of the city. That was the sensible thing to do. Yes—if it wasn't for Tania. It was after midnight before he had one constructive thought, but that thought was a good one; a damn good one. He knew the private phone number where he could reach The Reckoner, if anything important turned up. That is, anything important to The Reckoner. He remembered how The Reckoner had received some of his calls, when they were important only to Marty—and Tania.

Marty grinned. But this call would be important to The Reckoner. The Reckoner had once told him, and Marty had resented it terribly at the time, that some day, for his good service, his reward would be Tania. Marty would inform him diplomatically that if anything happened to Tania in his absence; that if she did not join him in his exile, then he would give to Lieutenant Bradley all the information he had concerning The Reckoner. Not much, maybe; not enough to destroy The Reckoner, but enough to destroy his aids—at least destroy Max Arnold.

Would The Reckoner act on that? Marty smiled as he reached for the phone. Max Arnold was important to The Reckoner.

**AS MARTY'S** hand stretched out for that phone, it rang—sharply, suddenly. Someone was calling him. Tania? He hoped so. It was quite possible, for she was in the room when Zee Clarke gave that number to Max Arnold.

But it wasn't Tania. It was Knight; the slow voice of his servant, Knight.

"I got the number from Miss Tania," Knight told him. "I couldn't go to the hotel because I was followed. But I'm an old lag at that game," (Marty had picked Knight up years before, on the streets of London) "and soon gave them the slip. I've been busy, sir, very busy; too busy to call. Now I have something to report. I want to tell you, sir, that if you don't hear from me again I'll be—be dead."

"Dead—dead! What happened? Knight, tell me!" Had the phone clicked; had Knight hung up, or—or—

But Knight was talking again.

"It's Miss Tania, sir. They've got her."

"Who—who? Rierson?"

"No, not him—now. Don Parks."

"Where are you?" Marty almost shouted the words, then caught himself and lowered his voice. "I'm coming."

"I'm up in the Bronx. I'll come—" And Knight gave a street corner. "I'll meet you there. Just hurry, sir, or I'll have to go alone."

"You know where she is; where Parks is?"

"No, sir, I don't." Despite that steady, polite "sir" of Knight's Marty caught the undertone of excitement. "But I think Mr. Rierson will tell me, and—"

"Rierson! Don't be a fool. He's the worst. Of course he won't tell you, Knight."

"You don't think so, sir? I think he will; I think he'll be very glad to. I understand your life may depend on it, and certainly Miss Tania's. Excuse me, sir."

There was a click, and silence.

The Reckoner, Max Arnold, Zee Clarke all were forgotten. Threats, cleverness, his great constructive thought were all gone. Just one thing now. To save Tania. And, Knight? What did he mean, Rierson would tell him.

Marty Day was acting while he was thinking. His hat and cane, nothing more as he sought that linen closet in his bedroom. The hat, so as not to make him conspicuous if seen on the streets, the cane—well, he gripped it firmly. He hoped that the might find a use for it that night; a deadly use for it.

He was through the linen closet, down that hall; his flash sending a pencil of light along the darkness. Then the window. It opened easily, shot upward. Marty snapped out his light. Yet there was no sudden darkness. A brighter light than his was shining in his face. Zee Clarke stood back in the blackness.

"What are you doing, Marty? You—"

"I've got to go," he told her quickly. "This seemed the best way, and—"

"It's Tania." And when, sensing trouble, Marty shook his head, "Why lie to me? Knight just called you up."

**MARTY** hung his cane in his sleeve, beneath his arm. "You lied to me then. You told me the phone was private." Both his hands were on the window sill; he was bracing himself to swing up.

"I couldn't let you make a fool of yourself," she said, and then, "Put a foot over that sill and I'll place a bullet in it."

"Zee!" He hesitated. "You'd shoot me? You! After what you said?"

"I'd put a bullet in your leg, anyway." She didn't raise her voice. It was very calm; very determined. "Don't you see, Marty? It is a trap, and—"

"You think so?" Marty dropped back to the floor. "I thought of that too, Zee. I thought of it. But—"

"Of course it is." She moved a step nearer now and lowered the light, but he could not see her plainly. Just a dull figure; a white arm, a white hand too, with something black in it; something black that was pointing toward him.

"But it was Knight's voice. It sounded like— Damn it, Zee!" Marty stepped closer to her. "You know Knight; you've heard him talk. What do you think?" He took another step. If he could get the woman off her guard! Just a quick lunge forward, a grab at the gun; then— He thought of his cane that he gripped firmly, but that would hurt. The twist of her wrist or the sudden pound of fine steel upon her delicate white knuckles! He didn't want to hurt her; didn't want—

"What do I think?" she said. "I think you take me for a fool. Stand back!" This as he moved another step. "You took a gun from me once, but I didn't want to shoot you then. Now—"

And Marty did it; he had to do it. The cane seemed to slip through the palm of his hand, along his fingers, stop suddenly as the curved handle facing upward reached the girl's wrist. It was doubtful if she saw it at all until the curved steel turned suddenly and shot down with the speed of a striking rattler. Just for a split second it encircled that wrist, then her hand was jerked toward the wall.

There was the single roar of a gun, the smell of powder in the small hall. The gun left her hand, hit the wall, bounced off it and thudded upon the floor. A dead silence, followed by a single surprised curse from the girl as her right hand went to her mouth. Then the cane swept back and twisted the flash from her left hand.

He heard the girl's sharp intake of breath as he jumped for the window; heard her words plainly too, as he stretched his body down from the stone sill.

"I forgot about that damned cane," she had said.

And that damned cane! The curved handle of it was hooked upon the heavy rough stone below the window, held there by the weight of Marty's body. Held perilously there, slipping toward the edge.

Quickly and easily Marty let his hands slide down that strong smooth steel. He looked up once and saw a blotch of whiteness that might have been a face. He drew up his body, let its full weight drop quickly. There was a whirring sound as the hidden springs of steel came alive. The cane seemed to jump into the air; the handle left the window. And Marty Day, knees bent, body relaxed, dropped easily to the grassy bank below.

**NO LIGHTS** popped up in that great stone mansion. The face was gone from the window. Gone! Why? Gone, because the woman was running down the stairs to head him off? Gone, because she was searching in that hall for the gun that had been twisted from her hand?

Reason told Marty that she would not shoot him. But instinct told him something else; pointed out to him, too, the stone wall and the street beyond, for Zee Clarke was a strange—a very strange and a very dangerous woman.

No shot crashed into the night, no voice cried hoarsely in the blackness. Just the darkness of the big house. But Zee Clarke had heard that message. Would she act on it? Would she notify The Reckoner; Max Arnold? Why should she? Marty nodded. There was a danger for him out there in the night and hence a danger to the others; a danger, at least, as Max Arnold would see it. Still, as he dashed down the street and flagged a cruising taxi he didn't hear a car roar from the drive of that old stone house.

Marty snapped his orders to the driver, promised a ten spot for speed and was thrown back on the seat as the chauffeur, having almost forgotten what a ten looked like, bent every effort to refresh his memory.

Marty sat on the edge of that seat, holding his cane tightly in both hands. Street lights flashed in and out on him; hundreds of them, perhaps, before he suddenly realized that he was a wanted murderer. Then he slunk back into a corner of the reeling cab. But such thoughts were nonsense. No one would see him to recognize him.

He looked back, watching for a speeding car; Zee Clarke coming in the same direction. But there was no car. He was fearful too of another kind of a car, a car with a screeching siren, a car with— He tried to smile. He knew now the feeling of other men, men he had hunted, men wanted for murder. He shook his head then. Did a murderer feel as he felt; one really guilty of murder? And then one thought. Not to be caught; not to be discovered before he reached Knight; reached Tania.

**THE BRONX** at last; the long, deserted street; the corner beyond that where he was to meet Knight.

"Don't you want to go to some definite place?" the driver said as Marty alighted before a great vacant lot overgrown with weeds, tumbled-down shacks far back.

"No!" Marty snapped, and handed the driver twenty instead of ten. "The extra money is for the speed back downtown," he said.

"Sure. Sure!" The driver pocketed the money, swung the car quickly, backed it once and turned around.

Marty glanced up and down that street. Not a soul; not even a cop. He walked briskly across the street from the deserted lot, and rounding the corner walked down a block lined with brick, walk-up apartments. On this street he was to meet Knight.

And he thought he saw him. No, the man wasn't Knight. He had a slouch, a shuffling to his walk, a bend to his shoulders, a furtiveness, as if he watched and feared; as if at any moment he would run for it, or dash into one of the numerous alleyways beside the buildings and disappear.

Was he watching Marty? And he was. Turning quickly, Marty saw the man pause down by the corner and look back over his shoulders, trying to study him in the darkness. Then he disappeared around that corner.

Was it just a coincidence? Was this just a drifter, a denizen of the night, curiously aroused by Marty's presence there on the lonely street? And another thought; a sudden, perhaps enlightening one. Was this man an emissary of Knight's; a man who was to take him to Knight, Knight fearing that Marty might be followed?

Marty nodded grimly. Well, he'd soon find out if this man had a real interest in him or if the interest was just in Marty's imagination; the panicky imagination of a hunted—yes, a haunted man.

Marty crossed the street, saw that the entire block as far as the corner was deserted, and stepped quickly down the few steps of an areaway. That was the second time in two nights that Marty had hidden in an areaway, but before spitting lead had rolled him in. Now—

His eyes narrowed, his lips set tight. He gripped his cane firmly as, lying there on those steps, he peered cautiously around the stone balustrade above the sunken basement entrance and saw the slouching figure approaching.

The man moved faster now. He looked up and down the street, across it even. Then he broke into a run—a nervous, tottering run. Marty nodded his satisfaction. The man had missed him and was alarmed.

His feet moved faster as he neared Marty, feet that seemed unused to such rapid motion. He reached Marty, stopped suddenly, swung around, made gurgling noises and clutched at his throat. The next instant he was jerked violently into that areaway, stumbled upon the steps and would have fallen had not Marty caught him.

Jerking the handle of his cane from the man's neck and slipping it over the crook in his arm was a single motion to Marty. Then his hands fastened tightly on the lapels of the man's jacket.

"Come! Out with it." Marty shook the man. "What— Why were you watching me?"

"Me—watching you? Yeah, Bo—that's it. 'The man with the cane,' the lad said. But I didn't think as how—"

"What 'lad' said?" Marty started to shake him again but stopped.

"I don't know, I don't know. He said to give you this note." The man opened a dirty hand in which was clutched a folded sheet torn from a note book. "He said you'd give me fifty dollars for it." And with a wink, "I guess that was hop talking, but I'd take ten."

Marty grasped the note from the man's hand, was reading it beneath his flash. And the first thing that caught his eye was the big "K"—that peculiar "K" of Knight's. The note read simply.

> I am trusting this man with the note. I have to. I did not dare to wait longer. Anyway, he don't know the lady's husband and can't tell him. But the lady is waiting for you at—here Knight gave a careful description of how to find the place—it's an old warehouse. She's there. Make it quick.
>
> K.

Marty nodded. Of course the fellow had read the note. But it wouldn't mean anything to him. Just a date with a woman, he'd think.

"Did you read this?" Marty peeled off five tens and shoved them into the grasping hand.

"Not me," said the man, "not me." He backed up the steps as Marty told him to be on his way. And when he reached the top step, "I'd of gone myself, governor, only I forgot to wear my soup-and-fish. Good luck with the lady. I hope her husband don't wake up and look around."

And the man was gone, clutching the money tightly, as if he expected someone to take it from him.

## CHAPTER NINE

# THE SINGLE SHOT

**K** **NIGHT WAS** clever, Marty thought as he hurried in the direction that was given him. Knight couldn't have done else, of course, if he had to leave. He couldn't very well get an envelope and seal it at that time of the morning. And Knight had to leave in a hurry. Why? One reason only. Tania was not only in danger, but immediate danger.

No other thoughts. Marty walked rapidly now; he dared not run. Even at that time of the morning there were several people abroad, and once he saw a cop. Did the cop see him? For a single moment Marty stopped dead, half started to slink toward an apartment, caught himself in time, and straightening his body, swung back his shoulders and walked down the street swinging his cane.

Turning the corner and out of the officer's line of vision Marty took advantage of the vacant lot. There was a path through it. He found it easily and his feet moved quickly. Sheds, stumps of trees threw strange shadows about him. Then the warehouse. A huge gloomy affair; ugly and incongruous against a background of row upon row of brick apartments. Close in the shadows of the huge squat building Marty moved. Broken windows that were boarded! Some with loose boards that could be jerked from their position; others with great gaping holes and broken glass, where neighborhood boys had already found an entrance. Plenty of places to enter but no light from within; at least, no light that Marty could find.

Time was passing and still he circled the building. Strange shadows! More than once Marty thought that he saw a figure in the darkness, and more than once he swung quickly as he felt sure he heard steps.

But always he discovered nothing. Nerves? Perhaps. But Marty did not like to admit that. He had never recognized nerves before, but now—

And he saw it. Sunken, between two sagging small outbuildings, was a narrow dirt passage, and at the end of that passage a door; a door that was partly open, Marty discovered when he picked his way carefully to it. He leaned close to the door and listened, pushed it gently, but stopped at once. Rotten wood groaned, then protested in an angry squeak.

Well, there was room for a body to slip through that opening. Maybe Knight's body already had. Marty turned sideways, jerked his torch into his left hand and squeezed through the narrow opening. A dark, damp, ill-smelling place; and silent, deadly silent! He stood still, listening. Then turning his torch toward the cold hard ground he sent a beam of light straight—straight— And he jumped back, then leaned forward again.

The light shone on the body of a man—a man bound hand and foot with strong rope. There was an ugly welt on his forehead, a gag across his mouth.

The watchman? Marty drew his knife and bent quickly, then hesitated. Watchman! The building didn't look as if it ever had a watchman. The man was breathing, all right. His nose was flat, his nostrils wide; there was no danger of suffocation there. Watchman! After all, he might be a watcher; a watcher for those above, who had the girl; had Tania. And Knight had surprised him?

**MARTY** moved his torch, biting into the darkness. There were steps; rotten, wooden steps leading to the floor above; broken, hanging, some even missing. For a moment only Marty turned and looked down at the bound man. He wished then that he had a gun; he wished that he had taken the gun from Zee Clarke, snatched it from the floor there in the narrow hall. But even as he made the wish, reason told him that such a move might have been disastrous. One that not only took time—time he could not spare—but one that might have prevented his making this trip tonight. Zee Clarke might have grabbed him, cried out; screamed a warning to others in that house.

Screamed! And Marty jerked erect, tossed up his torch and dashed toward those wooden steps. Would they hold him? Could he, at that speed, find and jump the missing steps; jump too the rotten ones that would give under his weight? Could he— But he didn't think of that as he dashed up those steps.

Scream! Yes, there had been a scream; a weird, eery scream of fear; perhaps horror. Just once. Short, sharp, terrible to Marty; and it died away. It was the scream of a girl; the girl, Tania.

Marty stopped; stopped because his head crashed against wood; wood that luckily gave slightly, or he would have been thrown back down those stairs. He felt the crack all right, but it knocked some sense into his head. It wouldn't help Tania any if he went stumbling, blundering into deadly gunfire—the gunfire of Don Parks.

Slowly now, very slowly Marty lifted the trap door above his head. And then Marty was out on the rough wooden floor, crawling along it, coming to his feet, moving more quickly across the open loft guided by a single light; sliver of light that came from a partly open door. A heavy wooden crate, then a wooden upright smacked him back. But he went on, reached that door and peered into the room beyond.

The first thing he saw was another door across the room from him, just an oblong well of blackness. Then he saw Tania. She was crouched there on the floor, her hands tied behind her back, her feet bound at the ankles; but she was not gagged. Great brown eyes were wide with fear—no, terror—and she was staring at something, fascinated. Marty saw the shadow on the floor, saw it move and become a man. The man was Don Parks; Parks, who was wanted for murder.

Parks ran his finger across the blade of a sharp knife as he looked at the girl. Then he placed the gun that was dangling from a finger of his left hand, upon a crate.

"Listen, sweetheart," he said as he leaned over her. "Can you write?" And when she only stared at him, "Damn it! can you write?"

"Yes. Why?" The words stuck in Tania's throat.

"Because," said Parks, bobbing his head, "if you don't tell me the name of The Reckoner you'll have to write it down for me later. Know why?" His face was very close to the girl's as Marty, gripping his cane tightly, slowly squeezed into that room.

"I'm an original man," Parks laughed hoarsely, his evil eyes on the girl; watching, even gloating over the effect of his words, so that he didn't hear the stealthy movement of Marty's body. "Can't guess why you won't talk? Well—" he jabbed the knife close to her mouth, even against her lips—"you can't talk without a tongue, sister."

QUICK thoughts raced through Marty's head. His hand that gripped the cane was steady. Could he throw that cane and strike Parks? Certainly. He knew that he could do that with a single motion of his right hand. But could he throw it so that it would strike Parks a paralyzing blow? Yes, he thought so. He had done it before; many times, perhaps during his years in the East, but never where so much hung in the balance; never where the deadly accuracy of his trained hand and wrist was so much needed. If he missed— But he couldn't altogether. He could follow it up with a rush. His right hand went up, the cane swished slightly through the air—and Parks turned his head. But too late, Marty thought. Then the cane never left his hand. A hand from behind grabbed his arm; something round and hard was jammed into his back and a voice said: "First, Knight comes here; then you. What's the racket, Mr. Day?"

Marty recognized the voice; recognized it as he was forced into the light of that room; recognized it as Don Parks reached out quickly and lifted his revolver from the crate. The voice behind him was that of Lieutenant Frank Bradley, but it was the voice of Don Parks that spoke now.

"Don't move, Mr. Marty Day," he sneered, "or I'll put a bullet between them pretty black eyes of yours."

Bradley's hand had left Marty's arm after jerking it to his side. Parks hadn't seen him at first, and now Bradley shot his gun along Marty's side and covered Parks.

"I don't think we'll have any shooting, Don," he said quietly. "Mr. Day is big and well built. I doubt if you could get a bullet through him that would hit me. If you want to get him, of course, why—"

And Parks didn't. His gun swung down quickly and the nose struck against the side of Tania's head.

"Bradley, eh?" Parks fairly sneered the words. "Drop your gun or the girl is blasted out!" And when no gun fell to the floor, "I'll do it all right. I know the racket; know that I'll be wanted for murder as soon as the evidence comes through. He'll tell you." He nodded toward Marty. "The Reckoner is going to produce it. Come! Drop that gun. I can't fry but once, you know."

"Yes, yes." Marty gasped the words as he stood there, a shield for Bradley and looked into the eyes of a killer. "Drop the gun, Bradley; let him go. You've got to, for the girl."

"I'll count three, Parks," said Bradley slowly. "Then I'll shoot. Believe that!"

"You—" Parks's gun stayed against the girl's head; his eyes were riveted on the gun Bradley held close to Marty's side. "I can see your hand, Bradley—the trigger finger. Just even tighten it, and—"

"One—" said Bradley very slowly.

"God!" cried Parks, "don't be a fool. You don't believe I mean it?"

"I've got my duty, mean it or not." Bradley's voice was very hard, very tense. But Marty knew the truth. He was going to shoot; going to shoot, and Tania would die. Marty didn't think, then, that the man who could save him; the man who might confess to the murder of Judge Ramdelfia, was going to die too. He thought only of Tania.

"Bradley—don't!" He fairly shrieked the words. Then he moved his body suddenly. Too late, he thought. The shot had come, echoing and re-echoing through that small room. Marty's eyes were held on Tania's face; Tania's dead face he feared. But it wasn't dead. Her eyes were staring straight up at Don Parks. Marty moved his head. Even as he looked, Parks was diving forward; diving straight toward the floor, the gun still grasped in his hand. But he didn't use it; couldn't use it. Marty realized the very second before Parks hit the floor that he was dead. He saw it for that single moment, saw those glassy, sightless, dead eyes.

"You got him." Marty grabbed Bradley by the arm. "Great shooting! I—"

Bradley tore himself loose. "You fool," he cried, "I didn't shoot. You blocked that. The shot came from the darkness of that door beyond; just behind him. I saw the flash. It was The Reckoner or—"

"Or Rierson," said Marty as he knelt at the girl's side and slashed at her ropes. "It couldn't have been The Reckoner; he didn't know. But Rierson feared Parks would talk. Rierson knew where he was." He thought of Knight's message and bit off his words. But there was no need to bite them off. Marty was talking to— Well, certainly not to Bradley. Lieutenant Bradley had jumped over the dead body of Parks and was out into the warehouse.

**MARTY** cut the girl free. She was trying to talk; finally her dry lips formed words. "He was the man who killed the judge, and now— You, Marty; you had better leave. Run for it while Bradley—"

And Bradley was back in the room, his gun swinging in his hand. "That ends the Parks case," he said with a shrug of his shoulders. "Too bad; we'd have roasted him sure."

"But my case! You—"

"No." Bradley looked up suddenly and he grinned. "It doesn't end yours; not by a jugful. Come on! We'd better get moving. Down to headquarters, of course." He answered the question in Marty's eyes. "If you expected that guy to help you out by confessing, you're certainly out of luck as far as he's concerned." And suddenly, "Your word of honor not to attempt to escape, Mr. Day, or I'll have to use handcuffs."

"No, I won't try to escape. And, Tania!"

Bradley shrugged. "She better come along." He looked hard at the girl. "She's not under arrest, but it's to her interest."

"I'll go where—where Marty goes."

"How did you know; get here?" Marty asked Bradley.

"Well," said Bradley, "a guy that signs his name with a big "K" picked out the wrong bird to give a note to. Oh, he wasn't a dick, but he does 'stool' occasionally for the boys; did for me when I used to work up this way; does a bit yet. Anyway, he got that note and buzzed me on the wire. A clever note, Mr. Day; just one bad line in it. Not a sure-fire line, but enough to get me out of bed and make me trot up to the Bronx. Then I hid across the street, recognized you and followed you. I'll admit I made a bull in coming in and grabbing your arm. But when I saw the guy wrapped up downstairs—well, I thought it was your racket."

"And the one bad line that made you suspect the note was for me?"

"Well," Bradley rubbed his chin, " 'suspect' is not the word. I earned my promotion by being persistent; not bright, just persistent. I follow up even the least sign of a clue. This bird who telephoned me said the guy who gave him the note told him to watch for a man with a cane. You always carry one, and—"

They were out in the loft now, walking toward the door, when a hand—in fact, two hands out of the darkness—grabbed Marty's sleeve. Marty turned, opened his mouth to speak and stopped. There, wedged between a packing case and the wall, was a man; a man who spoke; spoke though Marty could see a white cloth bound across his mouth.

"Don't talk, and cut my bonds—quick." The voice was the voice of Knight. Marty cut those bonds. They seemed loose, very loose. But Knight appeared very much frightened, and even took the knife from Marty's hand to hack more—much more than was necessary, Marty thought, to free himself.

"What the hell is this?" Bradley swung back. And, Knight, breathing heavily; apparently frightened into stuttering, tried to explain.

"I was following Miss Tania, to protect her, maybe, in Mr. Day's absence, when this man took her. I sent word for Mr. Day, and came here. I wanted to protect her. And that awful man caught me and struck me and tied me. Oh, sir—I hope, sir, he's dead."

What was the matter with Knight, Marty wondered. He had never seen him like that; never seen him in a blue funk before. Now—

But Bradley was saying: "He's dead all right; deader than hell." And as they went down the stairs to the street, "Damn it! quite a coincidence, this. The second time a lad has taken the lead when I—" And his words were lost, muffled in his throat.

## CHAPTER TEN

## KNIGHT AND DAY

THE POLICE system works smoothly and efficiently. A few minutes later a police car was at the warehouse and Bradley had given sharp orders about the body above, and to hold the bound man at the foot of the stairs.

"I'll be back before the photographers and medical examiner arrive," he told the police sergeant.

Five minutes after that Tania, Marty and Knight were waiting in a taxi while Bradley telephoned. Thoughts? Yes, many of them as Tania snuggled close to him. Funny, that! Bradley leaving him there on his honor. Not that he'd run out, but that Bradley would place such a trust in a man wanted for murder!

The taxi shot downtown, but not to headquarters. It stopped right before Marty's apartment house.

"You can pay the charge," said Bradley easily. "Then I'm going above with you. I've got a proposition to make."

Upstairs, Bradley lighted a cigar, willingly accepted the drink that Marty somewhat doubtfully offered him and threw himself into a big chair. After Knight served it and disappeared, "Let the young lady stay here with you." Bradley puffed lazily. "I've got a proposition to make, Mr. Day. You see, a certain man was murdered; a well-known judge. Before he died he made an accusation. I am the only one who heard it." He leaned forward and narrowed his eyes as he looked at Marty. "Now—for a consideration I'll forget that I heard it and we'll hand the murder on this Don Parks."

"He did it," said Marty. "He did it."

And Tania cut in sharply. "That's right. He killed Judge Ramdelfia. He told me so there when he threatened to—to—" and when Bradley grinned at her, "I'm willing to go on the stand and swear to that."

"Sure. Sure!" Bradley was affable. "And very natural of you too. But it wouldn't wash. The *ante-mortem* statement of the judge would go further with the jury; especially when there's a feeling with that jury that you love Mr. Day. Now," he sent rings of smoke toward the ceiling—"love's a beautiful thing. It softens the heart of even an old dick. Come! Give me the name of The Reckoner and I'll forget the judge ever made a certain statement."

"You. You!" Marty rasped. "After you would have let Tania die for what you call duty."

"Well—" Bradley reddened slightly—"I'm making you a simple proposition; not giving a lecture on the ethics of the department."

"Even if I did know," said Marty, "I—"

"Gangster's code!" Bradley sneered. And to the girl, "Do you want Mr. Day? I don't care who peeps. I want The Reckoner."

The girl shook her head. "I don't know—don't know." Her words were very low.

"Stubborn and foolish!" Bradley took his cigar from his mouth, looked long and steadily at the shreds on the end, and then, "Well— I'll smoke five minutes, by the clock."

"Then?" It was Tania who spoke.

"Then I'll lift that phone across the room and call headquarters, and turn Mr. Day in."

"You haven't told, yet, that the judge accused me?" Marty gasped. Strange thoughts were in his head. The cane beside his chair and, with a gulp, his word of honor to Bradley!

"No." Bradley looked at the clock. "It's my secret for four more minutes. I just let the boys know I wanted to talk to you. Why are you staring like that?"

Marty was staring. For directly behind where Bradley sat were curtains to a small conservatory, and those curtains were parted. And through the thin slit could be seen the eyes of Knight; steady, glaring, unfrightened now. But that wasn't what bothered Marty. It was something else. Knight's hand was through that curtain; a hand that held a gun; a deadly, black, heavy automatic.

**BRADLEY** half turned his head and gun and eyes disappeared. But they were there yet. Marty came to his feet. If he called out, Knight too would be arrested. If he didn't call out, Knight might shoot. And the phone rang.

Tania lifted the receiver, turned. "It's for you, Lieutenant. Police headquarters."

"Good!" Bradley came slowly to his feet, and as he walked to the phone Marty slipped between him and the curtains. Then, as Bradley's voice came to him, just a word here and there, he pushed through those curtains; confronted Knight.

"God! Knight. You mustn't; you can't. It—"

"It's his life or yours," Knight said. "I heard him say no one else knew. Maybe, just a clout on the head and—"

And from the other room the dull voice of Bradley. "Is that so? Yeah. I can't tell you now. Let me know everything he said; I'm listening."

"Knight," Marty whispered softly, "what happened? How did you find Tania?"

"Like I told you, I was following Tania," Knight said. "She went to Rierson's house and she didn't come out. I slipped around in the car I had hired to the block behind, was about to go through the yard back of Rierson's when men came. Three of them; two were carrying the girl. They put her in a car. One man stayed behind, and as the car drove away he turned back toward the Rierson house. I stuck a gun in his belly. It was Rierson, and—"

He stopped short. Tania had called. Bradley had parted the curtains.

"Come back in here," he said to Marty. "Any orders you want to give your servant can be given before me. I'm treating you pretty good; you think I'm a sap, maybe."

"You've been very decent; not the hard-boiled dick you've been painted. I—even if you don't understand why, I appreciate it."

"It's because I want The Reckoner; want him bad. Now, don't give me the line of the 'good he's doing.' A guy can't go around and shoot people right out of the electric chair. I'm not saying The Reckoner did it last time, with Razor Burke; but I am saying he did it this time."

"Why wasn't it Rierson? If Don Parks talked, it would have been the end of Rierson." Marty wished to defend The Reckoner. Anyway, he didn't see how The Reckoner could have gotten there on time; could even know of the warehouse.

"Rierson couldn't do it." Bradley poked a finger into Marty's chest. "Rierson couldn't have been there. I just got a message from headquarters. They found Rierson in that vacant lot not far from the warehouse. He was tied—tied hand and foot by an expert. Gagged too. And his face was beaten into a pulp."

"What does Rierson say?" Marty was stunned.

"He's just regained consciousness and states that he went out for a breath of air, had a gun stuck in his side, was pushed into a car, and the next thing he knew—a cop was putting a light down on his face. That is what Rierson says. But my guess is that The Reckoner kidnaped him and wanted him to talk; wanted him to tell him something; maybe made him glad to tell something." He looked at Tania.

"Glad to tell him something." The words rang familiarly in Marty's ears. But where— And Bradley was talking.

"Get ready, Mr. Marty Day." He shoved a hand into a hip pocket and jerked out steel cuffs. "Now—will you or will you not tell me the name of The Reckoner?" He half raised a hand. "No more speeches, no more denials. Simply yes or no."

Marty straightened slightly, felt Tania close to his side, and stretching out both hands, said: "No!"

Bradley looked him straight in the eyes for a long moment, and then, "Just one hand, Marty Day—just the right hand." He suddenly gripped it and shook hands with Marty. "Sometimes we cops have dirty jobs. I had one tonight. God, you must have thought me an awful fool to clown around with a guy wanted for murder!"

**HE DROPPED** Marty's hand and turned toward the door. Marty followed him, grabbed his shoulder, swung him around. "You're not arresting me; you're—you're letting me go free, knowing what—"

"Sure!" said Bradley. "Knowing exactly what. You see, the judge had raised his eyes and was looking over your shoulder when the shot came. It went right into his spine. He thought you had shot him in the stomach. The shock was great. He couldn't tell, of course."

"But how did you find out?" It was as if an iron hat, that had been screwed tightly on Marty's head, was suddenly released.

"The judge became conscious again and talked before the boys got there. When I told the judge he was shot through the back he knew you couldn't have done it. You see, the judge didn't know that Don Parks had been released, and he had never seen Parks; so he didn't know the man sent to his house to 'guard' him from you was Parks."

"Then you're not sure it was Parks?"

"But I am," said Bradley. "The judge pretty near slipped out on me, but I had an ambulance doctor jazz him up, and I wouldn't let them take him from the house until I got a picture of Parks there, for him to identify."

"But what made you think it was Parks?"

"You did, didn't you?" Bradley said. "Well—I get around a bit myself. I'll just take another drink of that stuff. It's good; damn good. No—no fizz water; I'll take it neat." And he did, walked toward the door, turned once and said: "You had a tough squeeze, Marty Day, and a damn good break. A guy mustn't expect too many breaks in life. She's not a bad-looking girl, and there's plenty of country around."

"Any other advice," Marty was standing with his arm around Tania. His smile was boyish again.

"Just a bit," said Bradley, and although his words had a ring to them, his eyes were very cold and his lips very hard. "You've got a nose and you've got a thumb—and there's The Reckoner."

The door slammed and Lieutenant Bradley was gone. Marty was no longer wanted for murder. Who killed Don Parks? The Reckoner could hardly have been there. It was impossible for Rierson to be there. And those words, "glad to tell." He remembered them; other things too. Knight bound in the warehouse; bound so loosely that a child might have jerked himself free! And Knight's anxiety; his eagerness to cut the ropes himself; to leave nothing that might—might—Marty swung suddenly.

"Knight!" he called sharply.

Knight came. Quiet; nothing of nervousness now that Bradley had gone.

"Knight—" Marty shot his words quickly—"over the phone you said Rierson would tell you where Tania was and—"

"And he did. He was most obliging." Knight nodded, and when Marty would have cut in, "He didn't know who I was, sir, but I—well, I persuaded him to tell. Indeed, he was glad to tell me."

"And the ropes then, in the warehouse when Tania was—"

"Miss Tania was about to die, sir; yes, sir. I heard you and the lieutenant talking about how The Reckoner or someone unknown shot this man, Parks. Very fortunate, sir. There was nothing else to do but kill him."

"But, Knight—" The snap was gone out of Marty's voice; there was a lump in his throat.

"You've been through a lot, sir. I wouldn't talk about it, if I may make so bold as to suggest it, sir." And his unemotional face breaking, his lips curving slightly, "May we forget the unpleasantness of this evening just as in—" And Knight's voice broke for the moment. Then, "Like in Arabia, wasn't it, sir? Just Knight and Day."

"Knight and Day." Marty repeated the words with perhaps more feeling than he ever had before.

Knight nodded, raised his head and sniffed. "I was getting up a little snack for you and Miss Tania," he said. "You'll excuse me, sir; I wouldn't want it to burn."

Knight gone—Marty didn't think much of the future. He thought only that he wasn't wanted for murder—and that he was alone with Tania.

# ANSWERED IN BLOOD

GARBED IN BLACK—A
SINISTER, SHIELDING
HOOD OVER HIS HEAD—
HE STOOD THERE—THE
RECKONER! AND IN THAT
TERRIBLE METALLIC
VOICE HE ISSUED HIS
DEATH COMMANDS. WHO
WAS THIS MASTER OF
MYSTERY? WHY DID
MEN HEED HIS ORDERS
BLINDLY, WALK INTO THE
MURDER TRAPS HE SET
KNOWING ESCAPE WAS
IMPOSSIBLE AS THEY
WENT?

# CHAPTER ONE

# THE DEATH THREAT

**M**ARTY DAY paced the upper level of the Grand Central Terminal. His black eyes flashed back and forth from the clock to the train gates, where the Boston express would leave in ten minutes. His tall erect figure stood out in the crowd. Across his arm was draped his ever present cane—the cobra cane, whose hidden springs could move strong thin steel with the rapidity of a rifle bullet.

There was a hum on his lips and a lightness in his heart; yet, a lightness that occasionally was lost in the sudden lump in his stomach that crept up into his throat. He wished Tania would come, so they could jump that damn train, make the ship at Boston and put water between themselves and The Reckoner.

He didn't know if he were in danger or not. He hardly thought so. Yet, he had disobeyed the summons of The Reckoner. The Reckoner! The unknown man; the hidden voice that had declared war on crime, and especially—war on Joseph E. Rierson, political leader, briber of officials, protector of criminals, and himself a cold-blooded murderer who stood above the law he controlled.

There had been excitement, money, adventure, and sometimes the feeling of a benefactor of mankind in Marty's joining forces with this Reckoner; taking his orders; accepting his money for carrying out those orders. And there was romance too—Tania Cordet.

And now he and Tania had decided to chuck it all, get married in Boston and sail for Europe where crime and hate and greed would be behind him.

**MARTY** snapped around. A hand was laid on his shoulder. He was looking straight into those unemotional eyes of Lieutenant Frank

"You'd give your life to see The Reckoner?... Well, look!"

Bradley, the detective who had so steadily stuck to the business of tracing down The Reckoner.

"I don't think she'll come," said Bradley. "I think you waited too long."

"You know who I'm waiting for?"

"Sure!" Bradley nodded, half turned toward the gates, watched the

guard slowly closing them. "You're waiting for the girl, Tania—and she's not coming. What are you going to do now?"

Marty hesitated, looked over the moving mass of people, bit his lip, fitted the steel handle of the cane tighter onto his arm and finally said: "I don't know. I don't know. What could—what could have happened to her?"

"I can hazard a guess on that."

"You think the—this Reckoner has her?"

"Well—no, I don't." Bradley stroked his chin. "And if he did I don't think it would be police business; that is, I don't think the girl is being held against her will." And suddenly, "Mr. Day, I advised you to quit this racket. You were going to take that advice."

"But Tania. If—if—"

Marty paused. His eyes widened. He grasped the tiny slip of wrinkled paper from Bradley's hand, smoothed it out, read the message on it.

Tania—
If you meet Marty Day he will never reach Boston. Either the police will remove him from the train or The Reckoner will remove him from—life.

The Reckoner.

"No, no!" Marty snapped the words. "He wouldn't dare. He wouldn't— If he did that I—I—" He looked at Bradley; stopped. After all, even though Bradley had proven himself a friend he was the law, and Marty Day had broken that law.

Bradley nodded.

"You were thinking, Mr. Marty Day," he said, "that if The Reckoner tossed you into jail; sent out information to the police of the activities he mixed you up in, why—you'd talk."

"Talk!" Marty tried to laugh. "Why, I don't even know who he is. I—" He looked at the detective. "You know, Bradley, I don't even admit there is such a man. I couldn't help the police any."

"You wouldn't you mean."

"Bradley," Marty said suddenly, "you're a hard man to understand. You're honest; fearless. You've done me many a good trick. Now, you're spending your entire time trying to get The Reckoner—The Reckoner, who is on your side; whose single purpose is to eliminate crime."

"And a single criminal, maybe?"

"And a single criminal. The most dangerous in the city—Joseph E. Rierson. You're not a fool, and you must know that by arresting The Reckoner you arrest the greatest menace to Joseph E. Rierson's control in this city."

"Sure!" said Bradley. "I know that; Rierson knows that. That's why he has used all his influence to get The Reckoner; that's why he has urged the police on in this hunt; that's why he has always advised me of what he learned concerning you. Rierson wants The Reckoner because he fears him; fears what he knows, what he'll do."

"And The Reckoner wants Rierson because he's a danger to society."

BRADLEY grinned. "Don't you believe that, Mr. Day. I'm not sure of the reason but I'm sure it isn't all altruistic. It may be money, it may be vengeance. My guess is that this unknown Reckoner is, in fact, a well known criminal. Someone whom Rierson has double-crossed; who hates him. Do you know what would happen if I went straight after Rierson? If I didn't get a bullet in my back I'd lose my job, and either way I wouldn't be much help to my family. You've got to take politics out of the Department and—" Bradley stopped; his eyes narrowed. "I'm on the trail of The Reckoner because he'll lead me straight to evidence against Rierson."

"Why"—Marty opened his eyes—"The Reckoner has given evidence to the police against Rierson. He's piling up information against crooked judges, racketeers, common gunmen—that Rierson protects. He's slowly undermining Rierson's power, giving Rierson's friends their first suspicion that maybe the Big Boss can't protect them after all. Then he'll get Rierson."

"And that's the vengeance." Bradley nodded. "He's letting Rierson know fear. But he has the evidence, now, that will convict Rierson. Why doesn't he use it?"

"How do you know he has it?"

"Because Rierson told me. Not in so many words," Bradley ran on, "but Rierson let me know in a round-about way that I would become an inspector shortly after The Reckoner is discovered—alive or dead."

"I see," said Marty.

"No, you don't," said Bradley. "I'm after Rierson; I hope to get him. He suspects it; and when that suspicion becomes a certainty I won't be working for the city."

"You, Bradley—you'd take a chance on Rierson! Why?"

"Maybe," said Bradley, "I'm just a guy who wants to be an inspector without crooked strings on him."

He turned away, but Marty gripped his arm. "That note to Tania!" he said. "Where did you get it?"

"Oh—that!" Bradley shrugged as he shoved it in a vest pocket. "I found it in Tania's apartment."

"And what," said Marty, "were you doing in Tania's apartment?"

"Checking up on a few things," Bradley told him. "We're coming to the showdown, Mr. Day."

"And why tell me all this?"

"Perhaps I rather like you and want to see you get from under before the fireworks start. Or—"

"Or—" said Marty.

"Or perhaps you can lead me to The Reckoner."

Marty laughed; at least he tried to laugh. "You've told me I'm a gentleman who's been swept into crime; now you want me to become a common criminal. A stool-pigeon. A squealer."

"Hell!" said Bradley. "You're talking like a book now. As you stand, you're just a sucker—a sucker for The Reckoner's schemes; and you're sticking because of the girl. Show me The Reckoner and I'll show you and Tania—an out. Don't you see, Mr. Day? Rierson wants to know who The Reckoner is. He's in a fair way to find out. If he discovers it before I do—*blooey*, things bust like that."

"It's your job," said Marty. "After all, I'm not a cop."

"But it's your life," said Bradley. "If The Reckoner has to close up shop he won't want his past coming back at him. He won't let Tania and you go now—alive, and he won't then. Another thing, Mr. Day. Max Arnold is your lawyer. Maybe The Reckoner saw to that, maybe he didn't." Bradley stroked his chin. "But it might interest you to know that Max Arnold used to be Rierson's lawyer some years ago. Rierson was just coming along then; just beginning to realize that the racket was the royal road to wealth and influence. They had some trouble. After Max Arnold's partner died—shot to death, by the way—their business relation ceased."

"And—" said Marty.

"Well, Max is your lawyer. Rierson is your enemy."

"So—what?"

"Max is a good lawyer. He'll work for anyone who pays him big money. Rierson likes good lawyers, and he can pay big money." And as Marty started to ask a question, "If you're thinking of a good place to eat dinner, try the Tavern Restaurant. Nice private rooms upstairs—but try it fast. You might be surprised and alarmed."

**TEN** minutes later Marty Day drove up to the Tavern Restaurant. Business was good, and several cars blocked his cab from moving to a position before the door. But Marty didn't encourage his driver to follow those cars as they moved in line. On the contrary, he ordered him to wait there by the curb. Joseph E. Rierson had stepped from the restaurant door and climbed into a taxi.

Marty could not believe it, at least after what Bradley had told him, that it was simply a coincidence that three minutes later the tall slim figure of Max Arnold also left the restaurant. And Marty could not be mistaken. Plainly, as the man turned and walked down the street, directly past his cab, Marty caught a good view of that sharp face; especially the beaklike nose.

Now—what? And Marty thought simply: Rierson had money. Max Arnold was a good lawyer. But also Max Arnold was close—very close to The Reckoner.

## CHAPTER TWO

## A PRICE FOR SILENCE

**K**NIGHT, MARTY'S servant, swung open the door before he could get his key in the lock. There was a warning in his eyes, barely audible words through lips that did not move.

"She's in there." Knight jerked his thumb back over his shoulder toward the living room.

"Who? Tania—Miss Tania?"

"No." Knight's voice was louder this time as feet crossed the floor behind him. "Mrs. Clarke. Mrs. Zee Clarke." And Marty thought that Knight's lips added, but silently, "The she-devil."

Zee Clarke, the girl with the amber eyes, stood almost in the center of that room when Marty went in. She was beautiful, of course; in that sinister way, Marty thought. And he didn't know. There was nothing in her face now to remind Marty of that night she had suggested that he kill a man.

"Marty," she said, "you're a fool. Twice now you've refused to answer the summons; the command of The Reckoner. I'm here to take you to him."

Marty stiffened. "I'm through with The Reckoner; through with Max Arnold; through with—with it all."

"Through with me too, eh? You know that I love you, Marty."

Marty stared down at her. He remembered the last time she had said that; remembered the look in her eyes, the closeness of her lips, the brush of hair across his cheek as she put her arms about him. Now she just stood there looking up at him, waiting for him to answer.

"You— Yes, Zee; you told me that."

"That's right." She nodded. "And you believe it?"

"Yes," Marty finally said. "And I believe that you believe it."

"Like that, eh?" She flipped a cigarette from her case with one hand and set fire to it before Marty could offer her a light. "I've come to take you to The Reckoner. It's your last chance. Don't be a fool, Marty. Go talk with him. I can't really believe you intended to run out—run out with Tania."

"I did," said Marty. "And it's not running out. I told The Reckoner when he called me on, the phone. I was straight and honest with him when I might have—yes, should have just slipped away. And how did he repay me? By threatening my life; by telling Tania that I would die. Maybe The Reckoner can send me to jail; frame me with the police by distorting and falsifying the work I did for him. But suppose I talked and—"

"You can't, Marty. That would strike at everyone but The Reckoner. At yourself; at Tania and—"

"If we left the country and—"

"But I would still be here. You must remember, Marty, that I killed a man here in your apartment; killed him that you might live; that Tania might live to take you from me. You can't talk."

"No, maybe not." Marty shook his head. "But neither can he deliver me to the police without bringing others into it. He wove his web too tight, Zee, for a single strand to be cut. But he could kill me."

"No," she said. "He can't kill you while I live."

"Zee"—Marty took both her hands—"you're a strange woman. Where do you fit? What power have you over The Reckoner? Why—" And dropping her hands, "Get out too, Zee. Things are boiling inside. Max Arnold! He—" And biting his lip, "Does The Reckoner thoroughly trust him?"

"More so, even, than he does me. He has to." She smiled slightly. "It's a mess, of course; as you say, Marty. A mess simply because I happen to believe that I love you. Otherwise— Well, there was the night that Max Arnold thought, perhaps, of putting a slug in your chest." She smiled sadly at him. "I know! It pains you to hear me talk so lightly of death; of killing. But remember—I am from another world. I have lived close to death; it can't make me shudder."

"Where is Tania?" Marty asked.

Zee Clarke smiled. "Tania is all right."

"What did he do with her?"

"Nothing." Her eyes went up. "Why should he? Besides, Max

Arnold is in love with her. He's older than you, Marty, and when love hits a man at that age it hits him hard."

"Tania and I," said Marty, "are going to be married. Nothing can stop that."

"Not even Tania!" Slender, expressive shoulders shrugged. "Why not talk to The Reckoner, Marty? It's your last chance." And before he could answer, "If The Reckoner can prevent Tania from running away with you by threatening your life, he could just as well force her into marriage by the same threat. You wouldn't want that; I wouldn't want that."

"You—you wouldn't!"

"Of course not," she said. "If I must recognize her as the reason you don't—" She left that sentence unfinished and tried, "Well, the real Tania may prove quite enough without the imaginary allurements with which you would adorn her were she the wife of another. Anyway, you must see and talk with The Reckoner if you would hope at all for Tania."

Marty set his lips tightly. "I'll see and talk with him," he said. "The same place; back of the little pawnshop?"

"No. That's out! Bradley suspects it. The Reckoner is at my house. Come!"

**THIS** time they entered Zee Clarke's house by the big front door. A butler admitted them; another servant took Marty's hat and coat. Zee smiled at him when he retained his stick.

"I know the cane trick," she told him, "and I know your standing alibi for always carrying it; an old wound in your leg that is apt to let you down at any moment. I shan't give it away. But here, you need not even fear The Reckoner."

"What power do you hold over him?" Marty asked.

She laughed softly.

"Perhaps the same power I hold over all men." The laugh died and she bit her lip. For a long time she stood by a curtained door to a room on the left. "Should I say 'most men'? No—all men. It is simply that I won't use that power on you. Funny, but I don't want you that way. Wait in there!" She flung open the curtains. "I'll tell The Reckoner that you are here; prepare him."

She turned and crossed the floor as Marty entered the library. The curtains closed behind him. Marty jarred erect. Max Arnold swung from a bookcase, faced him; smiled, nodded.

"Good evening." Arnold moved across the floor, pointed to a chair; to the cigars in the humidor on the polished table. "We haven't met in a few days. You should trust your lawyer, Mr. Day. I might have advised you against an elopement. Now"—close-set eyes came even closer together; fastened on Marty off the end of that beaklike nose— "it seems Mrs. Clarke has more influence with you. If I were a younger man I might envy you, Mr. Day; wanted by two such charming women. You will, of course, marry Mrs. Clarke."

"I will," said Marty, grasping his cane in both hands, "marry Tania."

"I see," said Max Arnold. "But if you continue in your present methods, you will, Mr. Day, be in no position to marry anyone."

"You mean—I will be dead?"

"Dead," said Max Arnold. "Quite dead. Why do you watch my hands like that?"

"The last time we met," said Marty, "I believe your intentions were to kill me—yourself."

"Orders!" Max Arnold shrugged his shoulders. "At that time you were wanted by the police for murder; a murder that time proved you didn't commit. But you were wanted by the police, and you might have talked."

"I had," said Marty, "nothing to talk about. I did not know and do not know who The Reckoner is. Your idea of eliminating me that night, Mr. Arnold, was purely personal. You are in love with Tania, so you warn The Reckoner against me; falsify my position and—"

"Tush, tush." Max Arnold made clicking sounds in his throat. "We mustn't quarrel; especially about the women—any woman. The Reckoner will not approve."

"Nor would The Reckoner approve of your—your associations."

"What do you mean?"

"I mean," said Marty very slowly, "your associate at dinner, tonight— at the Tavern Restaurant."

**MAX ARNOLD** spun suddenly. His face turned a quick red, then a sudden white. He leaned for a moment on the desk; went quickly to the curtains, flung them open, looked into the hall beyond and came back into the room again. He stood now very close to Marty. His breath came in quick, short gasps.

"If you breathe that to a soul I'll kill you."

Marty grinned. He took his words now from the words of Max Arnold.

"If I breathe that to a certain soul; the man who is waiting to receive me now, you will, Mr. Arnold, be in no position to kill anyone."

"I see." Max Arnold nodded slowly. "The price of your silence is the girl, Tania—eh?"

"Good God!" It was with an effort that Marty restrained himself from striking the man. "Tania is to decide her own life; her own marriage."

"And Zee Clarke?"

"Zee Clarke means nothing to me."

"But you mean something to her. I don't think you know the woman, Mr. Day. To you she's cold, hard, taking what she wants as her right. But inside—" small eyes centered to twin bright points; held Marty's. "Why, you'd think no more of Tania and her doll-like—"

"I'm not here to discuss either Tania or Zee Clarke with you," Marty said.

"But you are here to discuss with me the possibility of your telling The Reckoner that I was with Joseph E. Rierson. You can't understand that it might be a very harmless bit of law work, perhaps even a co-incidence that I met him there, or that you were mistaken in your belief that you saw me."

"It's not what I believe." Marty shrugged huge shoulders. "Rierson is The Reckoner's enemy. It's what The Reckoner might believe that should interest you."

"It never entered your head that perhaps The Reckoner sent me to him."

Again Marty's shoulders moved, but he watched those penetrating eyes.

"Then, of course, you would have no need of alarm and The Reckoner would not be interested in my little gossip."

"Only to the extent that I was indiscreet," Max Arnold started, stopped and said, "I'm a man who likes straight talking. What is the price of your silence?"

"The price of my silence, is Tania's happiness," Marty said, "the right of Tania to choose her own life; her own marriage."

"Very well." Max Arnold left the table and walked quickly down the length of the room, unlocked a door at the end and jarred it open. "Tania!" he called.

Tania came into the room. Small, erect, her steady brown eyes rested an Marty. For a moment she seemed to sway forward; about to run to him.

"Tania!" Marty stepped toward her—stopped. Max Arnold was between them.

"We are not, I imagine, to plead our separate merits and offerings for the lady's hand." Max smiled, and turning to the girl, "Mr. Day is rather a persistent suitor. He does not remember or does not understand a woman's right to change her mind. Will you tell him, Tania, that the elopement is off?"

TANIA opened her mouth twice before she spoke. "He knows that. You know that, Marty. That's why I didn't meet you."

"Yes. And I know more." Marty brushed Max Arnold aside and took Tania by both shoulders. "I know of the note; the threat you received."

"And I know too"—Tania faced him—"Zee Clarke, who—"

Marty laughed, a little wildly perhaps. "They've been telling you that, eh? About her! Why, she—"

"She takes what she wants." Tania jerked herself free and crossed the room, behind the table. "She—" And suddenly, "You were a fool to come here. Why didn't you go alone? Boston, London, Paris."

She stopped. Max Arnold had crossed to the curtains, flung them open. Zee Clarke stood there.

"Come in." Max Arnold bowed; his voice was mocking. "It's a long time since you have seen two men quarreling over a woman; over another woman. But the stage was set for it." Arnold laid a hand on her shoulder. "It must come to all women. You have spoken of my age without recognizing your own. You're cleverer, brighter, far superior in worldly ways to Tania. That she chooses me instead of Mr. Day leaves him free. Resentful, perhaps, but susceptible to all the many charms the years have taught you. Five years ago, perhaps—" Arnold shrugged his shoulders. "The truth hurts, doesn't it? But youth has slipped from you—"

"You beast!" Zee Clarke fairly snapped the words.

Marty took a step forward and caught her by the arm. Her whole body was trembling. "Don't believe him, Zee; don't pay any attention to him. You've got youth and beauty. It is just that— Well, Tania, to me—"

And Marty got no further. The woman turned, raised her right hand and with the open palm slapped him across the cheek. A bell buzzed in the library. She stood quietly a moment; then, as the bell buzzed again, her body trembled; her head shook as if she had just swallowed some particularly sour medicine. At length she spoke.

"You're rotten, Maxie," she said. "Plain rotten. But you're right— right, as you're always right. You can have the woman you want, and I—" She fastened those somber eyes on him suddenly. "You haven't forgotten our purpose here tonight."

"No." Max Arnold bent slightly. "And I haven't forgotten that, if you lack much in the charm of youth, your head contains brains that brilliant men—and only brilliant men could worship. Tonight The Reckoner speaks, perhaps, for the last time. You'll take Mr. Day above."

"Come!" Zee turned to Marty. There was nothing in her eyes to indicate love or hate.

"I'll want to see Tania before I go—and alone." Marty paused as Zee held open the curtains.

Zee Clarke laughed. "Your life," she said, "is in my hands tonight; yet you make a request like that." She let the curtains fall back, stood looking at him in the more brilliantly lighted hall. "Love and hate are very close—" She paused. "Very close tonight."

She led him up the broad stairs, turned onto the narrow ones to the right, passed along a corridor and paused before a door. Fitting a key in the lock she turned it; stood aside for Marty to enter. He would have spoken to her, but she shook her head.

## CHAPTER THREE

## $100,000 FOR MURDER

MARTY WENT inside, heard the doors close behind him; then paused, to take in the room under the dim light. Although the room was a beautifully furnished sitting room the arrangements for the interview with The Reckoner were much the same as those of the little pawn shop. In the pawnshop, a steel partition had reached down, shutting off the end of the room; here, heavy curtains were hung. In the pawnshop, a lamp had rested on a counter so it might shine directly in Marty's face; here, a similar lamp rested on a table where the two folds of the heavy drapes met.

Marty stepped forward and dropped into the chair close to the table. His cane was still held tightly in his hand. As if making himself at ease he poked the cane once or twice against the thick drapes. Just drapes, he thought. For just softness met the ferrule of the cane. And Marty had a wild idea.

Joseph E. Rierson was bending every effort, even to torture and murder, to discover the real identity of The Reckoner. Now—if he, Marty, could discover that identity, he was free and Tania was free. No more orders; no more commands; no more threats. The Reckoner went to great length to keep his identity a secret. Knowledge of his identity meant power—and power, to Marty, meant Tania. If she were giving him up, it was simply to save his life; nothing else.

But he'd see. He'd watch for the break; a chance perhaps to rip those curtains apart and look on the face of the man—

The soft glow of the shaded lamps went out and the hard glare of the lamp on the table shot suddenly into his face. Almost simultaneously with the sudden brightness came the voice that Marty knew so well; the grating mechanical words that might have been spoken by a man, a woman or a child. Nothing natural about that voice; nothing meant to be natural about it. Marty knew it wasn't a machine because it answered questions—questions it couldn't know he was going to ask.

"So, Mr. Day, you come at last. You have forgotten that I never make requests. They are all commands, and those who break those commands become enemies; and enemies are dangerous."

"I've been on the level with you," Marty said. "I told you flatly I didn't like your methods; the mess you were involving Tania and myself in; that I'd keep whatever confidences I had; that I felt I had earned the money you paid me and that I was through. Could anything be fairer than that?"

There was a hollow sound; it might have been a chuckle. Marty didn't know.

"But you came tonight."

"I came because of Tania."

"You want your reward, then."

"I want nothing," said Marty. "You brought Tania back by your threat to—to harm me; maybe your threat to expose her as you could expose me. Why not forget us, as we'll forget you? I want no reward."

"No? But I promised you such a reward. I promised you Tania. There, don't become so noble! Women; men; hate; love; greed. Such intrigues are going on now among my very closest associates. You love and hate and bicker, and what of my plans? Don't deny it! Even in this house tonight, trouble—trouble over a woman. Very well, Mr. Day, I forgive you everything. I offer you your big chance; I offer you Tania."

"For what?"

"You love her very much?"

Marty hesitated a long moment, and then, "Yes. You must know that."

"I do know that. Do you love her enough to kill a man?"

"Kill a man! Kill a man saving her?"

"Yes. Saving her from Max Arnold."

"By God!" said Marty, "if he harms her I'll strangle—"

"There, there! It's much simpler than that. We don't want Max killed." A moment's pause. "The time has come for the death of the greatest menace to society; the force behind all crime. I am giving you an opportunity of ridding the city of this man—Joseph E. Rierson."

"You're suggesting that I murder him?"

"The death of Rierson could not be called murder; simply justice and—"

"Vengeance!" echoed Marty.

"Vengeance?" There was a question in the voice. "Who put that idea into your head? Was it the police?"

"It was Bradley." Marty nodded. "And he hinted too, that your purpose is not entirely to aid society; that you fooled me; you played upon my stupid ideas of righting wrongs, protecting the weak. Well, maybe you have; but in so doing you've filled your own pocket and—"

"Where did you think the money came from that also filled your pocket?" The Reckoner snapped. "I have spent thousands; yes, hundreds of thousands. Isn't it right that these people who have preyed on society, now be taxed to protect that same society? But what of my proposition? In return for Rierson's death I give you Tania."

"Tania is not for sale, nor could she be bought through murder. If you have the evidence against Rierson—"

"There is no time for evidence. His death is necessary and imperative. Do you know what he is planning? The death of Tania; your death; the death of Max Arnold, and by God! I believe, the death of Zee Clarke. Don't you see?

"He is going to send through the underworld the names of those who aid The Reckoner; those who make secret war on criminals. And each one in that underworld; each public enemy who thinks he may be my next victim will strike. You understand now. Rierson must die that you people may live. It is to protect you that I send you on this mission tonight."

Marty's eyes narrowed. "You will send me on no mission of murder tonight."

"No?" The mechanical voice took on an edge; like a knife along a grindstone. "Rierson is turning your name and the names of others over to hired killers in the city tomorrow morning. So much money is offered for each one of you. I have planned things well; I have made it easy for you. There is little danger."

"If there is so little danger, why send me? Why not—"

The Reckoner laughed. "Because I trust you. Because I wish to reward you. But perhaps most of all, because the death of Rierson by your hand will allow me to set you and Tania free. With the death of Rierson, you will hardly be in a position to harm me later; you would hardly wish to be accused of murder. Your mission will be over; my mission will be over. Both of us will sleep contentedly, with the knowledge that the other cannot talk."

"Your single purpose, then, was vengeance on Rierson."

A long moment of silence, and then, "Correct. My single purpose— vengeance on Rierson."

"I should think you would want to be in at Rierson's death."

"Yes, yes. I will be in at Rierson's death."

Marty jarred slightly erect. For the moment the voice seemed human; at least, less grating. It— And then the feeling was gone. The Reckoner was talking again. Quickly, rasping once more.

"So, you have freedom and Tania. You will take her abroad. Not on the few dollars you planned to flee with, but with a fortune. One hundred thousand dollars in cash. Look!"

MARTY did look. The curtains parted, much as the steel partition at the pawn shop used to part. A white hand came through; a whitish yellow hand that always surprised Marty. It was so smooth, so shining; as if there were no lines in it, no veins in it; the skin drawn tightly, even smoothly across the knuckles.

"Twenty-five thousand tonight—here, in cash. The rest tomorrow."

Marty blinked in the light. Was it the light in his eyes that made that hand look so queer, so—but the money was real. He could see the green of the bills, the figures on the top bill. Five hundred. The money was dropped with a thud upon the table—and Marty acted.

He shot forward in the chair as the hand started back. His right hand, long trained to move quickly with that cane, moved as quickly without it. He caught the shining hand, gripped it tightly just as it slipped back through the curtains. And that was where he made his mistake. He had expected to follow that hand through the curtains, grip the body it belonged to, crush that body close to his before it could protect itself, and see the face of the man behind the curtains.

Marty did knock aside the curtains, hurling the lamp from the table. And he did follow that hand beyond the curtains, but only a few inches beyond it. Then his body pounded against something hard; something that gave slightly and sprang back. And the hand! It was slipping from his grasp. Frantically Marty tried to hold it; dug his nails into the skin—or was it skin?—and something gave. There was a rip and a snap. The hand was gone, slipping through a network of steel.

The lamp lay on the floor where it had fallen. The bulb was unbroken and its light now shone straight upon that lattice of steel. Two thin steel doors were locked together with a heavy brass padlock. And behind that lattice Marty saw The Reckoner, caught there in the full glare of the lamp.

Marty knew that what he saw would do him no good. The man was dressed in a long black robe such as a judge wears on the bench. There was a hood covering his head, or at least Marty saw only heavy black where the man's head should be. As to his size or general carriage! Well, The Reckoner took good care of that. His body was bent far backward and away from Marty; his knees seemed to give when he walked. Just a slouching, even slinking, figure.

The Reckoner half turned that lurching body sideways; a flash of white for a moment in the darkness beyond the reach of the lamp, that might have been a face; the wave of a hand that now seemed a very real hand—and The Reckoner was gone, passing through a door.

Marty straightened, stepped back and let the curtains fall, to hide again the network of steel. Bending, he lifted the lamp and placed it back on the table. It was then for the first time that he saw what he held in his hand. It was a torn bit of rubber glove; a finger and a thumb were missing. But the explanation of that peculiar hand, which had bothered Marty from the very first day he had seen it, was at least clear to him. The rubber glove had given the hand its shininess.

He had been a fool. He admitted that as he tucked his cane back over his arm and turned toward the door.

Many things had been left undone. He hadn't told The Reckoner about Max Arnold. Had he intended to tell him? He didn't know; he wasn't sure about that. Wasn't sure if he had made a promise to Arnold about that or not. But it was better so. He had something with which to threaten Arnold. That was true but it gave him little satisfaction. Max Arnold now knew something that would give him further reason to fear Marty.

**MARTY** would watch out for that. He'd go below, talk alone with Tania, get her to leave the house. Yes, he had been a fool. He might at least have pretended to concede to, or promise to think over, The Reckoner's proposition.

Rierson deserved to die. He recalled now Rierson's attempt to disfigure Tania for life by throwing acid in her face. For life? Probably for a few minutes of life. After that he would have killed both of them.

Marty reached the door, spun the knob. A moment of doubt, and the door opened. He was surprised at that. He thought that he might be locked in the room. Now he turned along the hall, reached the stairs, passed down them and stood on the landing looking at the large, well lighted reception hall below.

All quiet there. Just the butler standing at the foot of the stairs. Waiting there, very straight, very pompous, very dignified. And in his hands he held Marty's hat and coat.

"I'm sure, sir," the butler said when Marty reached the last step, "that Mrs. Clarke didn't expect you down so soon, or she would have waited."

"She left?" Mechanically Marty let the man help him into his coat.

"Yes, sir. She said she expected you'd follow them along to the theatre."

"What theatre?"

The man seemed surprised, genuinely surprised. "I don't know, sir. I understood you would know. But—really, Madame seemed to think you might be hours with the paintings. They're very valuable, as you know. That's why the steel doors are there."

"So that's why they are there." Marty looked at the man shrewdly. By no stretch of his imagination could he connect this overfed, overpompous, yet undoubtedly well trained butler with the intrigues of The Reckoner. He thought too that the steel grating was cleverly accounted for to other visitors. In a vague way he did remember paintings behind that steel.

"They have all gone?" Marty asked as he crossed to the front door.

"All three, sir. Mrs. Clarke, Miss Cordet and Mr. Arnold."

"And the other—other gentleman?" Marty put the question lightly.

"There was no other gentleman." The butler's eyes raised slightly, and then perhaps in a knowing way, as if he thought Marty might resent Mrs. Clarke's departure with a rival, "She took one of our cars, sir; no one called for the party. Shall I call a car for you?"

"No," said Marty, "I'll walk." He did think of going into the little library; even searching the house. But that would be stupid; ungrateful too, to Zee Clarke. It was a cinch that the servants, at least this particular one, had no suspicions of his mistress's activities. If The Reckoner had left the house, and Marty had no doubt that he had, then it was by some means unknown to the butler.

Marty was out the door when the butler stepped quickly forward. "This letter! Mrs. Clarke wished me to give it to you."

"Yes?" Marty took the square of white envelope. "You forgot it, eh?"

"Forgot it!" The man straightened. His stomach protruded as if he thought he were throwing out his chest. "Hardly, sir. I gave it to you exactly as directed. Good night, sir."

The butler disappeared and the door closed. Marty turned once, stopped, swung again, and going down the steps walked up the street. For the first time he remembered that in that room with the steel curtain was twenty-five thousand dollars in cash.

## CHAPTER FOUR

## MAX ARNOLD PAYS A VISIT

THE BIG Rolls pulled up just beyond the Biltmore Hotel and Max Arnold climbed out. He stretched in a hand and helped Tania to the sidewalk. "I guess," he said gruffly to the remaining occupant of the car, "that'll be all tonight. You'll be home if The Reckoner wants you, Zee."

Zee Clarke leaned from the car, beckoned to Arnold, and when he came closer, "Let me look at you, Max." She stretched up both her hands; her slender fingers went to either side of his face. "The devil's in you tonight. I've known you too long not to recognize the symptoms. What are you going to do?"

"I'm human," said Max Arnold. "The girl has thrown over Marty Day. We'll have an evening together."

"Max," she held his eyes, "you can't be in love with that chit, not—not after—"

"No?" Max Arnold spoke low so that the chauffeur heard nothing. "You've got the man you love. I've taken the competition off your hands. If you can't make good now— Well—"

"And those things you said to me!" Zee's voice was soft. "You meant them, Max? Age and—" She hesitated when he did not answer. "You admired me, Max—my brains, but you always laughed at love. I knew when it got you it would strike terribly. Be careful, Max. Be careful that you don't let anything happen to Marty Day."

"I think," said Max, "that Rierson will take that out of my hands." He hesitated a long moment, lifted his hands and drew the woman's fingers from his face, held them in a viselike grip. "I told you once I wouldn't let the man live who stood between me and the—the woman I loved."

"Yes—if you ever loved." Zee Clarke looked over Arnold's shoulder. "It's hard to believe—very hard to believe—that she'd be the one. There were times—"

"That's your pride," said Max Arnold.

"I don't know that I wish you to marry Tania. You—"

"Perhaps you'll get your wish." He started to close the door.

Zee Clarke spoke quickly. "You'll re-remember The Reckoner, Max, and you'll remember what the death of Marty Day will mean to him. You called me a serpent once. Remember that I can still strike like a serpent if Marty— Yes, and anticipate The Reckoner and act before he does. Don't make me strike at you, Max. I haven't withdrawn my protection. Don't forget that. Don't make a mistake, Max. Your hate and greed and passion and self-exaltation are stupendous and vital things when your reason guides them. Now don't let emotion kill that reason."

"No," Max Arnold said very slowly and very thoughtfully, "I hope not." And he slammed the door of the car so viciously that the chauffeur on the far side, behind the wheel, jerked in his seat. Zee Clarke was talking into the speaking tube. The car pulled slowly from the curb.

**MAX ARNOLD** turned and walked to Tania, who stood by the side of the building. "Well," he said, "you would marry me to save Marty Day?"

She didn't answer him.

He spoke to her again harshly. "Go to my apartment. Wait for me there. Johnson, my servant, will let you in." And when she started to move away he clutched her by the arm. "Don't ring Day up. Don't try to communicate with him in any way. You understand? You know what will happen to him."

"Yes." She spoke at length. "The Reckoner knows, understands—"

"The Reckoner spoke to you tonight before Marty Day came. My orders are his orders. He told you that."

"I brought Marty into it," Tania said slowly. "I'll get him out of it." And suddenly, "If anything should happen to Marty, I'll kill you."

"So, so—" Max Arnold pulled at her arm. Strong fingers tightened so that she winced with the pain, but she did not cry out. Then his fingers loosened, a hand slipped to her chin, tilted it up slightly. "You're very beautiful," he said, turned suddenly, and walking quickly down the block entered the hotel.

Max Arnold stood patiently by the desk while the room of Jacob Levine, Akron, Ohio, on the hotel register was called.

The clerk smiled. "You're to go right up, Mr. Arnold. Mr. Levine is expecting you."

The man who opened the door of 910 of the suite 910-912 was tall and thin.

"You're the lawyer man," he said, nodded, rubbed his chin. "That's right. I know you."

"That's right!" Max walked to the window. "Don't stand there like a fool. I want to see Joe; want to see him now."

"Keep your socks up." The man hummed softly, walked to another door and passed through it. Less than a minute later Joseph Ellison Rierson walked into the sitting room of the suite.

Max Arnold looked steadily at him.

"Well"—Rierson tapped his thick stubby fingers together before he raised his right hand to his flabby chin—"you've come to talk business?"

"I've come to do business, not talk it."

"Humph!" Little shoe-button eyes snapped into life. "Tonight?"

"Tonight," said Max Arnold. "I'll deliver the girl for you within the hour. The man later."

"Tonight?"

"Tonight."

**JOSEPH E. RIERSON'S** thick-set body moved slowly up and down the large room. Twice he turned and stood before Max Arnold, studying him. At length his thick lips moved and the blue lines in his face broke into ripples.

"The Reckoner is a very clever man; a very shrewd man. Aren't you afraid?" And without waiting for an answer, "Why do you do it?"

Max Arnold grinned. He said: "The same thing that dominates your life dominates mine. Money. I want it now."

"In advance, eh?"

"That's right." Arnold grinned. "You know what I promised you."

"Yes." Rierson nodded. "And I know how to handle you later if you fail."

"That's what has been bothering me," Arnold said. "You have never been slow about getting rid of people. Why now? This woman, Tania! She robbed you. She delivered the information that put you in the hands of The Reckoner. Why have you let her live? And the man, Day! Personally responsible for your dangerous position now."

"I've been in the hospital." Rierson spoke very slowly. "I wanted to wait—wait for something like this. I want to have them myself. I want to see them. I want them to know."

"But they've got to die," said Arnold. "It would—I've got to be sure of that."

"My friend," said Rierson, "you could not be more sure of anything. They don't know this man—this Reckoner?"

"No," said Max. "No one does."

"I thought—" Rierson hesitated. "This Clarke woman— Why, what's the matter?"

Max Arnold was on his feet. "You must not bother her," he said. And more slowly, "Don't make the game too dangerous for yourself, Joe. Some day, I promise you; maybe sooner than you think, I'll deliver The Reckoner to you."

Rierson's little eyes snapped. "I'd make you a wealthy man; I'd make you a millionaire. God Max, it's terrible! Who is he? A city official; a friend I meet on the street; one of my closest associates? You're close to this Reckoner, Max. You must—must suspect something. He's convicting and killing my men. I can't trust anyone. I should have stuck to you, Max—long ago. Now he's got the stuff on me, why don't he strike? I'll give you anything, Max. Anything. Any amount. I hate him. I hate this man, Marty Day. This woman. You're just a machine, Max. Just business—just money. With me—you wouldn't understand. I want vengeance."

"I understand," Max Arnold said very slowly. "Vengeance!"

For a long time the two men talked in a low voice, leaning forward, their heads close together. Finally Arnold came to his feet.

"You may see The Reckoner sooner than you think, Joe. Much sooner."

At the door he paused, looked back once at Rierson rubbing his hands. Then Arnold spoke again. "Watch this Marty Day," he said. "He's a fool, Joe, but a fool for courage."

There was a peculiar glint to his eyes; a twist to his lips, and Rierson noticing it said: "Maybe there's something more than money in it for you, eh, Max? Maybe vengeance, too."

"Maybe. For once in my life I wasn't quite careful enough, Joe. The Reckoner knows me but I don't know him. Marty Day and the girl know me. If they were all dead—all silent, things would be cleaned up for me."

"There's the Clarke woman," Rierson mused. "She'd know. She'd be alive."

"Yes," Max Arnold said very seriously. "But she's too beautiful to die, Joe—too beautiful."

"And me, too. I'd know." There was a laugh in Rierson's voice. "I'm not too beautiful to die, eh?"

Max Arnold grinned. At least, his teeth showed. "You won't talk, Joe."

"Hardly," said Rierson, "after tonight."

"Hardly," repeated Max Arnold, "after tonight."

## CHAPTER FIVE

## TANIA LEARNS THE TRUTH

**T**ANIA CORDET stood up when Max Arnold let himself into his apartment. There was a peculiar light in her eyes now as she crossed to Arnold; stood squarely in front of him.

"Max," she said, "what is it? You've changed. You're not so sure of yourself; not so certain. And, Max—I know the truth. You don't love me; don't even—"

He grabbed at her shoulders. "What do you mean?"

"I'm a woman," she said. "You don't love me and I don't care for you. You talk of marriage. At first I didn't know, but now I do. It's not love. It's hate. You hate Marty Day. You hate him and hope to make him suffer through me."

"Don't talk like a fool!" Arnold snapped. "Why would I hate him?"

And Tania knew. Suddenly she knew why Max hated Marty. Her brown eyes grew wide. "Because you're in love with Zee Clarke," she told him. "That's it. I've been blind and she's been blind. And—"

"And I've been blind." Max Arnold fairly snarled the words. "Do you think for a moment, that I could care for you when she—she— But she never knew. She—" He stopped, looked at the girl.

"No, she doesn't know." Tania nodded as if in understanding. "I thought that you hated her tonight, when you spoke to her like that. But now I know. It was the hurt love in you. It was— Max, Max don't do it. Marty doesn't love her—"

"But she loves him. I know. And all that stands between that love of hers for Marty is you, and her pride. When that pride goes, then only you. She'll sweep you aside. She'll—"

"Max—Max!" The girl pleaded with him again. "Don't do it. Don't do it!"

"Do it! Do what?"

"You intend to kill Marty Day. Don't, Max. Don't!"

Max Arnold stood looking down at her. Then he shook his head, rubbed a hand across his eyes, back through his hair, turned from her and reaching into a curtained recess lifted a decanter with fingers that trembled. He had difficulty in pouring the liquid into the glass. He spoke, half to himself. "She was right," he said. "She is always right. Not emotion; reason, reason."

He set the glass down on the table, shivered slightly, stretched his hand out before him and watched the fingers; saw that they were steady. When he spoke again his voice was calm.

"God! Tania," he said without turning his head, "what an imagination you've got. I'll show you how different it is from the truth. Get your coat! I'm taking you away."

"Where?"

"I'm taking you to Marty Day." He turned now and walked to her. His voice was soft and gentle. There was a slight catch in his throat; a catch that he had used often before a jury when he pleaded with them to send back that 'poor unfortunate to his mother.'"You guessed my secret, Tania. I'm sending you and Marty away. Don't thank me. It's not for you or for him. It's for myself. He's got youth and birth and courage. I've got nothing but what I've dragged up from the East Side streets with me. I'm giving him to you, Tania; giving him to you so that Zee Clarke may not have him."

"And The Reckoner? His threat to me about Marty."

"Leave that to me. I will take care of The Reckoner."

"But Rierson—"

"Rierson," said Max Arnold very slowly, "will be dead before morning." The girl looked at him. "Day is going to kill him tonight."

"No, no. I don't believe you."

"Maybe not." Max Arnold shrugged his shoulders as he walked to the door and opened it. "Come! We are going to meet Marty Day. It's up to you to convince him that the best interests of both of you rest on the death of Rierson."

**THE GIRL** didn't speak on the way down in the elevator. She didn't speak as they crossed the long hall of the apartment, to the street. She was silent, too, when they climbed into Max's car, which he drove himself. She had been wrong before; she'd be right this time. Flight was the only thing. She wouldn't hesitate about flight with Marty now. She had brought him back to save his life, and they wanted to make him a murderer.

She saw it all now. Excitement. Adventure. Romance! No. Just crime—sordid crime. That was what she was in. That was what she had dragged Marty into with her. And they would make him a murderer! She laughed at that thought, a little hysterically, and Max Arnold looked down at her. But she didn't talk. She wouldn't let him know the truth. So he thought he was taking her with him so that she would plead with Marty to kill a man! She shuddered slightly. Maybe her life had been such that Max would believe that; would believe that she would let the man she loved commit murder to save her. Well, she—

The car turned across to Riverside Drive, rolled slowly through the early evening traffic. Lights twinkled on the Hudson; distant, blurred flashes across the river. They passed the George Washington Bridge and continued to the end of the Drive.

Broadway. The Seventh Avenue subway became an elevated road. Then Kingsbridge, and they swung to the left and over to Riverdale Avenue. Up the hill almost opposite Van Cortlandt Park, until they reached a side road.

Tania would always remember the location of that side road. There was a man-hole in the street; a railing around it; a lantern, as if workmen had just left it.

She turned to Max Arnold to ask a question. The car suddenly stopped beside a torn, twisted wooden gate. There was a tiny flashlight in Arnold's hand; it slipped awkwardly and he juggled it. For a moment the light flashed upon his face; just for a single split second it held there. But in that split second the girl knew the truth. She read it in his face, in his burning eyes. She was going to her death.

Tania had known fear before, but never the same stark terror that gripped her then. She clutched at the handle of that door and screamed. Her piercing shriek cut into the silence of the country night.

One cry, that was all. Then the handle of the door slipped back; a hand tore her evening wrap from her shoulders, and she stumbled out onto the road, tripping over her long dress. But she didn't fall. Clutching up her dress she went dashing down that road toward the main highway—

**MAX ARNOLD** cursed, half stumbled from the car, looked at the running figure. Other men were there now. Two who ran quickly through the dilapidated gate and another, just a blurred figure, who stood for a moment on the steps of the house back among the trees.

"Get her, you fool!" Max Arnold fairly snarled as one of the men started questioning him. Then the figure came from the darkness; ran down the steps, was giving quick orders. The two men went in pursuit of the fleeing girl.

Rierson spoke to Arnold. "What happened? God, what a shriek! Lucky this place is so far from—"

"You were to be ready." Max cut in on him. "You didn't expect I'd drag her screaming from the car into the house!"

"I thought," said Rierson, "she'd be—well, in no condition to scream like that."

Max Arnold said simply: "This is no moving picture. You didn't expect me to knock her unconscious, tie her up and carry her from my apartment! Will they get her?"

"If she sticks to the road, unless some motorist picks her up," said Rierson.

"Get in the car," Arnold told him. "We'll drive along Riverdale Avenue. If she gets away now, everything is shot. She'll get in touch with Day and—"

He turned the car now; joggled over the rough road. "These men of yours, Joe—they know these woods?"

"Hell, no!" said Rierson. "They've never been here before tonight, but the girl hasn't either. If she sticks to the woods we can't—"

"She won't." Max nodded. "She's in a panic. And if she isn't she'll want to find a phone and warn Day. She'll hit the main road sure, and flag a passing car."

The car reached Riverdale Avenue. Max Arnold pulled to a stop close to the open man-hole, the light and the railing around it. A car hitting fifty came over the top of the hill, going toward Yonkers. Max switched off the lights of his car; watched the other shoot by. For a moment its headlight flashed on the bank across the road. A figure— the figure of a man pushed itself quickly behind a tree.

Joseph E. Rierson whistled. The figure came from the tree, ran down the bank, across the road and reached the car.

"Well, Fred." Rierson waited.

"It looked like a cinch." The man nodded his head. "Me and Rawley seen her plainly all along. Then the turn in the road, and we hit Riverdale Avenue. Like *that*"—the man snapped his fingers—"she was gone, and a car roaring by too. I don't see how she got across the road. There was only—"

Max Arnold grinned. "She didn't," he said, climbed from the car and walked over to the man-hole.

"Cripes!" said Fred, "you don't think she had time to climb down there and—"

"She didn't have time to do anything else." Max leaned over the iron railing around the hole and looked down. Then with a chuckle, "Look! She didn't climb; she jumped. She's unconscious and—" He broke off suddenly and clutched Rierson by the arm. "We've got to act quick—bind her and gag her. She's coming around."

"Here's Rawley," Fred said as a man slipped up on them. Then he threw a foot over the rail; threw it over just as the girl staggered to her feet, looked up. Looked straight into the round beady eyes of Rierson.

"You—you too? I knew it." The words were forced from her lips. "You're going to—to kill me?"

"And how!" smiled Rierson as he stared down into those wide brown eyes.

## CHAPTER SIX

## LAST ADVENTURE

**M**ARTY DAY waited until he was in his own apartment before he opened the long envelope the butler had thrust into his hand. Inside was another sealed envelope and clipped to that one was a note to him.

> Dear Marty:—
> I can trust to that misguided honor of yours not to open this sealed envelope and to only let it be opened in the event of your sure death.
> To read it now would do you no good. To keep it always on your

person, no matter what danger it may seem to be to others, is absolutely necessary. Do not put it in a safe. Do not hide it. Always keep it in your pocket no matter what your mission, nor how foolhardy you think such instructions are.

This envelope may contain your life and Tania's.

Zee Clarke.

Marty read the note through half a dozen times. Then he looked at the sealed envelope he held in his hand. Clearly printed on it were the words—

THE IDENTITY OF THE RECKONER CAN BE FOUND INSIDE THIS ENVELOPE IF OPENED ONLY BY THE PARTY IT IS INTENDED FOR.

Queer, that. Marty juggled the envelope in his hand. Of course he ought to open it. But he didn't; he just stood looking down at it. Zee Clarke. Strange woman! He hesitated for some time, then thrust the envelope into his jacket pocket. Knight had walked into the room.

"There was a telephone call." Knight's voice showed disapproval. "The Reckoner, sir. He said you're not to go out. There will be a message for you."

Marty nodded. "Anything else?"

"Only—that I'd chuck it, sir. It ain't the fun it started out to be. The cops are getting close. There's Rierson, who is only waiting to kill you comfortable like—and now The Reckoner himself who ain't so friendly. Just let us hop a boat, sir."

"And Tania?"

"Miss Tania's a woman, sir, and isn't rightly responsible for what she does."

"You'd leave Tania behind, eh?"

"No. I'd take her with us."

"But she won't go. That's to protect me, Knight."

"And quite right, from her point of view; that is, the woman's point of view. But I'd take her with us. If you would leave it to me, sir, I'd settle things for you."

"Just how?"

"Well, there's money in the bank. I'd invite Miss Tania over here and give her a bit of a drink; a drink that would surprise her. When she woke up later and wanted to sacrifice her life to save you—why,

I'd simply tell her that the captain couldn't turn the ship back. You went to all the trouble to get them passports, it's sensible to use them!"

Marty tried to smile. "We'd leave a mess behind us, Knight."

"You and me, sir, have often left messes behind us. And if you'll pardon my saying so, that's the place to leave a mess. Right smack behind you."

Marty looked across the room, looked down at his cane, pressed it suddenly down on the floor, released his hand from the rounded top and watched the cane jump suddenly into the air and make almost a perfect arc, to settle down across Knight's arm.

"Perfect, sir." Knight beamed. "Nerves all right, anyway."

"Yes." Marty nodded. "But the cane served no purpose tonight. A gun would have served me better."

"The trouble with the cane, sir, is—you've used it over and over on the same crowd or in the same circle. It's a weapon of offense or defense. A gun, now. Well, that's a weapon of elimination."

**MARTY** crossed to Knight and lifted the cane from his arm, adjusted his fingers carefully just below the curved handle. There was a tiny click, and from the inside of that rounded curve a razorlike blade appeared.

Knight was startled. "I never— You never even showed me that." Knight paled slightly. "What a horrible death that would be about a man's throat!"

"I know." Marty nodded. "I'd never use it; not even carry it—but it's the cane of all my canes that has the perfect balance. The maker put the blade there without my instructions. Just the slightest movement of the fingers and it would cut a man's throat. Too horrible to think of, of course, Knight. But it's there just the same and—" The phone rang sharply; rang again. Marty lifted it. Would it be The Reckoner or Tania?

It was The Reckoner.

"Don't talk. Listen!" said the mechanical voice. "Perhaps you are right, and murder—unless it be legal murder, will not end The Reckoner's career, nor will it end the career of Joseph Ellison Rierson. I have completed a case against him; evidence that will burn him to death in the electric chair. I was sure of that evidence, expected to have it in the hands of Lieutenant Bradley in the morning. Things went wrong; very wrong. Tonight you were listening to a disappointed man; a man who thought only of vengeance and forgot justice. Now a man is talking to you who is thinking of both. The slow suffering, the days and nights of waiting to go to the chair will satisfy my hatred. Are you listening?"

"I am listening. What has become of Tania?"

"Tania is quite safe. The man who was to sell me this final piece of evidence has sold me out; sold out his partner too. But this partner has heard the whole scheme and he was not a fool. He did not accuse his friend in blind rage. He came right to me and offered me the opportunity to right his partner's wrong, at a price. The partner, for the time being, has disappeared; but he had this evidence and will deliver it to Rierson tonight. But, there! You are not interested in the details. Will you go; be at the meeting of these two men and get this evidence?"

"It seems like dangerous work."

"Of course it's dangerous work," The Reckoner sneered. "Have I ever paid you large sums of money to do things that any common thug might do? You must be at their meeting, judge the proper time to strike, wait until the transaction has been made so that you will have only one man to face, and bring me that evidence. One hundred thousand dollars and—"

"I want no money from you; I will take no money from you. I simply want—"

"The girl, Tania, eh? Well, you shall have her, and—"

"I simply want her to be free to do as she pleases. No threats; no Max Arnold to control Tania's actions."

And when the mechanical voice chuckled, Marty said: "You're on the level with me in this? You'll keep your promise? This is the last thing you'll ever ask of me?"

"Success or failure; if you go alone and do your best, follow my instructions, this will be the last thing I will ever ask of you and Tania. I promise you that."

After that, instructions; minute details. Marty hung up the receiver.

"Knight," he said, "I will carry a gun with me tonight. You can't stick a cane in a man's stomach and make him hand over; at least, hand over documents that will roast him to death."

To himself he repeated his directions for finding the place where Rierson was to meet, alone, the man with the evidence.

"Riverdale Avenue. The road to the left, by the man-hole that is being fixed. Two hundred yards down toward the river, and the old house back behind a broken gate."

And the time! Well, Marty had a full hour yet.

A half hour later Marty snapped open the gun Knight gave him, examined it carefully and stuck it in his jacket pocket.

"If I might suggest a shoulder holster, that—"

"I don't intend to use it, Knight. Only play with it. It's different from a cane in that you don't have to know any tricks to use it."

"And you're not taking your cane tonight?"

"No." Marty shook his head then suddenly leaned over grabbed up his cane from behind the costumer. "I'd feel like a nudist without it, Knight. I'll take it along tonight as an ornament."

Knight watched that cane and shook his head. He knew that it was a trick, all done by those expert hands; even the moving muscles of Marty's arms. Yet, it seemed to Knight as if that cane moved itself; crept like a living thing down from Marty's wrist, to fit itself firmly, snugly, perhaps even affectionately in the crotch of his arm.

**MARTY** drove leisurely through the streets. His face was a little grim, his hands that grasped the wheel a little rigid. This was his last adventure. He was through with The Reckoner. He didn't exactly hate the man nor did he actually fear him. But he didn't admire him any more. And he hadn't told him about Max Arnold! Marty frowned. Up until lately he had always trusted Arnold. Yet, Arnold was a leader; not a man to be led. Why then had he bowed so long to the will of The Reckoner? It couldn't have been in the spirit of adventure; Arnold wouldn't fit into that kind of picture at all. It might have been money and it might have been fear.

Fear! That would be it.

The Reckoner could have discovered a wrong of Arnold's; forced Arnold to work with him on the threat of disclosing that wrong. It was so with Tania; it was so with Marty now. Once in, the ties were almost impossible to break. The Reckoner could lay his finger on each of his workers. None of those workers—at least, none that Marty knew—could lay a finger on The Reckoner.

Zee Clarke! Did she know? Or did she just suspect? The Reckoner had been there at her house.

No more thoughts. Marty had long since left the Drive behind, was across the draw-bridge at Kingsbridge, had swung left, then right, and was mounting the hill.

The directions were good; easy to follow. He might have passed that little side road if it wasn't for the man-hole and the lantern that hung upon a rail. Two hundred yards down that road Marty switched out his lights, drove slowly; his expensive motor just a purr in the stillness, his eyes piercing the darkness ahead as he picked out his way in the occasional splashes of moonlight through the trees.

And there was the house all right, not so far back from the broken gate. Dull; black; ominous.

Finding a grassy spot beneath the trees he carefully backed the car off the road to be sure of a quick get-away.

As Marty climbed from the car and stood peering through the trees at the blur of blackness that was the house, he felt the old thrill. Yes, he was through with The Reckoner, but he liked this sort of work. The happiness, the homes, the interests of many citizens would depend on him tonight. It was given to him to eliminate from the world's greatest city that city's greatest enemy. Joseph E. Rierson!

**IT WAS** such a feeling as this that had first driven him in with The Reckoner. Then Tania, of course, kept him there, even after he realized the danger to himself; the danger to others in the fast-growing power of The Reckoner, if that power should suddenly be turned to evil instead of good.

Where The Reckoner got all this information Marty didn't know, and he had quit trying to figure it out. In the beginning he had been doubtful of the explicit details of The Reckoner. Lately—well, The Reckoner's information had always been correct. Tonight The Reckoner had been more explicit even than usual. Every movement, to the smallest detail, had been carefully laid out for him by this encyclopedic mind of criminal activity. Well, he could trust him implicitly tonight, as he always had before. This was the big night; the final night. The Reckoner hated Rierson.

Marty studied the distance to the house; the spots of moonlight; the thick bush or a huge tree here and there. With quick, noiseless steps Marty ran from shadow to shadow until he reached that house, planted his body firmly against the worn boards, stood silently listening in the darkness.

Rierson hadn't come yet. The man who was to meet him hadn't come. But that was right, according to The Reckoner's instructions.

Marty moved along the side of that house, noted boards before the cellar windows; rotten boards. Then he found a loose one; felt of it with his cane. It gave slightly as that educated curved handle hooked under one edge.

There was the slightest sound of rotten wood crumbling and the squeak of a rusty nail being torn from that wood. Marty crouched low, swung his cane over his arm again and gripped the old board, made as little noise as possible.

The board came free. He dropped it against the house, ran a hand across the pane. Glass in some places; just torn ragged edges in others. The window gave beneath his pressure; swung back and upward.

There was room for Marty's six feet of well trained muscle, but just room. Little to spare as he stuck his feet through that window, turned his body and let himself slowly down into the cellar; his stomach, then his chest sliding through the opening.

No noise now. He braced his hands, held himself, lowered his body cautiously, his feet feeling for the cement floor.

Simple! Marty's toes touched the floor. He turned and faced utter blackness. Then the blackness was gone, suddenly pierced by blinding light; a light that shone directly into his eyes. A man laughed, a voice spoke, and two round hard objects were driven into Marty's sides.

"Don't move, Mr. Day," the voice said. Then, as the ceiling light flashed on, the man spoke the very thought Marty had just had. "Simple, very simple. You're a fool for courage, Mr. Day—but a fool just the same."

## CHAPTER SEVEN

## TORTURE AND DEATH

**M**ARTY DIDN'T speak. A man stood on either side of him. One dug a hand into Marty's pocket; found his gun. The other still kept a gun against his side. But it was Rierson whom Marty watched and it was Rierson who did the talking.

"No fear in your face yet!" His beady eyes popped. "Just stunned stupidity, eh? Well, we'll take you above and perhaps show you just a few things that will cause you a little emotion. I have a surprise for you, Mr. Day."

Marty's lips set grimly. His one thought was not a pleasant one. The Reckoner was through with him and had sent him to—to his death.

A man grabbed him roughly by the arm, hurled him forward, sent him stumbling toward the stairs. Another man was behind him, the gun against his back, and he was following Rierson up those steps; following the flash that was held in Rierson's hand.

But across Marty's arm he still held his cane, and in the handle of the cane was the deadly razorlike blade. For the first time in his life Marty was tempted to use it. There was no question that Rierson would kill him. He knew that. Now, a single movement of his fingers; a single jerk of his trained hand, and that curved handle would encircle Rierson's neck.

The man behind him would shoot, of course. Marty couldn't prevent that. But Rierson would be dead, his throat torn open in a single jerk; a single second. Marty's right hand crossed his chest, reached the handle of the cane—and stopped. For Rierson spoke, and in those few words saved his life.

"I am taking you to Tania," he said simply.

Tania! Marty's hand fell to his side.

Through the kitchen, along a musty-smelling hall they went. Stairs were there. A banister that showed dust; dust that was wet and caked. And up those stairs Marty followed Rierson.

They entered the room at the top. A button clicked, dull light flashed up; light that could not be seen from outside, for heavy dark cloth was nailed against the window; cloth that was lately put there, for it was clean and free from dust.

Across the room was a heavy curtain, musty and damp with age. It brushed Marty's face as he followed Rierson into the room beyond. And there Marty stopped dead. Every detail of that room was stamped upon his brain; accentuated rather than dimmed by the dullness of the single lamp and the glare of a crackling wood fire in an open grate.

Two windows, also covered with the new black cloth. A door to the left, which evidently led to the hall they had just come from; another door, slightly open; a single shelf and hooks along the wall for hanging clothes could be dimly seen. Just a closet, that. The worn furniture, the flat table with thick damp dust upon it; dust which was already beginning to dry from the warmth from the fire. The couch to the side of the mantel. The two chairs; one empty, the other—the other occupied.

Although Marty mentally digested every detail of that room, it was the occupant of that chair who held his eyes; sent the cold chill of horror in a single electric shock through his entire body.

Tania, bound hand and foot! Her gorgeous hair, shaggy; hanging down over her forehead. A cut upon her lips; blood that had dried upon her chin; wide brown eyes that dulled rather than brightened when she saw Marty.

**THE TWO** men acted quickly. Marty was swung around, his cane taken away. The fat hand of Rierson was holding the cane and he seemed to be examining it closely. Then Marty was thrust into the other chair, rope holding his body rigid; rope about his ankles, a heavy strip of it leading up and binding his hands tightly at the wrists. It was a good job; a thorough job.

Rierson spoke to the two men, followed them through the curtain as they departed. Dull whispers came from the room beyond. And Marty spoke.

"The Reckoner, Tania. He double-crossed me; you too. He's—well, he told me once that he had only friends and enemies. Enemies die. He trapped you, too?"

Tania shook her head. "The Reckoner didn't bring me here. It was Max Arnold. I nearly got away, in that instant that I knew the truth; saw death in his face. But, no—Marty. Max Arnold is close to The Reckoner. He knew of The Reckoner's plans for tonight and no doubt arranged with Rierson to wait for you here. He hates you, of course."

"Of course." Marty nodded. "Because of you—because he loves you and—"

"No." She shook her head. "Because he loves Zee Clarke. That's true, Marty. He admitted it to me. I was simply his dupe; partly to make her jealous, perhaps—but mostly, I think, to put her off her guard in protecting you. I—"

And she stopped. Rierson had come into the room. A man followed him. It was Max Arnold. Marty silently cursed himself for not telling The Reckoner his suspicions of Max Arnold.

"What a rotten beast you are," Marty started, and stopped. That was useless now.

"Tush, tush." Rierson shook the steel cane at Marty. "Max is simply disproving the old adage that a man can't serve two masters."

Max Arnold made a funny sound in his throat. If it was meant for a laugh, it died at once. "Just one master, Rierson," he said. "Myself!" And with an impatient wave of his hand, "Come on! Why all this talk. Get the—the business over with."

"But it's not business." Rierson shook his head. "The death of The Reckoner's hirelings for a while came under the head of business. The little lady started all the trouble. She worked as my secretary; learned of my connections; my friends; their secrets. And then she made it possible for our young hero, Mr. Day, to steal that information from my safe. In The Reckoner I see only the brain that conceived my ruin; in these two, the bodies of that brain. I am going to work upon those bodies, Max. I am going to draw a cry of agony for each of my friends. I am going to—"

"Bigger men than you have talked too much," Max cut in. "Bigger men than you have talked themselves even to death."

Rierson laughed, looked at Arnold. "If you haven't got the stomach for it, wait below. You have your money. The only stipulation was that they both must die; the means by which they die is left to me. A peculiar cane, this." Rierson turned his head and looked at Marty, then he threw the cane into the fire.

The cane struck the burning logs; the sizzling wood hid from all but Marty the sudden hum of the hidden springs. The cane twisted once, seemed to rise against the blaze like a curling rattlesnake, hung so a moment, and balancing on the end of the grate finally settled, the curved handle in the fire; the ferrule resting upon the stones before the open fireplace. And Marty felt a sinking in his stomach. The cane was not near; at least, not near enough to his bound feet.

"You're impatient, Max." Rierson half spun Arnold around, pushed him toward the hall. "Wait downstairs, with Fred and Rawley. I'm not entirely bent on vengeance; there's business in it, too. The Reckoner is in a fair way to ruin me now. But perhaps he will hesitate to go on with his persecution; perhaps the psychology of his name—of the fear he has inspired will backfire on him after tonight. I don't think that any living man—even The Reckoner—will be able to look on these two bodies and not fear the man who prepared them for him."

"You'd torture them then?"

Rierson laughed. He went to the fireplace, grasped the heavy tongs, thrust them deep into the blazing logs. "You see, Max, pain is both physical and mental. The physical to the girl will be the mental to the man. But, there! Leave a man who is growing old to his simple pleasures." And Rierson's laugh was natural as Max Arnold, with a single look back over his shoulders at the fireplace, passed through the door into the hall.

**RIERSON** crossed the room and stood before Tania and Marty. "I would not have believed it." He bobbed his head up and down so that his thick jowls rolled. "But I don't know when I have experienced such satisfaction." He leaned down, felt of the cords about Marty's wrists, then slipped the gun that dangled in his right hand into a jacket pocket. "The boys made a good job of you. You can see Tania well from your position there. You can see the brown of her eyes. And I presume too, Mr. Day, you can see the fire tongs with their two ends; the twin points that are coincidentally just the same distance apart as those two—" He stopped, bent forward, flipped Marty's jacket back further.

"They searched you, of course, but only for weapons. Now, what—" Fat fingers moved with swift and surprising dexterity into Marty's pocket and brought out the square white envelope. Until that moment Marty had forgotten it. Now he saw Rierson reading carefully the printed words. Rierson repeated them aloud.

" 'The identity of The Reckoner can be found inside this envelope if opened only by the party it is intended for.' The party it is intended for!" Rierson repeated. "Surely not you, Mr. Day. It's not opened; not—"

Rierson turned the envelope over, examined it carefully. Then breaking the seal, extracted a single sheet of paper. Marty could see plainly the small clear handwriting on that sheet. Twice Rierson read through that note, looked at the back of it. Then: "What does this mean?" he demanded of Marty.

Marty started to shake his head, and Rierson cut in.

"To be sure, it wasn't open. Now read it. Don't lie to me! What does it mean?" He held the letter close to Marty's eyes, watched his face, too, as Marty read it. And he saw surprise there; genuine surprise.

Dear Mr. Rierson:—
If this letter should fall into your hands, Marty Day is in trouble.

In plain words, one who should protect him has betrayed him. Do
not harm Marty Day.

If you will telephone the number on the top of this sheet the person
who answers that phone will disclose to you the name of The Reckoner for the life of Marty Day.

The Reckoner has enough evidence to convict you now. The name
of The Reckoner would produce that evidence and put it in your hands.
Do not let anyone but Marty Day know the contents of this letter.
That is very important to your life. Better make the call.

The letter was unsigned.

"Well"—Rierson's face was very close to Marty Day—"who gave
you that and why do you carry it?"

Marty hesitated. Then: "The letter came to me sealed, like that—with
instructions to carry it with me always. I don't know who sent it."

"The Reckoner?"

"I don't know," Marty lied.

Rierson jerked up Marty's head violently. Then with his open palm
he smacked him across the face. "The police! It's a trap?"

"You know I don't work with the police. I don't know."

Rierson hesitated. "You would advise me to call that number?"

"What do you think?" Marty said, but there was hope in his voice;
and seeing the crafty look in Rierson's eyes, "It's my life—and Tania's."

"Police or not; trap or not, it does not matter." Rierson leaned over
to the table, opened a box upon it and jerked out a phone, almost
touching Marty's head. "You see, this phone is only for temporary
use; tapped in on the wire—outside wire. I want you to hear the
conversation."

**RIERSON** slid around the table, lifted the receiver, called the
number, waited. He was so close that Marty could feel his hot breath
upon his cheek. And Marty watched the fire. Then his head suddenly raised. Clearly he heard the voice on the phone; he recognized
it too. It was Zee Clarke.

"Your name, please," Rierson said. "I—I got your note."

"Oh! This is Zee Clarke. It was a trap then. Marty is there?"

"That is correct. He is here. Who— Let me have the name you
were to give me."

Zee Clarke laughed.

"I'm not a fool," she said. "First I will have to talk to Marty Day and know that he is alive and well. Max Arnold, of course, sold him out to you. There! Don't tell me about it. Let me tell you just what you are to do to get from me the name of The Reckoner. I won't betray this Reckoner to his death, if that's what you think. But I will let you know who he is, have him meet you, and in exchange for Marty Day's life he will turn over to you all the evidence he has collected. Here's your chance to escape the hot seat, Mr. Rierson. There will be victory for neither you or The Reckoner; just a draw."

"The Reckoner must be very fond of this Marty Day if you can make him do all this."

"It is not The Reckoner who is fond of Marty Day," the woman said. "Do you agree? I will come to talk with you."

"You expect me to tell you where I am; where I have this Marty Day?"

"Hell, man! I have only to call The Reckoner, tell him that Marty Day is a prisoner of yours. He will, of course, know where he sent him."

"If you did—if I—Day would be dead before any help could come."

"And that's why"—Zee Clarke's voice was smooth as glass—"I want to come and see you; want you and not The Reckoner to tell me where you are. It will be while I am with you that I will telephone The Reckoner; tell him that my life rests in his hands; that he must send the evidence he holds against you to you or I will disclose his identity."

"Yes?" Rierson was thinking.

"You know what you could do with the knowledge of that identity unless you and The Reckoner reached an agreement. The Reckoner is hated and feared in the entire city. His identity would mean his death by a hundred bullets before morning."

"God! It would—it would." Rierson nodded his agreement. Thick lips smacked; beady eyes sparkled.

"And," said Zee Clarke, "you wouldn't roast to death."

The sparkle left Rierson's eyes, his lips closed tight. He was silent so long that the woman spoke again.

"It's a chance, of course. But if I didn't come alone or if I—"

"I know," said Rierson. "It takes only a second to kill a man; just a second. You understand that."

"Yes." And after a pause, "If the man is there—Max Arnold, who betrayed The Reckoner's friend, I can arrange to save him from the wrath of The Reckoner too."

Rierson hesitated, finally said: "That doesn't interest me—only him. All right. Drive up Broadway, and turn after you cross the bridge at Kingsbridge. Then go up Riverdale Avenue. Watch the side roads to the left. Stop when you see a man-hole with a light over it. A man of mine will meet you there. God help you if you don't mean what you say."

"And I have your word that no harm will come to me?"

"My word, lady. If you disclose to me the name of The Reckoner, you have my word; my fortune; and my everlasting protection."

"Good! Now put Marty Day on."

Rierson nodded, held the phone close to Marty's lips.

Marty spoke quickly. "Don't come, Zee. He intends to kill us. And you, with your knowledge; he'd torture you until—"

"Sure!" said the voice of Zee Clarke. "That's in the mind of Rierson, all right. But he never could make me talk unless I wanted to talk. I'll be there."

**THE RECEIVER** clicked. Rierson laid the phone back in the box. "So she won't talk." Rierson looked down at the now glowing tongs. "All women talk," he said, and walked to the curtained room, looked carefully into it and finally entered. Marty heard his feet across the floor, then he heard him call, "Rawley!"

Crooks, thieves, murderers. Romance! But Marty couldn't laugh. Max Arnold had betrayed him. Now Rierson didn't care what happened to Max Arnold. But Rierson didn't return immediately to that room. Once he heard Rierson say: "Stick below, Max. I've got a private word for Rawley about guarding the outside of the house. No, no; I have done nothing about them yet. Things are delayed for a moment."

Marty Day tried to cheer Tania. He told her that Zee Clarke would get in touch with The Reckoner; maybe the police. She knew that Max Arnold had trapped them.

Tania shook her head. "No, Marty," she said. "The Reckoner will not like Zee Clarke interfering in this. The Reckoner would not dare use the police. They are as dangerous to him as they would be to Rierson. We can't lie to ourselves any longer, Marty. Many of The Reckoner's acts have been good acts; but men have died; men, maybe who deserved death. But the law will look on it as murder. No. You defied The Reckoner; I would have left him. He will not raise his hand to save us tonight."

<h1 style="text-align:center">CHAPTER EIGHT</h1>

<h1 style="text-align:center">THE RECKONER</h1>

**I** **T SEEMED** a long time before Zee Clarke came. Then that hall door opened and she just slid into the room. Rierson closed the door behind her. She barely looked at Tania, smiled and nodded at Marty and went directly to the fire.

She poked at Marty's cane with her foot, knocking it further from the grate, so that the paint that covered the steel and made it appear an ordinary walking stick dripped upon the stones. Then she clasped her hands behind her back and spoke to Rierson.

"Your man," she said, "was just a bit rough in his search." Her amber eyes flashed, her thin lips curved. "He is not a man to handle women; at least, in the way of business."

Rierson nodded, said: "Sit down."

"I prefer to do my business standing. I am here to produce The Reckoner and make a deal with you. You understand that."

"No." Rierson shook his head. "You understand that, but I don't. You are here to tell me who The Reckoner is." He looked long and earnestly at her. "You are a very beautiful woman, Mrs. Clarke; far too beautiful to die. Far too beautiful to remain silent."

She laughed. "Don't be a fool, Rierson," she said. "I wouldn't have come unless I was sure."

"You weren't followed," said Rierson. "At least, after you reached the side road. We have a friend of yours here. Yes. Max Arnold. He knows you are here now, but he doesn't know why. Max!" Rierson turned to the curtained room.

Max Arnold came into the room. He stood looking at Zee Clarke. At length he said: "You were a fool to come, Zee. You loved him that much?" He nodded his head at Marty.

"Max"—Zee Clarke spoke slowly—"I couldn't let you do this. Everything you ever obtained was through reason. Now I'm not going to let you ruin it all by emotion. Do you know why I'm here?"

"Yes." Max Arnold looked at her steadily. "You are here to betray

The Reckoner for the man you love—Marty Day, and you speak to me of emotion overcoming reason! I am afraid, Zee, you have walked to your own death."

"Sensible, Max." Rierson nodded.

"You don't understand, Max." Zee shook her head. "I explained it all to Rierson. I'm afraid he doesn't intend to keep his word to me. I want you to suggest that he does; insist that he does."

"Yes!" Max Arnold sneered.

"Yes." Zee nodded very seriously. There was no fear in her eyes, no trembling in her voice; her words were very clear. "I am going to the telephone and call The Reckoner, Max. I am going to tell him that he is to make a deal with Rierson, all that evidence he has against Rierson for our freedom. If he won't make good I will disclose to Rierson the name of The Reckoner. So you see, Max, The Reckoner must come here tonight."

"I see," said Max. "Rierson gets the name of The Reckoner. What's to prevent him later from giving that name to the underworld?"

"The Reckoner must make that deal with him." Zee nodded. "Must arrange that the evidence against him is squashed so long as Rierson does not divulge The Reckoner's real identity. You see, I have come prepared."

"Except for one thing," Rierson snapped in. "This evidence against me will not be made public before morning, certainly. And before morning, Mrs. Clarke, you will have watched the two you came to save die slowly, and will have decided to talk. You will understand exactly what they suffered before they died."

"You—you don't want to go through with the bargain?"

"Hardly!" said Rierson.

"God, Max!" Zee Clarke turned suddenly on Arnold. "How could you have done this? What made you destroy everything; everything I had built up in you? How could—"

**AND TANIA** spoke. The words just shot from her mouth. For the moment she had forgotten that the thing was real. It was as if she watched a play. As if— But her words rang through the room.

"Max Arnold did all this because he loved—loved you, Zee Clarke."

"Me?" Zee Clarke laughed as she looked at Tania. Then she turned and looked at Arnold. Her eyes were bright; her lips still parted, and the laugh died in her throat. She bent closer. Her eyes burnt into Max Arnold's eyes. Her words were just a spoken thought.

"It's true, Max. It's true."

She was swaying forward when Rierson raised an arm and knocked her back.

"Go below, Max," he said, and there was no lightness in his voice. "Don't be a fool about women. Remember—I have two men watching downstairs." And as he pushed Max Arnold back toward the curtain, "If you want the woman, and she'll talk—you'll have her later." And Rierson looked at Zee Clarke now. "Well, well— Max, look at her. I guess, after all, it's you—not Day. Look at her!" And pushing Max through the door that led to the hall and locking it after him, "She'll have a double reason to talk now."

Zee Clarke, seemingly stunned, was saying: "He loved me enough; wanted me enough to kill—kill them both, and make it look as if Rierson did—"

"Get back there." Rierson held a gun in his right hand. With his left he struck Zee Clarke brutally across the mouth, knocking her onto the long couch. "If you make a fuss I'll call the two men from downstairs to tie you up too." He half turned, keeping his eyes on the woman as he gripped the tongs; lifted them from the fire.

"Well," Rierson stood close to Marty but spoke to the woman, "do you talk?"

"And you won't make the deal?" Zee Clarke brushed a hand across his mouth.

"No. And you're not going to tell The Reckoner anything."

"The Reckoner," she said, "has already received my message."

"His name?"

And Marty jerked his head back. The red hot tongs were close to his face; to his eyes. Another thrust and blindness; agonizing blindness.

"If The Reckoner doesn't act on my message at once I will give you his name." Zee Clarke almost shouted the words, yet Marty thought there was not exactly panic in her voice.

Rierson's little eyes snapped. To him the woman was breaking up, as all must break up—all had broken up—who faced Rierson. His voice was almost as loud as the woman's.

"His name?" he cried out.

"His name—" A voice suddenly echoed the words of Rierson. It was a mechanical voice, a rasping voice. Like the dull scraping voice on a phonograph played with a worn needle.

**MARTY** jerked so suddenly that for a moment the tongs touched his cheek, but for a moment only. Rierson's stubby fingers opened and the tongs slipped from them, struck Marty's knee, fell to the floor. For that voice was the voice of The Reckoner, and the body that owned that voice suddenly parted the curtains and stood in the room.

The black robe; the black hood over the head; the two slits that were eyes; even the peculiar, shiny hands which Marty knew now were gloves. And in the right hand was a gun; a heavy automatic that was directed straight at the body of Joseph E. Rierson.

The black figure moved slowly, ominously, until its back was to Marty Day and Tania. But his right hand could still be partly seen and the black gun was plainly visible as it covered unwaveringly the bulky form of Rierson.

Rierson suddenly came to life; at least he found speech. "Fred! Rawley! Max!" he cried out loudly and wildly.

The Reckoner laughed. "You want my name? You want to find me? Don't cry out for Fred, Rawley and Max. They can not hear you."

"You—you— They are dead?"

"No, not dead. Only men who must die, die; and men who know me. Step forward, Rierson. Keep your hands visible. There! That's right." This as Rierson took two steps forward; mechanical movements; maybe unconscious movements. "Now, Rierson"—the metallic voice ground out the words—"you wanted to know me. Raise your right hand—so. Lift the hood. You would give your life even to see the face of The Reckoner. Well, look!"

Rierson's breath came in fast, uneven gasps. His right hand jerked up as if it were lifted by an invisible force. For a moment it hovered about the blackness of The Reckoner's hood, then it thrust that hood up and back over The Reckoner's head.

Marty could see that; could see the black hood flop over and rest on top of The Reckoner's head. He couldn't see the man's face but Rierson could. Plainly came Rierson's startled cry; plainly came his words.

"You—you! I never thought; never—"

Rierson's hand shot beneath his jacket with a quickness that must have been carried over from his earlier days as a gunman and a killer.

A shot rang out. Rierson's left hand clutched at his chest and he staggered back. Plainly Marty saw his face; the livid blue veins, the horrible, malignant, little shoe-button eyes. Then Rierson's gun crashed, yellow-blue flame spurted. The Reckoner's body shook. Then another shot.

Rierson's hand dropped to his side, his fingers seemed to relax, open, almost gently, slowly. A great hole, with rough, powder-smeared edges appeared just above the bridge of his nose. His eyes popped; his mouth hung open. The black-robed figure raised a hand and jerked the hood back over his face. Then he turned as Rierson crashed face downward on the floor.

A dead silence in that room. Marty and Tania could not move. Zee Clarke seemed to be frozen there on the couch. Death had been sudden; sure, since The Reckoner had entered that room. Now Tania was safe; he was safe. They—

The breath sucked back into Marty's throat. The Reckoner moved suddenly, menacingly; the black hood hiding his face. But the menace was not in that hood. It was in that right hand; the shining right hand that suddenly raised the revolver and clapped it hard against Marty's temple.

Zee Clarke came to life. She bounded from the couch; flung herself against the hooded figure, knocking his arm aside, driving him from before the fireplace.

"No. Not now. You can't—you can't!"

"They know. They know." The rasping voice had a human note; perhaps a natural note now.

"No." Zee Clarke clung to his arm. "They don't know; they can't be sure—ever sure. Rierson is dead and— Then you'll have to kill me too; kill me first."

"You—you!" The gun suddenly disappeared some place in the folds of that black judicial robe. Both The Reckoner's hands shot out and fastened on the girl's throat.

Distinctly Marty heard her say: "Very well, if you can. I'd rather be dead than know you were simply a murderer, after—"

**AND THROUGH** it all Marty sat strapped in the chair and did nothing—nothing but listen to others plan his death and Tania's death, and now Zee Clarke's death. For Zee Clarke had either lost her strength or didn't care, or— But she lay passive, still, while those rubber-gloved fingers closed about her throat; tightened there. The Reckoner was going to leave no loose ends behind him.

It was at that moment that Marty's eyes fastened upon his cane; the cane that had been out of his reach, even if—if— And the cane was no longer out of his reach. It had dropped further from the grate, so that only its curved handle was clinging to the edge now. Had the heat moved it; had a fallen log moved it? And Marty suddenly remembered. Zee Clarke had moved it. Zee Clarke, who knew the use he could make of that cane.

The Reckoner cried out sharply: "I can't—can't kill you, Zee; not now. But they must—"

And Marty and The Reckoner acted almost in the same few seconds. The Reckoner threw the girl from him; hurled her across the room and back onto the couch again.

As for Marty! His bound feet shot out; one foot touched that cane. The curved handle turned, hidden springs hissed under the sudden pressure of his foot and the cane bounded straight up and into his tied hands.

Hot! The steel burnt into his flesh. He set his teeth grimly. But the pain did not stop him; it only made his deft, sure, long-practiced movements the quicker. A single pressure of his fingers and a prayer that the heat had not harmed delicate mechanism. Then the click of the blade jumping into place; a blade that cut the rope that held his wrists as if it were mere thread. After that Marty's movements were all seemingly a single motion, as the hooded figure peered through the slits in the mask and watched, stunned for a moment, while Marty's hand twirled.

Marty simply reversed the cane, let his fingers slip down close to the ferrule which was not so hot, and with a quick upward jerk tore that blade through the rope that had held his ankles.

And Marty was free; free and out of the chair, flinging his body toward The Reckoner as The Reckoner's gun jumped into his hand again. But this time The Reckoner's finger did not close upon the trigger. The cane slipped forward; wrenched the gun from his hand, the sharp blade which still protruded from the curved handle drawing blood from his wrist.

The Reckoner backed suddenly away. Marty jerked the cobra cane back over his arm. The heat did not at once penetrate the sleeve of his jacket.

"At last," Marty could not keep the gloating out of his voice, "I'm going to get a look at the face of the man—"

Marty stopped. The Reckoner's crouching body straightened; moved backward, close to the open closet door.

Footsteps on the stairs outside; heavy, running feet; the shouting of men. Why hadn't Marty thought of it before? The men below! Rierson's friends were coming. And in Marty's moment of hesitation, indecision, The Reckoner backed quickly into the closet and jerked the door closed behind him. A lock clicked.

Pounding on the door; a body hurled against it, and Marty had bent quickly and lifted Rierson's gun from the floor; that was the nearer to his hand. Zee Clarke was getting slowly from the couch when Marty swung, gun raised, and the door to the hall burst open.

A gun cracked, plaster crashed from the wall above the fireplace. Men were in the room; men who were strangers to Marty. Then a voice spoke behind him. Marty's gun dropped to his side. The fight for life was over; his life, Tania's life. Marty turned and faced the man who had come through the curtains; the same curtains that The Reckoner had come through. It was Lieutenant Frank Bradley.

**TANIA** was quickly freed, but she could not stand at once. It was necessary to restore the circulation to her aching feet. Bradley had just risen from the side of Rierson.

He looked at Marty; at the gun still dangling in his hand.

"So you plugged him, eh? Finally got him. Well, he kidnaped the girl. There, don't tell me! I guess you can make out a pretty good case. I wouldn't have found the house if it wasn't for the shots and perhaps the car I saw turn out of the road."

"I didn't kill him," Marty said. "You wanted The Reckoner. Well, maybe it was self-defense, but The Reckoner killed Rierson tonight. I guess it's—it's—"

Zee Clarke laughed. "Don't be a fool, Marty," she cut in quickly. "Bradley must know the truth. You trusted him enough tonight; at least, enough to insist that I telephone him your message that Tania was held a prisoner here and that you were coming to make a deal with Rierson."

"Sure!" Bradley smiled over at Marty. "All the breaks will be your way tonight, Mr. Day. Of course, if Mrs. Clarke could have told me exactly where the house was—why, I might have made it in time to prevent the shooting."

"But The Reckoner—" Marty started and stopped. Zee Clarke's amber eyes were on him; warning eyes. He tried to piece things together. Zee Clarke had telephoned Bradley in his name. Why? To be sure! To protect herself if things went wrong. No, not exactly that. To protect all of them, of course. Now her eyes said, as plain as if she spoke the words, "Protect The Reckoner and he will protect you. Disclose him and he will—" Well, if The Reckoner talked, he could make it very unpleasant for him—for Tania. In plain English Zee's eyes said, "We are all saved together or we all sink together." But the closet! Surely the police would— And Zee Clarke spoke.

"Marty—as you know—Lieutenant, has an exaggerated sense of honor." She shrugged her shoulders. "I knew my way just as far as I told you. The repaired man-hole was my sign post too. But I had luck in locating the house. I sneaked in." She raised her head, exposed her slender white throat. "Rierson's fingers were on my throat when I shot him. I had to—"

A detective spoke from across the room.

"The closet door is locked and the key gone." The man paused and leaned down; then straightening, said in a low voice, "I can hear someone breathing heavily inside there, like—like—"

"Hell!" said Bradley, drawing his gun again and pointing to the closet door. "Quit the brain work and pull that damn door off its hinges. I brought you along for beef, not brains, Haviland. Let's see the beef work."

Every pair of eyes turned toward that door. Detective Haviland grasped the knob, pulled once and only once. The lock came from the rotten wood almost at the first effort. Haviland jarred back. For a moment, darkness; then a figure.

Marty's eyes fairly popped. Things were to be cleared up now. Just as soon as Bradley tore the black hood from—

But no black-clad figure came from that closet. The hood was gone, the black robe was gone. The man was dressed in a plain blue business suit. No mask covered his face, no rubber gloves disguised his hands. He just took two steps forward, then his knees gave. Bradley stretched out a hand and supported him; helped him to the couch.

Marty stared for a long time at the man upon the couch. The blood was dripping slowly through the fingers of a hand he held close against his chest. At length Marty spoke.

"You—you!" He fairly gasped the words. "Max Arnold! You were—are—"

Zee Clarke snapped in quickly. "Where did you think Max went after Rierson shot him? Did you think the door led to another room? Poor Max. He did everything he could to—to—"

And for the first time Zee Clarke broke down. She threw herself down beside Max Arnold; her arms were about his neck.

"Max—Max! Not now! You can't die now, when I—when we—when we just found out. Max, don't. Max!"

## CHAPTER NINE

## NOT SO DUMB

**I**T WAS close to two hours later when the doctor left Zee Clarke's house. Before he left he spoke to Zee and Marty.

"Just a flesh wound." He smiled encouragingly. "Two inches closer, maybe, and then— But he'll be around in a week. Nothing but loss of blood. I'll drop in tomorrow. Don't move Mr. Arnold to his own home yet."

Alone in the sitting room, with the door closed to the little bedroom where Max Arnold was, Zee gripped Marty by the arm.

"I'm not asking you to believe that Max is telling the truth when he says he never really intended to harm you and Tania. But I saved your life tonight; saved Tania's life tonight, and discovered something I never dreamed was possible. He loves me, Marty—and I guess I always loved him but never realized it, because it wasn't—didn't seem even a remote hope. Max and love didn't fit at all. His purpose was vengeance, maybe; the downfall of Rierson. No, it wasn't all for society, of course. But, even so, it served society well."

"Max Arnold was The Reckoner," Marty mused.

"Yes." She nodded. "He'll be around in a week and defend me at the trial, if there is a trial. But, here!" She shoved a thick envelope into his hand. "There's the evidence against Rierson; it involves many others. It will make Bradley the envy of every man on the force; make him an inspector. He's a smart man—Bradley; a bright man. Too bright to stir up a lot of trouble for himself. Go and talk to him now."

Marty turned to the hall and stopped. "The two men in that house; Rierson's friends. What became of them?"

"Max told me. He had prepared everything. He had another car out back; two men in it. He just got Rierson's men, Fred and Rawley, together in the kitchen. It was easy for Max to put a gun on them; they thought he was Rierson's friend, of course. Then Max turned them over to his men. They were driven to the city and let go. Rierson is dead. Dead men have no friends. No, they won't talk.

"Don't be too hard on Max, Marty. He can't harm you now. Rierson killed his partner; only Max knew that. And that partner was the only living thing Max ever cared for until—" She stopped, grasped Marty by both shoulders. "I guess I told you the truth, Marty, when I said I get anything; any man I want." She threw her arms suddenly about Marty and kissed him. "After all, it was Max I really wanted."

Downstairs Lieutenant Frank Bradley paced back and forth. He led Marty to a distant corner, far from the uniformed men who stood at the door.

"You got all that evidence, eh?" He stroked his chin, whistled as he ran his eyes over the documents that envelope contained. "I wonder if I'm a fool to go through with it. But, hell, you're a good skate, and I'd like to be an inspector."

"Rierson is dead," Marty said. "There is information that will clean up the worst of the crooked politicians, lawyers, judges and such like in the city. It's a big thing, Bradley. And in return, you simply make it easy for us. After all, you've got proof of nothing, and—" Marty straightened. "I'll promise you this, Bradley. The Reckoner is through. If he ever enters into criminal life again—why, I'll tell you who he is."

"Will you?" Bradley grinned from ear to ear; his voice was sarcastic. "Well, now— Mr. Day, that's mighty white of you; mighty decent of you." And the grin disappearing and his mouth grim and hard, he pounded a finger against Marty's chest. "It isn't so much slipping from my duty that bothers me; the evidence you gave me is worth that and the stripes of an inspector can soothe the most festering conscience. But I do hate to be considered dumb; just plain dumb." The finger against Marty's chest pounded harder now. "By the way, I wrapped that robe and hood in a newspaper and gave it to Tania. Better burn them."

**MARTY** didn't know just what to say and he didn't know for certain if Bradley knew who The Reckoner was; simply suspected who he was or just knew that he had actually been at the house up at Riverdale. So Marty only said: "The killing of Rierson was self-defense. I'll take the blame for it if you think—"

"Hell, no!" Bradley said. "That's all arranged. "I'll keep the cops here until the D.A. shows up. But let Zee Clarke take the blame. Now mind you—I don't think there will be an arrest. But if there *should* be a trial—why, that Mrs. Clarke's got the eyes and—yes, the legs—for it. But—"

Bradley stopped. Tania had opened the door that led to the library.

"There you are!" nodded Bradley as with some difficulty he thrust the large envelope into his pocket. "I'll make this evidence public slowly, as a hard-working cop should. Don't forget to burn the outfit. People are queer and might get to thinking that a lad who called himself The Reckoner shed them in that closet."

But Lieutenant Bradley was smiling as Marty crossed the huge reception hall and entered the library.

**TANIA'S** eyes were radiant; bright; alive. She followed Marty's eyes to Knight, who sat upon the floor, a can of paint and a thin brush still upon a sheet of paper. He was admiring a bit of painting he had been doing. The result of his efforts stood against the flat desk.

"Knight brought your things over," Tania explained. "Zee thought the police might keep us here all night. But finding the paint was his own idea. I told him about the cane and that you were through with adventure—romance."

Marty looked at Knight. Knight spoke.

"I told her, sir," Knight said, "that you never will be through with romance as long as you have her. As for adventure! Well, sir; that's in your blood—in your cane. There!" He held the cane up by the ferrule. "It's as good as ever, if you should find it necessary to stick it behind the district attorney's ears tonight."

Marty and Tania looked at each other. The girl took two steps forward and met Marty. For a moment she hesitated, looked toward the spot where Knight had been. A door closed softly. They were alone.

www.ingramcontent.com/pod-product-compliance
Lightning Source LLC
Chambersburg PA
CBHW061634050726
47502CB00012B/2169